# ELVIS
# & COWBOY
# CHARLIE

## (The "what if" Novel)

## by
## Gary
## McCarthy

# Elvis & Cowboy Charlie

## Written by **Gary McCarthy**

## Canyon Country Books

Layout and Design by Laura Ashton
laura@gitflorida.com

**www.canyoncountrybooks.com**

*Elvis & Cowboy Charlie* **by Gary McCarthy
is available on Amazon and other online
booksellers, as a Kindle ebook, and from Gary at:
www.canyoncountrybooks.com.**

ISBN: 978-1499635232

First Printing

Printed in the United States of America

# CANYON COUNTRY BOOKS
## Gary McCarthy

*Gold & Lace*

*Isaac Beard & Sons*

*Sisters of the Wyoming Mountains: Book I*
*Sisters of the Wyoming Plains: Book II*

*Our American West*
*Volumes I through IV*

## National Park Series Novels:

*Yellowstone Thunder*
*Yosemite Thunder*
*Mesa Verde Thunder*
*Grand Canyon Thunder*
*River Thunder*

*Joaquín Murieta Was My Friend*

*Maddie O'Brien's Wild Turkeys*
*Maddie O'Brien's Christmas Donkeys*

Published by
## Canyon Country Books

**www.canyoncountrybooks.com**

*To Elvis fans all over the world*
*and for Michael Lacapa, a great Native American storyteller,*
*who told me the wonderful, wise and funny "Coyote" stories*
*used in this "what if" novel.*

*Elvis & Michael*
*R.I.P.*

# Elvis & Cowboy Charlie

## The "What if" Novel

by

## Gary McCarthy

## *Foreword*

When Elvis Aaron Presley died on August 16, 1977 at the age of only forty-two, like millions of his fans I asked...how could such a tragedy have happened to the greatest rock & roll singer of all time? Why, I wondered, hadn't someone or something changed Elvis' fatal trajectory? And then, because I couldn't accept his untimely death, as a novelist and huge Elvis fan I began to wonder...**what if?**

**What if** a young half-breed and his beautiful, free-spirited sister met Elvis by chance at an All-Indian Rodeo in Winslow, Arizona and completely changed his life? **What if** Cowboy Charlie Coyote, his sister Stella and his Hopi grandmother Lucy Yoyetewa understood the only way Elvis could possibly enjoy a long, healthful life was to turn his back on fame and fortune?

This is my Elvis tribute and story. I wrote it for all The King's devoted fans whom I'm certain have also wondered...**what if?**

*Gary McCarthy in Arizona, 2014*

# Route 66 just West of Winslow, Arizona

## Summer, 1972

The afternoon sky was dark with thunderheads and the war in Vietnam was suddenly finished with the fall of Saigon. President Nixon came back from China, a fella named George Wallace was shot and paralyzed while the news was all about some political wreck called Watergate.

None of it concerned me in the least. I was a tall, slender twenty-year-old cowboy whose father was a Navajo rancher and whose mother was a white vanishing act...someone I couldn't even remember. Our family owned a big patch of sagebrush a little southwest of Winslow called Coyote Ranch where it took fifty acres to feed one cow; we were poor and without electricity or running water...we'd never had it so we didn't miss it. We had a generator and a windmill and we listened to the radio...whenever the reception was good... and we'd listen to anything and everything to fill our evening hours. I had worked other ranches in Arizona and New Mexico and was considered a *real* cowboy, a top hand with a good head on his broad shoulders and a fella who could sing nicer than anyone else around a campfire. In short, I was content with my lot to be a cowboy for the rest of my life. I didn't care about money, and women were still an exciting mystery to me though I sure got the looks from the cowgirls. But I'd seen what they'd done to other cowboys and at that time they did not seem to be worth their bother.

Politics and the outside world meant nothing that summer of 1972; what *did* concern me was my first taste of rodeo. My father had been a professional bull and bronc rider and famous...especially among those who competed at the All-Indian Rodeos springing up around the Southwest. But he'd gotten busted up so many times that he was a physical wreck at forty so I'd agreed with my Hopi grandmother Lucy Yoyetewa that being a working ranch cowboy was fine...but rodeo cowboy was not.

Still, after being pestered for years, Father got me mad enough to try bull riding and now, as I was about to ride my first bull, I was wishing I was anywhere but on top of Buzzard. Our rodeo had started out with the wild horse event where they turned out five or six mustangs and teams of three caught, saddled and then rode them to a standstill. It was a big crowd favorite and got everyone in the mood for the more serious action. My father had roped our mustang, Homer Yazzie had saddled the crazed beast and I'd ridden it to a stop. We'd won ten dollars and managed not to get stomped, kicked or bitten. But now it was time for the bull riding and I have to admit I was worried.

The crowd was big for our kind of local, All-Indian Rodeo, maybe two hundred in the stands and fifty or sixty more hanging around the pens. And as I climbed up on the bucking chutes I saw a long, white limousine swing into the rodeo grounds and a man get out of the back seat. I was too worried to pay him or the limousine any attention even when someone started yelling that it was Elvis Presley and the small grandstands began to empty so that us bull riders were momentarily forgotten. That was fine because I figured no one was going to see me get bucked off and possibly stomped.

In an All-Indian Rodeo, I knew that everything that can go wrong, will go wrong. You can enter for five dollars an event, but there isn't any prize money, just ribbons and shiny belt buckles. I'd bucked out some rank horses, but this was the real thing and the bull I'd drawn looked bigger to me than a hay barn and acted meaner than a teased snake. He was a Brahma and Holstein cross with a humped back and eyes as cold as agates. Buzzard was his name and he had long, banana-shaped horns and his entire body was marked with scabby scars. He weighed in at close to two thousand pounds. Our Navajo stock contractor said that before Buzzard got older and a little arthritic he'd bucked off all the best rodeo cowboys. I was also told that this black bull was a devil when he got a cowboy on the ground or hung up in his bucking rigging. But now Buzzard was supposed to be as easy to ride as Grandma's rocking chair. Pa was helping me settle in and getting my gloved hand right.

"Elvis just arrived," a cowboy said. "I got to go see him."

"He probably ain't even real...just some doped-up phony," another cowboy said. "What the hell would Elvis Presley be doing here?"

"Beats me."

"Charlie," my father snapped. "Put that Elvis crap out of your mind and focus on this ride!"

"Yes sir."

"Relax in the shoulders, Son, and don't let this old bull beat you before the ride; he probably can't jump higher than a dog's back."

"I...I expect not, but he sure is big!"

"Yeah," Father agreed, "but you were lucky to draw Buzzard first because he probably won't have the strength to buck and score points for the next rider who draws his number. Just get your spurs working and score some points for the judge. When the whistle blows, come off high and smooth like I taught you."

Father finished with my hand and then pounded on my shoulder. "I'll be in the arena waitin' for ya, Cowboy Charlie."

Buzzard was as hard and still as a marble statue in the chute; he'd done this a thousand times. I could feel the sweat popping out under my shirt despite the day's rawness. My heart was beating fast and my mouth was as dry as the nearby Painted Desert. I wanted to be someplace else but knew that I had to make this ride…my first and only professional bull ride. Rodeo was still in Father's blood and he said it was also in mine, but right now my veins were running ice water. To make things worse there was trouble out in the arena. Eddie Shook was drunk again and arguing with the judges. I wished they would just whack him in the head and cart him away so I could get my ride over with.

The only person more worried than me was my Hopi grandmother. She and Father had been arguing for months about my rodeo riding and it was one of the only times I'd seen her lose.

"I'll be your coach and your banker," Father had told me a hundred times. "When I was winning big I squandered my talent and money. Now I got nothing to show but aches and pains. For you, Charlie, things will be different."

I wanted them to be *real* different. I wanted to be a writer and singer of western songs, but Father didn't think that there was any money in it except for the few and the very lucky. He told me that most musicians died young and hard like poor Hank Williams.

"You okay, Charlie?"

I twisted around to see Homer Yazzie. I liked Homer but he had a way of talking you to death or messing around with things left best alone. Like now as he reached down the chute and readjusted my bucking rope.

"I always had to redo your Pa's wrap," he rumbled. "I can't tell you how many more paydays he'd have earned if I'd have been along to help him when he was winning."

"Just wish me luck and stay back. And what's going on in the arena?"

"Aw, you know how Eddie gets. He's just drunk again and having fun."

"Man," I breathed, "he sure picked a bad time to get drunk and start arguing."

"Now remember that Buzzard tends to jump out and spin to the right three times. After that he keeps bucking straight until the whistle blows. I talked to the stock contractor who told me that Buzzard performed poorly last time out and he's afraid this bull won't even put on a show. He says that if Buzzard just trots out into the arena that he's bound for hamburger heaven, probably wind up at McDonalds."

For a moment, I almost felt sorry for my bull as I watched Eddie being

9

kicked and shoved out of the arena. Suddenly, Buzzard's ears began to twitch. He stamped his massive front hooves and wiggled his leathery hide.

Homer's eyes lit up and he whispered, "Here we go, Cowboy Charlie Coyote!"

I managed to screw my hat down tight and give a nod as the gate swung open. I caught a glimpse of Father out in the arena; he was yelling and trying to kick and shove Eddie under the arena fence. I also saw Grandmother in the stands screaming at me as Buzzard exploded out of the bucking chute. I tried to remember what Homer had said about two...or was it three spins to the right? Suddenly, Buzzard was really bucking and slinging his head so hard that I was immediately blinded by a long, sticky stream of green slobber...or at least I hoped it was slobber and not shit. I felt my testicles being crushed like grapes and I bellowed in pain as my body seemed to be yanked apart. My arm felt torn out of my shoulder and I saw my hand still caught under the rope. I forgot about trying to keep one arm up and tried to release my hand, but it was no use as I was hurled toward the ground then yanked up short and sent jerking and flopping alongside the huge bull. Buzzard's horns found my head and my ribs and I was sure I was about to die.

From a great distance I heard people yelling at me to get loose, or tear free or some other such nonsense. I had no greater wish in my life than to be free, but I was helpless. Then Father was beside me, clawing at my gloved hand and trying to rip me free. I can still see that monster bull bawling and slinging snot a moment before I was hurled to the ground.

Father jumped between me and Buzzard and when he screamed it was like nothin' I've ever heard from any human. I saw him lifted high in the air with a horn jutting out of his back and I swear that Grandmother howled in horror. When Father hit the ground I crawled to his side.

His hand clamped on my wrist and I felt all of his fading life-force flowing into my body as he whispered, "Charlie, be...Hopi but also *Navajo!* Learn about those peoples *then* decide. Stella, too," he added as his hand loosened its death grip on my wrist.

Blood pumped from his mouth like water from a deep well and then I heard the death rattle in his throat and saw his body go still.

I looked up and saw Buzzard charging us with his bloody horns sweeping just over the dirt and I tensed expecting to die. Only later did I learn that none other than Elvis Presley and Homer Yazzie had saved my life by jumping in front of Buzzard and distracting that bull.

Only right then I didn't know it was Elvis. I thought he was just another rodeo Indian with long, black hair. I was crying for Father while Grandmother was singing Hopi prayers and sprinkling pollen on me with sacred stone-ground corn. I floated in a fiery red sea, then sank and didn't wake up until I was in the back of Elvis' Cadillac limousine.

"Clear the arena!" the announcer kept yelling.

I didn't know then that Elvis had been on his way to Hollywood by car rather than by his jet airplane because of bad weather and a recent scare. He'd had trouble breathing and had to direct his pilot to make an emergency landing in Dallas. He'd seen the highway sign pointing to our rodeo and stopped because he had a little Cherokee blood and was curious about the spirituality of most Indians. All I knew was that we fish-tailed it out of the arena headed for the hospital way off in Flagstaff. As the powerful Cadillac kept gathering speed, Elvis kept shouting over the seat, "Hang on Cowboy Charlie Coyote... hang on!"

Then Elvis began to sing so softly that I could hear his famous voice over Grandmother's Hopi death chants and the whine of the new Cadillac's tires on Route 66. It was probably ten miles down the road that I realized Elvis was singing, *There will be peace in the valley....somedayyy.*

# Chapter 2

"Charlie!"

I heard Stella calling my name over and over and it seemed to be coming from a long, long ways off.

"Charlie, can you hear me?"

"Yeah."

I didn't want to open my eyes because the last vision I had was of Father hanging on Buzzard's horns. But then I heard Grandmother talking and that lifted me back to the happy times. I never learned to speak much Hopi but I'd heard plenty of coyote stories that amused and entertained me all during my childhood and since my white mother had disappeared without a trace, those stories were our only spiritual connection.

"Charlie, wake up!" Grandmother whispered in my ear. "Come back to us from the other world."

I saw my sister and her eyelashes glistened in the bright overhead hospital lights. Grandmother, however, was as calm as a sunny summer morning.

"Charlie, do you remember what happened?" Stella asked.

"Buzzard killed Pa instead of me."

"That's right. He died saving your life. It's what he wanted to do."

"I know."

"It wasn't your fault." Stella's voice cracked and it took her several moments to continue. "Homer Yazzie is telling everyone that he is responsible because he wrapped your hand too tightly."

"That's not true! It was nobody's fault but my own. I wasn't good enough to ride Buzzard and that's what got Father killed."

Grandma wagged her head back and forth making her turquoise necklace rattle like dice. "Your father is not dead. His spirit will always be with us."

Her black eyes rolled up toward the ceiling fan and we all stared at it spinning round and round. I could feel its gentle breeze on my face and hear its soft hum. *Maybe,* I thought, *Father is in that fan's wind speaking to me right now.*

"How long have I been in here?"

"Five days." Stella glanced at Grandmother. "You had better tell him."

"Tell me what?" I asked.

Grandmother took my hand in her own brown, leathery one and choked, "We buried your father on our Coyote Ranch."

"That means we'll probably lose it to the bank."

"Father had some money stashed away," Stella told me. "Five thousand dollars."

"This is not the time to speak of money," Grandmother said.

Stella continued. "The rodeo crowd took up a collection. They filled two cowboy hats with cash and turquoise and silver jewelry. Mickey Blue even gave us a horse to sell that ought to bring at least a hundred dollars."

"Tell me it's not that old roan gelding with the white eyes."

"That's the one."

"We'll be lucky to get thirty dollars for that crow-bait," I said, "but it was nice of Mickey anyway."

"No more money talk!" Grandmother snapped. "Now we speak of what the doctor said about your head."

I tried to reach up and examine my head, but my right arm had a needle in it and my left felt too heavy to lift. "What's wrong, Grandmother?"

"The surgeon had to screw a little piece of tin against your skull to protect your brain."

My eyes must have bugged because Stella blurted, "It's not tin! It's a nice, shiny stainless steel plate they used to cover the drill hole they made to relieve pressure on your brain. They say that your skin and hair will probably grow back over the plate so that nobody will even know you have it."

"'Probably'!" I cried, appalled by the image. "So if I don't wear a hat I'll send flashing signals to the sun! Like kids using mirrors to send messages on the Hopi mesas?"

"Hush now," Grandmother gently instructed. "Your hair will grow back fast, but the surgeon said you should never ride horses or bulls again."

"I don't care about the bulls but I won't stop riding our horses. I'm a working cowboy and we have a cattle ranch. We have calves to rope and brand next spring and the only way to do that is atop a horse."

"Charlie," Grandma said, "don't worry so much about the doctor's instructions. "You can ride well-broken horses, but no more rodeo bulls."

I had already decided that I wouldn't ride the bulls again. "Fair enough," I gladly agreed. I turned to my sister. "I didn't mean to shout at you but I have to work horseback or we'll lose our ranch sure as sundown."

"Father's money will carry us the better part of a year. And the donations will help. I'll look for a town job to bring in extra money."

I bit back a quick objection. Over the years Father had sometimes been forced to take outside work in order to keep Coyote Ranch afloat. He'd clerked in a hardware store and later loaded trucks at a feed store owned by Mr. Jenkins over in Holbrook. But he'd always quit the minute he figured he had a nest-egg which he hid in a bean can in our back yard. For the Coyote family, a "town job" was something only to be taken when things were desperate…like when cattle prices were rock-bottom or feed costs or death losses wiped out our profits. Father had always encouraged me to work summers at other ranches because he thought I'd learn things that he didn't know and we needed the extra cash. But a permanent town job had never been a part of our thinking.

"Stella," I told her, "you're going to be needed at home for awhile."

My sister changed the subject. "Do you even remember the handsome man who showed up in the rodeo arena then rushed us in his big, shiny car to this hospital?"

"Naw, not really." I knew that she wanted to tell me it was Elvis Presley so I played dumb.

Stella smiled that big smile that drove cowboys wild. "You won't believe this."

"Try me."

"It was Elvis Presley."

"No!"

"Grandmother, tell him it was Elvis Presley and that I wasn't dreaming."

"It was him alright. I saw his picture once."

"What would a famous man be doing at our rodeo?"

"I know it's hard to believe," Stella said, the words tumbling from her lips. "But Elvis was on his way to Hollywood when he saw the roadside sign saying that we were having our rodeo so he decided to stop and watch. And then he saw you and Father get gored so he offered his limousine to take you all the way here to this big hospital in Flagstaff. He said his Cadillac could go 120 miles an hour…so of course we took up the offer. And Elvis felt so bad about Father dying bravely and you having surgery that he promised to keep in touch. And he really meant it!"

"How do you know?"

"Because he called this hospital just yesterday to check up on you."

None of this made a lick of sense to me. I was starting to wonder if Stella had been the one that had had her skull operated on, but I just said, "Why would a man like that care about me?"

"Because he is kind and has Indian blood in him. Elvis said that his mother's great-great-grandmother was a full-blooded Cherokee so that's why he cares."

It was my experience that almost every white man I'd ever known had taken up the now popular idea that they were part Indian. Maybe white men had stopped watching Indians doing all those awful things in the Hollywood movies. I didn't know and didn't much care, but if Elvis being part Cherokee was going to help us keep Coyote Ranch then what was the harm?

"Isn't that wonderful how Elvis is one of us!" Stella gushed.

I couldn't completely share her enthusiasm because I'd never known any white people who were concerned about Indians. "What I know for sure is that Father is dead, our ranch is mortgaged and I've got the lid of a tin can screwed into my skull. How much is this hospital stuff going to cost?"

Both women took a deep breath and then Grandmother said, "Charlie feels awful, but he's right. We can't depend on anybody but ourselves." She got up to leave. "Charlie needs rest so we have to go now."

Stella kissed my cheek and headed out the door.

"Grandma," I called, "was it *really* Elvis Presley and not just some imposter? There are probably a lot of 'em that pretend to be him growing long sideburns and wearing fancy clothes and driving big cars."

Grandmother wasn't a big woman, barely five feet tall but she had a presence that made you believe what she had to say. "What matters now is that you get strong and don't ever ride bulls again."

"For sure I won't," I vowed as tears filled my eyes. "I just still can't believe that Father is *dead.*"

"Only his body is dead. Not his spirit which never dies."

Then Grandmother was gone.

I was in that Flagstaff hospital almost three weeks during my slow recovery. Most mornings Dr. Hodges would remove my head bandages and ask me questions just to make sure that my brain was still working. He would say things like, "Cowboy Charlie, how many fingers am I holding up? Or, count backwards from fifty, very quickly."

I didn't mind because the cloudiness in my head had been slowly clearing. What really concerned me was how we were going to pay our medical bills when Elvis lost interest in us. I didn't want Grandmother to worry about it but Stella was another matter and although I didn't push her for answers I could see that she was losing weight. I knew that both she and Grandmother were working much too hard trying to do their own chores in addition to the ones that Father and I normally took care of. I wanted to get out of the hospital and back to work, but the doctors wouldn't allow it. I started wondering if they made more money the longer I stayed. I sure hoped that wasn't the case…but

I didn't trust white people all that much.

One afternoon, the head nurse announced, "Cowboy Charlie, you have a very special phone call." There wasn't a phone in my room so they had to help me down the hallway to the visitor's lounge. I noticed that all the nurses were staring at me. I picked up the phone and said, "This is Charlie Coyote."

"Charlie, it's Elvis Presley. How are you feeling?"

"Well…better every day, Mr. Presley."

In the back of my mind I was sure it was a spoof being played by one of my friends calling from Winslow. They had a wicked sense of humor and probably figured it was time to pull one over on me…to make me laugh again. And so, amused and deciding to play along with them, I replied, "Fine! And how are you hangin' today?"

Wild laughter.

"Glad to hear that you've kept your sense of humor, Cowboy Charlie Coyote. I'm fine. The weather hardly ever changes here in Las Vegas. My big album recently recorded live at Madison Square Garden is off the charts and I also just recorded *Burning Love* which is going right to the top. Best song I've had in years. I'll be coming back through Flagstaff. Will you still be in the hospital?"

"I don't know."

"Can't you ask someone?"

I shouted down the hallway to the nurse's station. "Mrs. Hudson, Elvis Presley wants to know when I'm getting out of here."

"Tell Mr. Presley that you are ready to leave as soon as you sign your payment and discharge papers."

Her reply nearly floored me because I could not have imagined how one of my friends had gotten the nurses to go along with this silly game. But they obviously had so I took a deep breath. "Mr. Presley, the nurses say I can leave when you arrive."

"Oh, that's great! I'll be by to pick you up and I'm sure sorry to hear that your father passed. I've never seen anyone braver. You ought to be real proud of him."

This wasn't sounding at all like a joke anymore. I suddenly realized it really was Elvis.

"Hello, Charlie."

He was wearing blue suede shoes, a pink shirt, black pants and enough gold to fill Fort Knox. But there was something about him that shocked me and I quickly realized it was the puffiness in his face and his sallow complexion.

Elvis just didn't look healthy, but I figured it was because he was exhausted from all the recording sessions.

"The hospital administrator says you're cleared to go," Elvis told me. "My limousine is waiting outside. Let's get out of here. Hospitals give me the spooks."

"Where are we going?"

"I promised your grandmother and sister that I'd deliver you home today. I'll wait out in the lounge until you get dressed. They got a television there."

"Yes, sir."

*"Elvis,"* he gently corrected before he disappeared.

The moment Elvis was out of sight I slammed the door and got dressed fast then ran my fingers through my black hair, stuffed my toiletries in a bag and reached for my coat.

"Goodbye, Cowboy Charlie," a nurse said as I burst out of my room. "Stay away from those rodeo bulls!"

"I sure will," I yelled over my shoulder.

When I got to the lounge, my surgeon and an important looking fella in a suit were talking to Elvis. The man spotted me and said, "My name is Fred Peterson and I'm the hospital administrator. How are you feeling, Mr. Coyote?"

"Just fine, Sir."

There was a mob waiting for Elvis in the lobby, but we pushed through with the help of the hospital staff. Next thing I knew we were in the back seat of the limo and squealing out of the parking lot.

"Charlie," Elvis said, "this is my friend and driver, Mark Lane."

Mark was a powerful and handsome man with broad shoulders. He smiled in his rear view mirror and said, "Nice to finally meet you, Charlie, and I'm sorry about your father. I lost my own a few years back so I know how bad it feels."

"Thanks."

Elvis expelled a deep breath and turned on some hillbilly music as we sped down Route 66 toward Coyote Ranch. I watched the sagebrush swim past in a blur and when I thought about what had happened to me and Father and what was happening now, I wondered if anything was real. One thing I did know for sure was that my life had changed because of Elvis Presley and it would never be the same again.

# *Chapter 3*

"So how far is it to your ranch?" Elvis asked.

"It's a ways."

"I talked to Stella and she said exactly the same thing." Elvis grinned. "So what is 'a ways'?"

I hesitated, even though I knew exactly how many miles. The trouble was that I wasn't sure that Elvis or Mark would be willing to drive over washboard dirt roads to my home after leaving Route 66.

But I couldn't avoid the question so I said, "Maybe two hours away."

"How's the road?"

There was no avoiding the truth. If they started down the dusty road, they'd soon discover that it was awful. "It's potholed in some places, rocky in others. We have a few dry washes to cross."

"We can do that," Mark said matter-of-factly although I couldn't imagine that this car had ever been off the pavement. "No problem."

"I hope not," I said, deciding to be honest about my reservations. "But if this long car goes down into a steep wash, we could bottom out and be stuck. We use pickup trucks in this country."

"We'll be fine," Mark promised.

Elvis nodded, not looking a bit worried. "Just tell Mark when we get near your turnoff."

We traveled east a good long while before I directed Mark where to turn. We hit the washboard and started bouncing so hard that we had to slow down. Elvis didn't seem to notice the jostling.

"What happened to your mother, Charlie?"

"She disappeared not too long after I was born."

"You mean like she just vanished?"

"That's right." I really didn't want to talk about it and neither my father or grandmother had ever wanted to talk about it either. Something bad had happened and I think everyone thought the subject was best avoided. But it had always troubled me and I knew the mystery of our mother bothered Stella even more.

"I loved my mother, but she passed on when I was in the army. Mother always knew that she'd die at the age of only forty-two. I was drafted or I'd never have left her in such poor health."

"I heard about you being in the army. Was it bad?"

"No. I made sergeant and the guys treated me just like everyone else. Not a bad life. I'm proud to be a veteran and to have served my country. I met Priscilla in Germany. We were married in 1967 and had our only child, Lisa Marie, the next year. I love 'em both…but it didn't work out. My wife and I were separated not long ago. She fell in love with her damned karate instructor."

"Once I saw a picture of you and your wife. She's beautiful."

"Yes, but we don't see each other much anymore." Elvis shook his head and suddenly looked real sad. "Anyway, do you miss your mother?"

"I probably would if I'd ever known her."

"Yeah, that makes sense. But I'm sure you miss your dad."

I couldn't answer because a painful knot suddenly filled my throat.

"My dad is still alive and we get along a lot better than we used to. I take care of Vernon and he looks after a lot of my business."

"That's good."

I suddenly was remembering all the times my Father had yanked me out of bad scrapes. I couldn't imagine how I'd manage without his steady hand and knowledge of day-to-day ranching.

"I had an older brother," Elvis said in a voice I could barely hear over the gravel pounding the undersides of the Cadillac. "He died stillborn just before I was…born. His name is Jesse Garon and we are identical twins. I still think of him often, mostly in the hours before dawn when I can't seem to sleep."

Elvis shook his head as if trying to dispel something that was haunting him. "Charlie, don't be spooked when I tell you that I can remember lying safe in my mother's womb before Jesse and I were born. My twin brother and I were closer than anything and we still are."

I had never heard anyone talk like that and could not think of a single thing to say.

"And I often dream of Jesse and me doing things together."

I swallowed hard and managed to ask, "What kind of things?"

"Oh, nothing special. Sometimes I dream that we're just a couple of dirt-poor kids playing in Tupelo, Mississippi where we were born in a little shotgun shack my father built. Once in a while I dream about us performing together on stage. We'd really have been something because he had a voice as good as mine, but he wasn't much of a musician."

I snuck a sideways glance at Elvis because his strange talk was starting to make me feel uneasy. I'd never heard of anyone talking like that and frankly, it made the hair on the back of my neck rise.

"You probably won't believe this…nobody else does either, but Jesse and I are closer than living brothers. I just can't understand why I was the one that was chosen to live and he was the one that was stillborn. I became rich and famous, but poor Jesse never had his fair chance."

Elvis swallowed hard and took a deep breath. "Sometimes I honestly wish that it had been Jesse who had lived instead of me."

"Why?"

"'Cause," Elvis answered, his voice cracking, "I'm convinced that Jesse would have become a famous gospel singer. He'd be saving souls while most Christian folks believe I'm leading the young astray with my rock and roll music and gyrations."

"That's not true."

"Why, it is, sometimes."

I had to turn away because Elvis' expression was tragic. He asked Mark to find some gospel music on the radio. After I listened to that a while, I had to say that I was not too impressed with all the screaming and carrying on.

"You don't like that music, do you, Charlie?"

"No sir, I guess I like country-western and rock'n roll a whole lot better."

"Gospel music is Negro music from the heart of Dixie. It's the kind of music that I grew up hearing and singing."

"You grew up with Negros?"

"That's right. They're very spiritual…just like Indians. They got rhythm in their bones and music runs way down deep in their souls. Many of them are my friends."

We listened to his gospel music until the radio's reception faded and then Elvis sang "Amazing Grace" and suddenly, everything that had happened at the rodeo came rushing right back to me. I saw my father as plainly as if he were with us now. The memory of his death and the gospel music nearly brought me to tears. And when Elvis was finished singing he looked at me with a sorrowful smile. "Just remember, Charlie, your father, like my mother, will always be walking at our side. Jesus loves us and so do they…always and forever."

"I'm sure that is true."

And so while we sat side by side I gazed out the smoky glassed window at the high desert country of my birth. I thought about Father and all the fence posts along the road reminded me of him and how we'd fought to put every one of them deep and solid in the ground before we'd strung the barbed wire. On a bitterly cold winter morning when I was about eight, I'd ripped open my forearm on the wire and the blood had ran down from under the old Levis' coat across my hand. My father had told me then that the freezing weather would make the wound heal clean and fast...and it did.

In our biggest section I'd watched my Navajo father ride a handsome young sorrel gelding with his long, black hair tied back in a ponytail that stuck out from under the brim of his hat. Even then it struck me that he rode like a man that was born to the saddle and was always in perfect union with his horse. And over by the dry wash under a pinyon pine I'd watched him struggle to pull a dead calf from its mother's womb and then he said a little prayer for the calf's spirit and petted the young cow until it closed its eyes to sleep and die.

The nearness of Coyote Ranch brought back emotions in me so strong that I struggled to breathe. Finally I said, "It won't be long now."

But I had forgotten to tell Mark about the steep wash just up ahead and the limousine bottomed out with a terrible noise from underneath. Mark slammed on the brakes and put the Cadillac into neutral. And there we sat with the limousine's muffler rattling like the exhaust pipe on an old John Deere tractor. Mark twisted around looking upset. "Elvis, I'm sure sorry. I didn't see that one coming. And now we've torn off the muffler."

"It doesn't matter," Elvis told him not looking a bit upset. "I'm far more interested in this country than our car. So ease 'er out of here and let's keep going."

Mark put the Cadillac back in gear and we eased out of the wash, muffler dragging and roaring so loud that even inside the limousine the sound was like standing next to a passing locomotive.

"It was my fault," I offered. "I should have warned Mark. The truth is that this country is awful hard on mufflers. The shops in Winslow and Holbrook do a big business in tires and mufflers."

"Charlie," Elvis said, "is this country any good at all for raising corn or tobacco?"

Given what had just happened, his question momentarily caught me off guard. "Nope," I answered, "we grow alfalfa, some Hopi corn and a few other crops but mostly it's too dry and the growing season is too short for productive farming. That's why we're all ranchers. Sheep and cattle...but if there were a market for rattlesnakes, we could do a sight better."

It was a joke that was often told and usually got a laugh, but Elvis seemed to be too lost in his thoughts to notice. "That's too bad, though it's what I'd suspected. But there are a lot of starving people in this world and this is big country. You could feed half of China off this much Tennessee farmland."

"I expect so," I said.

"Back down in the South, all this would be cut up into little fields and it would be farmed. We don't let good earth go fallow back where I come from. It's planted in cotton, corn and tobacco…whatever will make a cash crop. Charlie, have you ever visited Tennessee?"

"I've never even been out of Arizona."

Mark turned back to look at us. "Elvis, should we go on? The road is getting even rougher. I hate to tear this limousine up."

"What else is there to do?" Elvis turned his attention back to me. "Would you like to travel and maybe move someplace else?"

"Nope," I answered without even hesitating. "I've seen the Grand Canyon and the Petrified Forest and I can't imagine anything being handsomer. And lots of people come from hundreds of miles to see that big meteor crater we passed awhile back. Why, I've found arrowheads and fossils and there are drawings on the rocks from some of Grandmother's people and only God knows how old they are. Those rocks tell stories…but even Grandmother says that no one knows exactly what the stories are about."

"That's probably for the best," Elvis said. "That way you can look at them and everyone gets to make up their own stories off of the rock drawings."

"I never thought of it that way, but you're right."

"Do you think that it was the ancestors of the Navajo or the Hopi?"

"Probably both. I know both claim 'em all."

"What are the differences between the Hopi and the Navajo?" Elvis asked. "Somebody told me that they were old enemies. Is that true?"

"We were once, but not anymore. In fact our tribes are even starting to intermarry but our customs and lifestyles are completely different."

I could tell that Elvis was genuinely interested, but the truth was that I didn't feel qualified to answer his questions. And, I remembered my father's plea to learn more about the Hopi and the Navajo. The memory of his dying request was still much too painful so I stammered, "You need to talk to my grandmother about those things because I don't know all that much about it."

He laughed. "When I was your age all I could think about was music and girls."

"I think about girls a lot," I confessed. "But also about horses and ranch work."

"Are you a real good cowboy?"

"I'm learning all the time to be a better one, but most people think I'm handy, especially with breaking horses."

Elvis was silent for a moment. "Cowboy Charlie, I expect there will come a time when you become more interested in your Indian blood lines. I've done some research on my Cherokee blood and those were a prosperous, well-educated people until they were driven off their lands and exiled to reservations. Some were never caught, but most lost everything. They even had their own alphabet and I'm proud to have them in my family on my mother's side."

I wanted to tell Elvis about what little I knew about my parents and how I'd been told that their marriage had caused a big fight and then banishment by the Hopi. I wanted to tell him how Grandmother cried when she gazed off toward the Hopi Mesas with eyes far too old and weak to see that far. But I couldn't find the proper words. Besides, what would Elvis think of my family if he knew that we had been forever cast out by those spiritual people for reasons that had never been thoroughly explained…and that my mother was like a ghost in my mind? Also, I had been taught by Father that some things were far better kept as secrets. So, instead of saying any of those important things I changed the subject.

"Elvis, one of the main differences between the Hopi and the Navajo is that Navajo are livestock tenders while the Hopi are corn farmers. You rarely find a Hopi family that doesn't plant a couple of acres of corn or a Navajo family that doesn't have a few sheep, goats, cattle and horses."

"I love to ride horses," Elvis said. "I once played a half breed in a movie called *Charro* and I did all my own horseback riding. I was killed in the end, but the Hollywood people said that was one of my better roles which isn't saying much."

"I didn't see that one."

"Aw," Elvis said, quietly, "you aren't missing all that much. I quit making films a few years ago. I did more than thirty and never got any good scripts; most of the songs I had to sing in 'em were stupid."

"Then why'd you do so many?"

"I made a million dollars a movie!" Elvis laughed. "I guess that was reason enough, huh?"

I couldn't even wrap my mind around that much money. "I'd say so."

Elvis suddenly spotted one of our big, horned cows and got excited. "Who owns that wild red and black cow?"

"Uh…we do."

"Mark, stop this car and shut off the engine!"

The limousine skidded to a stop and Elvis jumped out and marched toward the surprised cow that stared at him and then snorted warily.

"Elvis," I called, climbing out but staying back. "Some of these old cows can be ornery and…."

But just as I was saying that, the old girl lifted her tail, farted and then trotted off with her eyeballs rolling around in her head.

Elvis began to laugh and when he finally was able to speak, he said, "Charlie, it's just good to finally see a female who has the sense to run away from me!"

We watched as the cow stopped about fifty feet away and turned to stare at us suspiciously. She was a cross between a Hereford and a probably a Mexican cow of undetermined background and maybe her lineage was royal enough even to go back to the bull rings in Spain. I didn't think she'd charge us or the limousine, but some of these wild old girls got a little crazy out on this tough rangeland.

"Charlie, have you ever roped and branded that one?"

"Sure have. That CR brand stands for Coyote Ranch." I couldn't conceal my pride.

"How many acres does your family own?"

"We have title to about three thousand and we have another two thousand with a Bureau of Land Management grazing permit. Most Arizona ranchers lease more public grazing land than they own."

"I see." Elvis pivoted completely around. He looked up at our buttery blue sky and took in a deep breath of sage. "You really feel like you've stepped back a couple hundred years out here by yourself. I can't hear the highway and there's not even a vapor trail in the sky. And everything is so quiet!"

"Except for your limo," I said.

My Coyote family lived about ten miles off Route 66 and surrounded by the only world I ever knew or loved. It was a land bursting with grama and bunch grass, twisted scrub pine, sage, red rocks and a forever blue sky. It was the land where my father now lay buried. It was also the land where Grandmother and I would lie and maybe Stella, too. I loved this land and when I closed my eyes I thought of how it should never change.

I stammered, trying to put those thoughts into words but Elvis put his little finger to his lips and whispered, "Shhh, listen to that silence."

Mark and I knew enough to keep still while Elvis savored the quiet. He wore a peaceful expression I hadn't seen until then.

"Ahh," he finally sighed. "We'd better get moving. It'll soon be sundown. How much farther, Charlie?"

"A couple of miles."

Both Elvis and Mark shook their heads and the driver said, "Boy, you Coyotes sure live out in Nowhereville."

I thought that was kind of funny, but said, "For me, it's the only way to live."

Mark dropped down on the dirt road and rolled onto his back. I thought it a shame that he'd get his suit dirty, but that was none of my business. When he'd looked around under the big car, he stood up and said, "I'm afraid the muffler is torn almost completely off and is dragging."

To my surprise, Elvis just shrugged. "Don't worry about it. There's no one out here to complain about our noise. Isn't that right, Charlie?"

"Yep."

When Mark gunned the engine and the limousine rocketed forward, Elvis laughed and called, "Sounds just like an Army tank I drove in Germany. Stomp 'er and make this big sucker fly!"

We accelerated, gravel striking the underbelly like machine gun bullets. I sure didn't approve or see the big hurry. We could tear out the transmission but I decided to keep my mouth shut as we careened down the rutted, gravelly road chased by a towering rooster tail of dust.

# Chapter 4

I was nervous about what Elvis would say when he saw our house because it was beyond humble. A lot of people might even call it a shack. But we had all lived in it quite a few years and called it home. Father had built it as a one-room cabin several years before Stella was born. My parents had moved here with nothing more than an old truck and stock trailer, six head of cattle, two horses and big dreams. Over the years Father had added on a kitchen and then boxed in our bedrooms. We got our water from a spring that flowed only a hundred feet north of our cabin. Eventually, we dug a well, added a pump and put in some plumbing so in the winter we could use the indoor facilities. But in the good weather, we still used the old one-seater outhouse. Pa said that there was no sense in using a septic when you could use a hole in the ground. Grandmother thought differently, and had no intention of bothering herself with the flies, spiders and smell. We still heated our water on a wood-burning stove.

There were three small bedrooms now, one for Grandma one for Stella and of course the third one was for Father. I slept in the attic loft and didn't mind that at all. The heat off the stove settled in among the rafters and I was warmer in the winter than any of them down below, but it was hotter than hell in the summer and so I usually slept on the front porch. My loft was about ten by sixteen feet and I had it fixed up with cowhide rugs on the floor and rodeo posters nailed to the walls between the places where I hung my jeans, shirts and coats. Father had always liked to keep his door open at night except on the coldest winter nights, but Grandma and Stella kept theirs shut because of Father's snoring. Since my loft was right over his bedroom, it could get pretty loud at night, but I was a good sleeper after working outdoors all day. Now, I was thinking how much I'd miss Father's snoring and how I had come to think of it as part of the night.

"Our place is just over the next hill," I shouted over the limousine's rattling thunder. "But our house sure isn't very impressive."

Elvis smiled. "Neither was the one in Tupelo, Mississippi where I was born. My daddy built a two-room shotgun shack way back in 1934. It wasn't much bigger inside than this Cadillac, but it was ours free and clear."

I was relieved to hear that Elvis came from a poor beginning. "We have some good outbuildings and cottonwoods planted long ago around the yard give us shade and protection from the wind."

"I like trees," Mark said. "They add a lot to a place; especially one as bleak as this."

"Sure do," Elvis agreed.

We shot over the crest of a hill and down into a valley which was maybe two hundred acres of pasture grass surrounded by red rocks and pinyons. A few of our cattle were grazing and I had to admit that under the clear turquoise colored sky it made for a fine picture.

"You own all of this?" Mark asked.

"Yes we do," I told him. "And we've got an option to buy more land to the south…a lot more, in fact."

"You ought to do it," Elvis said.

We passed horse corrals and then our corrals and workshop where Father had spent a lot of his time working on tractors, trucks and machinery. He'd even taught me how to weld and overhaul a gas engine, but I didn't care for the work. Father always reminded me that ranching was more about fixing broken machinery than riding tall in the saddle. I'd seen enough broken machinery littering ranches to know that he was right. Most of us small cattle and sheep ranchers were too far from town to haul in every piece of busted equipment and good farm and ranch mechanics were rare and high-priced. So, if you were handy with tools and could weld, you could get by on the cheap. That's what us Coyotes had been doing as long as I could remember.

Because of the missing muffler, we burst into the ranch yard sounding like a string of firecrackers going off along with some big-bore rifles. Chickens scattered, most flying straight up into the cottonwood trees and our spooked horses almost busted down the corral. The moment we rattled to a stop, Grandmother and Stella appeared on the porch where we spent most of our free time in good weather.

The engine died. I jumped out into a dust cloud and the silence would have been impressive if not for the chickens giving us hell from on high.

"Not exactly blue Hawaii, huh?" Mark said, grinning at his boss.

"It looks just fine to me," Elvis replied, opening the door just as Rip, my dog, came to give us his usual smell-over.

"Dog, get out of here!"

"Aw, he's fine," Elvis said, laying a hand on Rip's handsome head. "He's just happy to see you."

"Welcome home, little brother."

I had to admit that Stella was looking unusually fine. She was wearing her usual tight Levi's and she'd polished her boots and tied her long black hair back with a colorful scarf and even put on lipstick...which I thought was going a little overboard for my homecoming.

"Nice to be home," I told her, meaning it from the bottom of my heart.

Stella detoured around me and then gave Elvis a big hug and then a wet kiss on the cheek. "Mr. Presley, we'll never be able to repay you for taking care of Charlie's hospital bills. We can't thank you enough."

"It was my pleasure," Elvis said, trying to disengage. "How you doin', Miss Lucy?"

Grandma stepped forward and shook his hand. "You are a very generous man."

"Why thank you." Looking embarrassed, Elvis quickly changed the subject. "This valley and your ranchland are even prettier than I'd imagined."

"Would you like me to show you around?" Stella gushed.

I thought my sister was being pushy so I snapped, "What is there for Elvis to see that he can't see from right here in the yard?"

Stella's face darkened with anger but before she could speak, Elvis said, "I'd enjoy a ranch tour."

My sister nearly swooned.

"If you want, we could even saddle a couple of horses and go for a ride."

I couldn't believe my ears. Stella was embarrassing me by making a complete fool of herself. So I tried to rescue her dignity by saying, "I'm sure that Elvis would rather sit on the porch and have a glass of lemonade."

"I'm tired of sitting. I'd enjoy a horseback ride while there is still daylight."

"Then you shall have it!" Stella cried like a fawning schoolgirl. She snatched Elvis by the hand and nearly jerked him off his feet.

"Maybe you'd like to ride along with them?" Grandmother suggested to Mark.

"No, Ma'am. I'd as soon sit in one of those rocking chairs up on your porch and enjoy a glass of your lemonade."

Grandmother looked at me. "Charlie," she said, cocking her little head one way and then the other like a cactus wren, "you look a little peaked to me. I'm going to fatten you up starting tonight with chili and cornbread."

"Good." I was eager to have something spicy after all that bland, tasteless food I'd choked down at the hospital.

I spotted some fresh stacks of hay. "How'd we get that last cutting of hay?"

Grandmother looked pleased. "Our neighbors came in when we were off visiting you at the hospital. They cut, raked, baled and stacked it in just three days. I know who did it and I'll be sending them something nice in appreciation."

"I didn't know that Elvis paid my hospital bills."

"Do you think they'd have set you free without paying?"

None of us had ever been in a hospital before so I shrugged and said, "Maybe not." I turned to Mark. "Does Elvis do this sort of thing often?"

"All the time," the driver said with a grin. "He constantly talks about what it was like being dirt poor. He'll also be paying for your medical follow-ups and tests."

"Does Elvis know how much that might cost?" I had to ask.

"He doesn't know…or care. He'll just have all your bills sent to Memphis for his accountants to pay. He won't even think about it and neither should you."

I couldn't comprehend anyone not worrying about their bills. All my life I'd heard lessons preached about being thrifty and how to save your pennies, nickels and dimes. And there were still plenty of times when we had less than twenty dollars in our cookie jar so Elvis' lack of concern about money was a major puzzlement even though I knew he was very rich. I guess when you had that much money it was like having a whole boxcar of Butterfinger candy bars and by that I mean that a person could only enjoy so many in a lifetime.

I used my cane to hobble up on the porch and collapse in a rocking chair. Mark sat down too as Grandmother Lucy went inside to get us some lemonade. When she returned with full glasses the chauffeur gazed around and shook his head.

"What?" I asked.

"I just never thought I'd be bringing my boss to a place like this, Cowboy Charlie. Not that there's anything wrong with it, mind you. But it's so far out in the boonies."

Grandmother sat our glasses of lemonade down. "What are the 'boonies'?"

"It means the sticks…a way out place like this ranch."

The man seemed restless and wearing that uniform made him appear odd out here and uncomfortable outside his dust-covered Cadillac.

"We like it just fine," Grandmother said, a little testiness in her voice.

"Don't get me wrong," Mark said quickly. "I admire you for having so much land. Hollywood is a place of fantasy and flakes and Memphis isn't much better. Elvis is mobbed by fans day and night and there's always someone with their hands out for a favor or money. Did you know that he often uses a double to fool the screamers and autograph seekers? Even that usually fails. His fans are sharp."

I wasn't sure that I understood. "Mark, are you saying that you use someone that *looks* and *sounds* like Elvis to trick folks?"

"That's right...only up close you can always tell it isn't him. Nobody is as handsome and there's that voice that's impossible to imitate. People mob Elvis wherever he goes. He's a prisoner in his own Graceland Mansion and he has to sneak out just to get into some country and to see everyday sights."

"But...but he's out in public now," I argued.

Mark laughed outright and made a sweeping gesture with his hand. "Charlie, do you call *this* being in public!"

"No," I conceded, "I guess not."

"Look, I don't want you folks to misunderstand. I'm happy to be here and so is Elvis. And, if I can be completely honest, this place would be his salvation."

"What's that mean?" I asked.

"It means this fresh air would do wonders for Elvis' health and state of mind."

"His health seems okay to me," Grandmother offered.

"Oh, but I wish that were true. You see, Elvis is a walking pharmacy. He can't sleep then he can't wake up because he takes so many pills. I've been his driver for years now and he feels worse and worse as time goes by. But no one can tell him so."

Mark lowered his voice and his expression grew serious. "And you must promise not to repeat what I've just told you. The truth is, I'm really worried about the man and it has nothing to do with the fact that he pays me so well. I'd be happy to lose my job if Elvis changed directions and found a way back to good health."

"I promise I won't say a word."

"Did you notice that his fingers tremble just slightly?"

"Come to think of it," Grandmother said, "I did. I thought maybe he was just drinking too much coffee and was nervous."

"He ain't naturally a bit nervous," Mark said. "But I can see Elvis changing month to month and not for the better. It's a crying shame."

"With all of his money, why doesn't Elvis take a real vacation out West?" I asked.

"I used to ask that very same question, Charlie. But the more that I've been around him the more I realize that Elvis loves to be the center of attention and having his friends around at all hours of the day and night. Most of them are good, but there are some that are just pure blood-suckers who want to party and sponge off his generosity."

I nodded, trying to form a picture of Elvis' day-to-day existence and it was not one I liked. "What's Elvis do in the daytime when he's not recording songs?"

"He's a night owl who normally sleeps most of the day. That's one of the reasons why Elvis quit making movies. He did thirty or thirty-one in the sixties and almost ruined his voice, his health and what should have been a good marriage to a fine lady."

Mark steepled his fingers and rested his chin on them as he watched a raven wheel around in the sky with its mate. They flew in perfect unison, dipping and soaring and playing. We all watched the ravens until they disappeared.

"Yep," Mark said, "if Elvis would stay in a place as peaceful as your Coyote Ranch it would do him a world of good."

"Well," Grandmother said, "we have an extra bed now that my son...is gone."

"That's right," I added. "I know my father would have been proud to have Elvis stay and rest with us. But if he needs a little exercise, this is the perfect place because there is always ranch work."

"Maybe Elvis really could spend an extra day or two," Mark agreed.

"And you too," Grandmother quickly added.

"Thanks, but no thanks. I'm a city man born and bred. I don't like the wide open spaces and I'm already getting a little antsy with all this space around me. I don't suppose you have a television set?"

"Nope," Grandmother said, folding her arms. "And I don't ever want one, either."

"Well," Mark told her, "I'm a news junkie. I can't stand not knowing what's going on all around the world."

"But this is the world too!"

"Sure it is, but it's your world, ma'am. Not mine." The driver closed his eyes and took a couple of deep breaths. "I can smell the sagebrush and the trees and that's nice, but I would far rather smell a bagel in a city bakery."

Grandmother shot me a sideways look that said she was plenty disgusted. But that was just her...she thought even Winslow and Holbrook were too crowded and that Flagstaff had gone to the dogs with all the people and cars. So without bothering to argue, she went back into her kitchen.

I leaned back in the chair just happy to be home. The clouds were turning crimson across a forever sunset. Somewhere a mockingbird was singing sweetly and a few cows were mooing out on the range near a water tank. Maybe I dozed off for a few minutes, but I awoke suddenly when I heard hoof beats that told me that Elvis and my sister had returned.

The light was fading fast, more deep blue than black and I could hear and just make out the silhouettes of Elvis and Stella out by the corral. *I wonder what they're talking about?*

31

Just then Grandmother appeared. "You leave them be, Charlie. Stella is pretty excited about Elvis."

Mark cleared his throat. "Your granddaughter is mighty attractive, and Elvis loves pretty women, but Stella would be wise not to get too lovesick over him."

I snorted. "Warning Stella about something is like waving a red blanket in front of a fighting bull. It just makes her all the more determined. I've watched her break the heart of about every cowboy in this county and danged if I don't think she usually does it on purpose."

"Charlie! That's enough of that kind of talk. Stella is your sister and she loves you."

"I know. I know. And anyway, here they finally come."

Stella looked nearly giddy as she and Elvis strolled up to the porch. The last rays of sundown played on her hair...made it gilt-edged and beautiful. And of course, in his own way, Elvis was also beautiful and I say that in a manly, sensitive kind of way.

He was maybe fifteen years older than my sister and they made a striking couple.

"Grandmother," my sister said, purposefully ignoring me, "Elvis would like to stay overnight and go for a longer ride in the morning."

"Mark," Elvis said, "you might want to drive back to Flagstaff this evening and get that muffler repaired tomorrow."

"Alright, but it could take more than a day. I think more than the muffler is messed up underneath. We hit those washes pretty fast and when we bottomed out the last time and ...."

"Take however much time you need," Elvis interrupted. "We can't drive all the way back to Nashville with that thing roaring. I'll need my suitcase."

"And your guitar," Stella quickly added.

Mark climbed out of his chair. "I'd best be leaving right now."

"What about supper?" Grandmother asked.

"No time for that, I'm afraid."

"The least you can do is to take along a few things to eat on your way back to Flagstaff. I can give you big slices of my cornbread with butter, cinnamon and powdered sugar on top."

The driver's face split up in a wide grin. "That sounds just fine, ma'am!"

# *Chapter 5*

Fifteen minutes later, Grandmother had food on the table. The chili was delicious, but the conversation made me want to gag. It was dominated by Stella babbling on and on to Elvis about how great it was to raise cattle and sheep, pigs too, if you liked pork, and the chickens were always a part of the scenery. You needed their eggs and it sure would be nice to have a milk cow instead of having to settle for that awful canned milk that tasted so wretched. Powdered milk was better…but nothing was as delicious as fresh milk straight from the cow.

And then she went on and on about how the Arizona sunsets and sunrises were so spectacular and the seasons changed and how you could hear elk bugling out in the sagebrush just before dawn. And there were eagles on the wing and Canadian geese flying north and south and on and on and on with her silly and non-stop talk. Why, you'd think we lived in someplace like Yellowstone which I'd never visited but had seen pictures of in old magazines. And we didn't have nearby lakes or rivers…just the Colorado and it was always so muddy it would float horseshoes.

Elvis just listened and nodded. Grandma was suffering and so was I, so when we finished eating we beat a hasty retreat back to the front porch and I was hoping for some silence.

Elvis walked out in the yard and gazed up at the sky. I could tell that he was amazed and filled by wonder over all the high country stars. He and Stella wasted a lot of time trying to find the Big Dipper and some other constellations. All of a sudden I would have thought Stella had a graduate degree in astronomy! The truth was that she was completely winging it and wouldn't know the difference between Ursa Major and the Seven Sisters. I was willing to bet that she couldn't even point out the North Star, but knew better than to toss her that challenge with Elvis craning his neck up at her side.

Finally either Elvis' neck started to ache or he just got tired of stars because he turned to us back on the porch and said, "Mrs. Yoyestewa, I was hoping you'd tell me a story that has to deal with your Indian people. Stella tells me that you know a great many such stories."

"Which one do you want to hear?" Grandmother loved telling stories and

33

we all liked to listen because they changed with each telling as she creatively added little twists and turns to keep up our interest.

"Whichever one you'd like to tell."

"I will tell a *Coyote* story," Grandma said, her eyes wide and wise. "Maybe it will even hold a lesson for you!"

"For me?" Elvis asked with surprise.

"Yes."

"Then let's hear it."

I had to smile because I could guess which one of Grandmother's stories we were about to hear. She knew dozens, but this was one of our favorites.

"Grandmother!" Stella wailed. "Please not that one!"

"I will tell him the story I want to tell," Grandmother said stubbornly.

Stella groaned and stomped into the kitchen and Grandmother began one of her best stories.

*A long, long time ago, Coyote was out in these hills and smelled a cooking fire. Thinking he would find roasting meat he started toward this smoke, but it was many, many miles away and so the hour grew late before he arrived at the campfire surrounded by white men. Because they were friendly, they invited Coyote to share their scraps and leftover food. This made Coyote very happy and he ate well. By and by they sat around the campfire and began to talk. Coyote liked to howl, but he could talk very well, too. And when one of the white men said that he was strong, Coyote bragged that he...by golly... was also very strong. When another man bragged that he was smart, Coyote boasted that he too was very smart and so it went with Coyote bragging all evening until finally one of the men told Coyote about this huge snake that ran back and forth across the country. It was so big and so long that anyone who killed it surely would be considered the bravest, smartest and strongest of all animals.*

*"I could easily kill that snake," Coyote boasted. "I can kill any snake."*

*"Not this snake," the man argued shaking his head. "It is so big that it would frighten even you away."*

*Coyote howled with laughter and then he grew serious and said, "No snake can frighten Coyote. Where is this stupid snake? Tell me and I will kill it just to prove how strong and brave I am."*

*So the white man gave Coyote directions. Full of himself, Coyote left the camp and ran all the rest of that night to the place where he would find and kill that snake. But by then it was almost daylight and Coyote was very tired and footsore so he lay down behind a bush and went to sleep.*

*When the sun arose, Coyote was awakened by a very loud thunder. He jumped up and stared because he saw that the snake was so long that its trail ran in both directions as far as the eye could see. It was far, far longer than anything Coyote had ever even imagined. And the snake had fire and smoke coming out of its nostrils!*

*Oh, my, thought Coyote, jumping back behind his bush to hide. This is indeed a very large snake. How can I kill such a big snake?*

*Coyote sat and watched until all of Snake had passed. And then he wondered if it would return. After a long while he convinced himself that Snake had seen him acting strong and brave and had decided to run away in fear. Yes, the more Coyote thought about that the surer he became that Snake was afraid of him and that lifted his spirits. But late that same afternoon when Coyote was napping again Snake reappeared from the opposite direction and again Coyote saw smoke and fire coming from Snake's nostrils. He decided that he would sneak up on Snake and attack him from behind. Yes, that was the smartest way to do it!*

*So he crept down close by where Snake would pass feeling the earth shake under its great weight and as Snake smoked and breathed fire Coyote let its head pass and then jumped out and tried to bite Snake from behind! But he lost his footing and....oh, my, Snake cut off his tail!*

*Coyote howled and howled and whimpered and cried. He ran around and around in circles because it hurt so bad, but he did find his poor, bloody tail. Coyote wept because it had been such a beautiful tail. He wondered if he could possibly save it because everyone would laugh at a coyote without a long, beautiful tail. Finally, Coyote fell asleep beside the tracks of Snake cradling his lost tail.*

*He awoke suddenly to see Snake coming back! Angry for what Snake had done to his tail, Coyote jumped at Snake's ugly, smoking face, teeth snapping.*

*But you know what, Elvis? Snake ran right over Coyote and cut off his... his head!*

Grandmother stopped, her little shoulders shaking with suppressed laughter. I was biting back my own whoops, but Elvis looked confused. "That's it? That's the end of the story? Snake just killed Coyote."

"Sure," Grandmother told him. "And the moral of the story is…don't lose your head over a little tail!"

We all broke into gales of laughter.

Elvis and Stella went riding early the next morning and they didn't return until late that afternoon. I was in my rocking chair talking ranch work with

Grandmother when they galloped up to the house. Stella had never looked happier and I had to admit that Elvis also appeared happy and relaxed. He'd gotten a little sun on his face and his cheeks were pink from an early tan. I watched them tie their horses to a hitching rail and said, "Looks like you both enjoyed your ride."

Elvis nodded. "This is God's country, Charlie. Maybe He didn't quite finish it by giving it a lot of water, but I have a feeling He likes it just the way He left it and so do I. And I'm beginning to understand why you people love it out here so much. We rode up to the pines where you could see for a hundred miles in any direction. Stella even roped a calf and we checked it over just to make sure that it was healthy."

My sister laughed. "And you should have seen Elvis tackle that little fella!"

Elvis looked down at his clothes. "I got cow-shit smeared all over my pants and I don't smell too good, either. But Stella told me just to wash them out in the stock tank and spread them over a sagebush to dry. It worked out fine."

My cheeks suddenly warmed as I wondered about Elvis without pants around Stella.

"That's what took us so long," Stella explained while avoiding our questioning eyes. "Well," she added quickly, "we'd best take care of these horses. We rode them many miles today."

"Good idea," I wisecracked.

My sister nailed me with a killer grin.

When they'd led the sweaty horses off, I turned to Grandmother. "What do you think really happened out there today?"

"Charlie! Don't even ask."

So I didn't. That evening we ate beef roast, boiled potatoes and canned spinach and afterward we went out on the porch while Elvis sang and strummed an old guitar I'd never got around to learning how to chord. He sang songs he thought we'd especially like. "Love me Tender," "Don't be Cruel," "Old Shep" and a whole bunch of gospel music. Elvis was better than anyone I'd ever heard on a cheap, hard-to-tune guitar and I enjoyed his playing nearly as much as I enjoyed his singing. He asked us to sing along as he played so we joined right in and sang some popular western tunes recorded by Hank Williams, Earnest Tubbs, Patsy Cline and Johnny Cash, among others.

The stars came out and the moon cast a golden glow on our ranch yard. The chickens were roosted, the dog asleep under our porch and I have to admit that I don't think I've ever had a happier time in my life. Sitting with Elvis and having him all to ourselves was like a dream…like magic and I never wanted the evening to end.

This famous man from Nashville had a voice that could make you laugh or bring tears to your eyes. I had always enjoyed his singing on the radio, but it wasn't until he was singing all by himself, sometimes without even playing that I realized that he was a true genius. You hear all the time about musicians and how some get all the breaks and some don't...as if that was the single most important thing concerning success in show business. But that evening I decided that it was not...when you heard a talent like Elvis Presley you knew in your heart that he had to be discovered sooner or later. I was in awe of the man's gift. Stella always thought she could sing but couldn't carry a tune in a milk bucket. I, on the other hand, really did have a fine voice and I was not bashful about using it when I was out on the range by myself. And, to be honest, I'd sung more than one Elvis song in my time...a lot more in fact.

"Charlie," Elvis said, stopping right in the middle of a great western standard called "You Are My Sunshine,"—"you have a fine voice."

"Oh, compared to yours, I'm pretty bad."

"You'd be good enough to be a lead singer in almost any band."

I was so thrilled by this compliment I turned about three shades of red before I managed to say, "Thank you!"

Stella, no doubt jealous said, "Charlie caterwauls all over the ranch. I swear he chases the birds off the trees and the chipmunks underground with his singing. Why, you can hear...."

"Stella," Grandmother said sharply, coming to my rescue. "That's enough. Charlie has a fine voice and he writes good songs, too."

Elvis raised his eyebrows in question. "Is that right?"

I squirmed. "Well, I don't write music so I just put my feelings to words."

"You *should* put them to music," Elvis urged. "You don't have to be able to read music, but it helps. Why, I know plenty of good singers who can pick a melody up with just simple guitar chords."

"Maybe someday," I said lamely. "Lot of times I'm so tired after working the cattle that I just want to listen to music on the radio. Music like yours and Eddie Arnold, Buck Owens and the like."

"I understand," Elvis said, making me feel that he really did understand. "But how about me teaching you a few chords and progressions on this guitar. Easy things that will take you a long ways with songs."

I didn't even try to hide my excitement. "Would you!"

"Why sure." He picked up the guitar and fiddled with the tuning a little. "Watch this."

"I'm going inside," Stella announced stiffly. "Our kitchen needs cleaning."

I could tell that Stella was really miffed that I was suddenly the object of

Elvis' attention. Normally, she wouldn't have minded much…but it was pretty clear to me and Grandmother that she was hungry for Elvis and really wasn't even interested in sharing him with us.

A few minutes later it was also clear that my sister wasn't showing any mercy on the dishes, pots and pans from the way it sounded.

Elvis grinned. "That girl sure is a worker!"

"Yes she is," I agreed, winking at Grandmother who rolled her brown eyes.

That night, Elvis taught me how to play the chords, C, A-, F and G7. He went over and over them even putting my fingers on the strings and saying, "If you can learn this sequence smoothly, you'll be amazed at all the fine songs you can play. You won't dazzle any professional guitar players, but with your fine voice, no one will notice that you're not a real picker."

"Do you mean it?"

"Well of course! When I was just a little kid, I wanted a bicycle but we were so poor my father gave me a cheap guitar, one far worse than this. Dad bought it at a hardware store in Tupelo. He told me that since it cost so much and took nearly all the money out of our cookie jar, he'd be real disappointed if I just messed around with it and didn't really learn to play. I listened, still thinking how much I'd rather have a bike. But you know, getting that guitar so young was one of the best things that ever happened to me. It taught me the important lesson that things in our lives that might at first seem a big disappointment, often turn into a lucky break."

He grinned. "And just maybe, Charlie, it'll be that way for you not being able to rodeo anymore."

"I'm not sure that's true."

"You aren't thinking of riding bulls anymore with that plate in your skull, are you?"

"Well, no, but I might make money doing other events like calf or steer roping. I'm a good roper and I still think I could do okay riding broncs."

"Man," Elvis said, "you aren't making sense!"

I was hurt by that comment. "Maybe that's because you don't understand some things about me or this life we work so hard at keeping any more than I understand your life."

"Maybe you're right about that." Elvis ran his forefinger across the top of the guitar. "But I recognize good people when I see them and I sure can recognize bravery. And I also realize that it's good to try to understand people different than ourselves."

"Meaning?"

"Well, for example when I grew up in Tupelo as a kid I used to play and sing a lot of gospels and I was around Negros and they gave me their special love of music. When I was dirt poor, I learned a lot about humility. When I was a truck driver I earned just thirty-five dollars a week working for Crown Electric Company. My family was facing eviction, but I learned to take matters into my own two hands and follow my dreams. Sometimes they work out, sometimes not. I was lucky, but I worked real hard to make my dream of being a singer and performer come true."

Elvis picked up the guitar and sang a little of a song that went, *You gotta follow that dream wherever that dream may lead you, you gotta follow that dream to....* He stopped playing and sat silently for a moment clearly lost in his thoughts about where he'd come from and where he might be headed.

"Elvis, I...I don't really have a dream," I finally blurted. "My father was well known in rodeo and he thought I could be even better. I guess he told me that so many times when I was growing up around here that I imagined I'd become a rodeo star...a world champion."

"Or you could become a singer," Elvis suggested. "You have the voice and the looks: you ought to think about learning how to play this guitar better. If you do, I'll see that you get a quality guitar...probably a Martin... and I'll show you how to do a little pickin.'"

I inhaled and closed my eyes. I could almost see myself up on the stage with dozens of pretty and screaming girls wanting to touch my pants legs and taste my kissing. Just the thought of it made me feel special.

"Or maybe," Elvis said, "you could be a famous songwriter."

Right then I was making dreams I'd never imagined possible. I could almost see myself on stage and performing with the likes of Johnny Cash, Jim Reeves, and Charlie Pride. I slept so well that night that I slept late and when I pulled on my clothes and dashed into the kitchen hoping to have some coffee with Elvis, he was already riding off with my sister.

"Grandmother," I complained, "where is she taking him this time?"

"I have no idea," Grandmother replied as she watched them from the porch. "But I do know that Elvis Presley will take your sister anywhere he wants."

I needed to say more, but something in Grandmother's expression told me to stay quiet. I studied her old, weather-beaten face and saw worry. That was unusual because neither Grandmother nor my father had been long on worrying. They just put their heads down and took care of business. Like Elvis said he always told the musicians and other people who worked for him. *TCB* was his motto and I had no doubt that he followed it religiously.

"Is everything alright, Grandmother?"

She watched them gallop our horses across the pasture and into the cottonwoods. "I sure hope so," she said more to herself than to me. "But I'm mighty worried about your sister."

"She'll be fine. Elvis is a gentleman."

"Oh, I know that," she said, working up a smile. "But I'm not so sure that Stella is a lady and *that's* what has me worried."

My eyes widened, but I didn't have a single word to add so I went inside and poured a cup of coffee and started thinking about all the chores that I needed to do if we were to keep this ranch up and running.

# *Chapter 6*

When Elvis left our ranch, Stella went to her bedroom in mourning. I didn't feel good about Elvis leaving, but I tried to keep my spirits up and I was determined to start practicing on my guitar. The steel strings hurt, but Elvis promised that if I spent some time everyday holding down the strings, pretty soon the pain would go away. He'd also taught me how to tune the guitar and that made it sound much better.

I was certain that we hadn't seen the last of Elvis. He'd stayed two whole days on Coyote Ranch and when Mark finally did return he'd remarked that Elvis hadn't laughed so easy or looked so rested in months.

"How long is Stella going to keep up that moping and crying?" I asked Grandmother when my sister could still be heard through the cheap door to her bedroom.

"I don't know. I tried to warn her about Elvis leaving but she wouldn't listen. Stella has the lovesick blues."

"Lovesick Blues" is the name of a song."

"No matter," she snapped, "that's what your sister has real bad."

"Well, we *all* miss Elvis, but that doesn't mean we should go off the deep end."

"You don't understand women, Charlie."

"I guess not," I said, heading outside, "but Elvis said he'd come back some day and he will."

Two days later, I chanced upon my sister hiding out in the barn. "What are you doing here?" I asked, squinting through the gloom.

Her head snapped up and she pressed something dark to her breast and I could tell she was trying to hide it.

"Come on, Stella, what have you got?"

"Dammit, Charlie, I'm reading."

"Reading what?"

She gave me one of her long, weary sighs that was supposed to mean that my question was boring beyond her belief. "Alright, you deserve to know. This is a diary that I found yesterday hidden in the bottom of Father's dresser drawer."

41

Father had always kept his door closed. I didn't think it possible he would have written a diary and I said so.

"Charlie, it was written by our *mother!*"

I felt my heart stop for a moment and somehow I realized that so many things about my mother were at last going to be known. *What was she like? How did she get out here from the East and why did she stay and marry our father.* I swallowed hard and managed to ask. "Have you read it?"

"No."

The idea of reading my white mother's thoughts filled me with hope but also dread. "Then we should burn it. There might be things in there that we were never supposed to learn."

Stella gazed at me as if I were crazy, then her face softened. "Charlie, we hardly know anything about our mother. I need you to share this with me."

Stella opened the diary and held it to a crack of light piercing the barn's wall. It was all that I could do not to run away, but something made me stand as if my feet were fence posts set deep in Mother Earth.

*October 6, 1945*

*Dear Diary, I am never returning to modern society. Not after what war has done to our country. On August 6, we dropped an atomic bomb on Hiroshima, Japan, killing hundreds of thousands of innocent people. Then we dropped another three days later on Nagasaki with equally horrible consequences. How could our country do such a terrible thing in order to claim victory?*

*I desperately seek peace and simplicity. I want to grow corn with the Hopi, to work in their fields and to rise with the sun and to lay my head down on a husk mat and sleep through starry Arizona nights. In the short time that I have lived among the Hopi, I have experienced a rebirth working with the soil and understanding the sacredness of corn. In the winter, when it is too cold to work the fields, I want to write a book about the Hopi. I am a very good photographer and I must show this life in pictures. I have found a small, stone house where I will live on this reservation and I will do everything I can to earn the trust of the Hopi. My parents have always been rich so they cannot possibly understand my feelings and the sense of purpose I seek in my life. They have threatened to disinherit me, but I do not care. This is the only path that shines for me now that the outside world has gone mad and power hungry.*

*I just learned that a formal document of surrender is to be signed in Tokyo Bay aboard some battleship. This news fills everyone with happiness, but somewhere inside me I believe that this has left a bloodstain on our national morality and it will NOT be the last "great war". If we must as human beings war with each other, then I want no part of that and will live and die among these peaceful, spiritual people. A deep soul-sadness has overcome me.*

Stella closed the diary and it took her several moments to speak while I struggled to understand what I'd heard. My mother had been fresh out of college and a seeker of wisdom and peace. Her maiden name was Ellen Allen and she had come to the West and discovered the Hopi who still lived on their three mesas largely untouched by modernization and the white culture. Mother had lived for a time on First Mesa receiving money from her wealthy New York parents. The Allens had been appalled and furious about their daughter's new sense of mission and had soon disinherited her. To make matters worse, while she was living among them, there had been a "love triangle" where two strong men fought for her hand and her heart. Father had won, but from that time on there had been bad blood among him and the Hopi. My father's own father had been a Navajo, but Grandmother had never explained why she had married the man and I knew that she never would. So Stella and I were a strange mix…a quarter Navajo, a quarter Hopi and half white…sometimes it seemed that we were blood-grounded to absolutely nothing.

Once, when I was ten years old Father had taken us up on the Hopi mesas. I recall our old Chevy truck overheating as we climbed ever higher over their cornfields on a narrow, winding road that was terrifying because of the sharp drop-off. Father had stopped the truck and lifted the hood to cool the engine. He'd ordered us out of the truck to look at the land below, past the cornfields, past the red rock flats and far out to forever. I saw towering mesas jutting out of the hard land and black cones which my father said were old volcanoes, still not dead.

"And can you see those high, snow-capped mountains?" Grandmother had asked, pointing to the west. "They are the San Francisco Peaks where the Hopi messengers we call kachinas go to sleep and gain powers."

"Where is our Coyote Ranch?" I had asked.

"Out there," she said, pointing to the southwest.

"I wish we were there now," Stella had said. "I am afraid of what these people might do to Father. I have always heard about the bad blood caused by my mother."

"It was not your mother's fault," Father had insisted, trying to keep the anger out of his voice. "Blood was shed and all the blame for it was on me… not her."

I remember pleading with Father to find a place to turn the Chevy truck around so that we could leave, but he would not do it.

43

In a dusty village whose name I have forgotten the Hopi heard our noisy truck and came out to stare. Father and Grandmother got out and told Stella and me to join them. "These are good people. Don't speak unless spoken to," Grandmother had warned.

I remember being so scared I was afraid that I might piss in my pants. A huge dog raced toward us with raised hackles. Father and Grandmother froze and we cowered behind them. My eyes were jumping all over the place. The Hopi people on that high, narrow mesa were living in rock houses, with blankets for their doors. There were many levels and many children and none of them were smiling. I had been wearing good Levi's and boots and kids my age were dressed poorly.

A group of stern-faced men had come out of the rock houses, gathered and talked, some making angry gestures toward Father. But Father had stood still and proud...waiting, although for what I was not sure. I had just wanted to run away. I had thought the huge dog would tear my legs off or that these angry looking people might grab us all and throw us over the side of the mesa to feed their corn far, far below.

When the men had seemed to reach a verdict, they came forward, without friendliness in their faces. Suddenly, angry words had spewed from their mouths and the men began to shove us back toward our truck.

My father yelled back at the men...*in Navajo!* Some of them began to strike him with their fists and his nose was broken. Blood ran like a river down over his mouth and onto his best white shirt. Grandmother was not struck, but she was spit upon. Stella and I bolted for the truck and threw ourselves inside trembling and almost crying.

I remember that the truck struggled to start. The Hopi, even the women and children began to pelt us with rocks. Stella had screamed, but then I looked into her eyes and saw that she was not afraid anymore but filled with a rage... like a cornered animal ready to fight and...if necessary...die.

I had been so proud of her and so ashamed because of my own fear.

The truck had finally started. Father popped the clutch and stomped the gas. The truck spun around in a complete circle and it had sprayed the Hopi with rocks and gravel. A pack of dogs attacked the truck tires and I had felt the Chevy bump up and knew that we'd run over one. Father shouted and laughed crazily and then we had shot back down off the mesa and none of us had ever looked back.

"That is not like my Hopi," Grandmother had told us that night. "They are a good, gentle people."

"No they're not!" Stella had cried. "They were *horrible!* They wanted to kill us."

Father had raised a hand. His face was purple and his eyes ringed with black. He looked stricken and wounded. "The Hopi *are* good people. They will never forgive me, but they shouldn't blame you for what happened before your time."

"I never want to go back there," I had choked. And then, Grandmother began to cry.

All those memories came rushing back to me in the dark barn filled with shifting sunlight and shadow. "Stella, I don't want to hear any more in that diary about the goodness of the Hopi people! And I don't want to know any more what is in that diary."

"But it is only by knowing how much our mother loved those Hopi that we can be whole."

"I'm already whole, dammit!"

"You think you are, Charlie, but you are not and neither am I." She lovingly patted the diary. "The words of our mother will make us stronger and more forgiving. We will no longer have any fear in our hearts...and we will forgive the Hopi and know them as part of us. Let me read just a few more entries before you go."

I wanted to say no, but just couldn't.

*December 11, 1945*

*Dear Diary, The main Hopi ceremonies run from January to August. I have learned that between April and June there is a kachina dance performed in one of the Hopi villages nearly every weekend. I greatly admire the beautiful kachina dolls and have asked many of these people to teach me how to make them. But I learned that this is considered a man's work. And to think I always believed that dolls were for girls!*

*December 21, 1945*

*Dear Diary, Today I was devastated to learn that women are also forbidden to plant and harvest the beautifully multi-colored Hopi corn that transcends the simple definition of food for these people. Corn is life here and when I asked to help and take part in the next fall harvest, I was again scolded and told this also was man's work. How can that be when working with the soil is so life affirming? I need to plant and tend to the fields to see life regenerated...even to know hope. What can I do about this? Perhaps no one would object if I plant a small garden next to the old stone house that I have taken to living in.*

*January 23, 1946*

*Dear Diary, One of the elders, a very old man who I did not believe could see so well caught me taking photographs of a nearby burial ceremony. Suddenly he began to screech like an owl and all the men of the village came running. I was very afraid that I would be hurt, but instead they took my camera and bashed it to pieces. I cowered before their wrath and they made it known in no uncertain terms that I was never to take pictures of anything in the village again. But now, without a camera and with them all watching me with suspicion how am I to create a book that celebrates their Hopi ways? I have only paper and pencil and they do not even want me to draw…but I will not give up this dream! The world needs to know how these people live in peace and harmony so their right thinking becomes the salvation of mankind.*

"Why did she believe that the Hopi could save mankind!" I cried, the anger in my voice surprising even me. "We both have Hopi friends and they quarrel and fight as much as anyone."

"Maybe they got along better back then."

I had my doubts. Even worse, I was starting to think that Mother had not been right in the head. That she was like the hippies I'd heard about who practiced love and smoked a lot of dope and did nothing but sit around and talk about finding truth and inner peace. And I was even beginning to wonder what Father had seen in her. Father had always spoken so lovingly about Mother; now I was questioning why. What truths was she seeking and maybe she had been a little insane and had even run away from an asylum back in New York. All these thoughts were shaking me to my core.

"Stella, I've heard enough for tonight."

"I'm going to read just a few more short entries. I can't put this down quite yet, but you can go if you have to."

To have left then would have looked cowardly so I had to stay. I sat down on a bale of hay and tried to compose myself for what I thought would be more troubling revelations concerning our mother.

*February 8, 1946*

*Dear Diary, All Hopi men belong to secret religious societies called "clans" which define a Hopi's identity. Members spend a great deal of time down in their kivas singing and dancing, fasting and praying. It is forbidden for a woman to enter a kiva and I was warned not to even go near one of the ladders that lead down into their dark, secret interiors. Each clan has its own secret songs, dances and purpose. For example, the Snake Clan is said to have special powers with snakes which help bring more rain. When I said that I did not understand how snakes could bring rain, I was instructed that it was better I should not know.*

*March 15, 1946*

*Dear Diary, Hopi society is so complex and confusing! My only friend Molly tried to explain how all the clans are independent, but interconnected. This is hard for me to understand, but she explained it several times. For example, a child is born into his mother's clan, not his father's. That child will call all his mother's sisters Mother instead of Aunt. Furthermore, all of his mother's brothers are uncles. And only uncles can discipline and teach a child the Hopi ways. When the child enters adulthood, they cannot marry anyone who is in the same clan as themselves or even a closely related clan. Molly's explanation and her English is not the best, but when I asked her what would happen if two young people fell in love but were forbidden to marry because of the clan complication, she shrugged her shoulders and said, "That would be just too bad." So I guess romantic love is not allowed here unless the younger men and women are very aware of the clan connection. I find this distressing to say the least!*

No more distressing than I did. I stomped out of the barn. Most of my friends were Navajo, but I also liked my Hopi friends. They were not a bit like the Hopi leaders I remembered as a ten-year-old that day when my father had taken us up on the mesa seeking peace and forgiveness. Neither Stella nor I knew what he had done although we'd talked often of it in secret. But now I was thinking he killed or badly injured a Hopi man up there on First Mesa. That just *had* to be the truth of it...Father had fought a Hopi over love for Mother.

"Will we ever find out what *really* happened to our white mother long ago?" I managed to ask Stella. "Because to tell you the truth, I'm not sure I want to know."

"But we *must*."

I didn't agree but I realized my older sister would never rest until she and I at last knew the full truth about our dead mother. "Charlie, I need you with me on this."

I couldn't refuse Stella. "It sure sounds like she was a romantic."

"Of course she was! Don't you absolutely admire her hopes? Can't you feel how much our mother loved?"

I felt overwhelmed by those questions. I'd always tried to push our mother far back in my mind. Not once had Father spoken of his courtship with our mother and I knew it was because he was nearly crushed by guilt and remorse. "Maybe we ought to go have supper."

"Charlie, look at it like this…if I can love Elvis as unconditionally as Mother loved our father and the Hopi, then Elvis will one day return to marry me."

Stella sounded desperate and her words made no sense at all. I said, "Do you remember that Grandmother once told us that our mother fell into a deep darkness?"

"I remember."

"And what if that diary causes us to fall into that same darkness?"

"It won't."

"You can't be sure," I said, walking out of the barn.

Stella didn't follow me. And she didn't show up for supper, either. I caught Grandmother looking out the window at the barn. I knew my sister was still there thinking about our mother and maybe reading her diary.

Late that night, when Stella still didn't come to the house, I couldn't stand it anymore. I crept out to learn more about what happened to my mother long ago on the Hopi Reservation. When Stella looked at me I saw she had been crying. I went over to her and draped my arm around her shoulders.

"Is it that bad?" I asked.

"It's…it's sad but beautiful, Charlie."

*March 17, 1946*

*Dear Diary, I have met Phillip. I will not write his last name in this diary, but I can say that he belongs to the Tobacco Clan. He is extremely shy and gentle and he has played his flute for me. His music is so haunting and beautiful that it sends chills up and down my spine. Phillip drives a truck for the social services agency delivering meals to the old and the sick. His English is not good, but I'm sure if we see each other for awhile it will quickly improve. What on earth would my wealthy parents say if they knew I was being courted by a Hopi man who lives alone in a crumbling rock house? I think they would call me crazy. I want to learn more about Hopi from Phillip, but realize I must not press him too hard or fast or he will shun me. I have held his hand and we have gazed into each other's eyes in the moonlight. I wonder if we will one day become lovers.*

"Father never mentioned this Philip," I said quietly.

"I know. And in just a moment and after a few more pages," Stella said, "now you will learn why."

*May 6, 1946*

*Dear Diary, Molly showed me how to make piki yesterday. It is the traditional Hopi food made of blue corn, finely ground and then mixed with water and a pinch of wood ashes. This somewhat watery paste is spread across a hot, slick cooking stone. Molly says these stones are so smooth because they are handed down from one generation of women to the next and more prized by the Hopi women than gold. When the piki is poured across the hot, black stone it becomes thin and dark and Molly turned it with her fingers. When it is ready then she folds it up into little rolls and places it in a basket to be used in ceremonies and family gatherings. Piki is delicious but when I tried to turn it on the hot rock I blistered my fingertips! It hurts so badly. I asked Molly how come her fingertips did not burn and then blister like mine...but she did not know. I think the Hopi women ought to use spatulas to turn the piki.*

*May 12, 1946*

*Dear Diary, I am in trouble again! Ruben Begay has caught my eye and made my heart flutter. He is without question one of the handsomest men I have ever seen and also one of the tallest. His mother is Hopi, but his father was a Navajo and he took the Navajo name!*

I took in a sharp breath. "Stella, do you know what this means!"

"Of course I do," she said, biting her lip. "It means that Father's real first name was Ruben and that he changed his last name from Begay to Coyote." Stella's hand flew to her mouth and her eyes grew wide. "How could we not have known!"

"The Hopi are secretive people, Stella. The Navajo, too. Unlike white people they don't wear their secrets on their sleeves and tell anyone who will listen about their pasts. It makes perfect sense to me," I said, nodding my head with absolute conviction.

"I agree," Stella whispered. "Why would our father change his last name to *Coyote?*"

"If he stole our mother from a Hopi, maybe the Hopi gave him that name because Coyote is thought of as a trickster and...and a thief."

"You're probably right," Stella whispered. "Or maybe our father changed his last name out of guilt...or as a reminder of what he'd done to deserve the hatred of the Hopi people."

"Or *spite,*" I said, knowing our father better than Stella ever had. "We'll never know for sure, Stella."

Right then in the barn I thought as hard as I've ever thought about Father.

He had always been a quiet man, not one to talk about himself. He would tell you about cattle and horses, but mostly about the rodeo life he had once loved and been so good at. He would tell the same stories of bucking horses and bulls over and over and of the riders and ropers he had known and admired, liked and fought. Father would talk about the sun and the moon and the stars…but he would never talk about his background and because Grandmother would not either, both Stella and I had long since learned that there were dark secrets best not brought to light.

*But now I knew that I was really a Begay; probably the most common name and biggest family on the entire Navajo Reservation.*

"I would rather be Charlie Coyote than Charlie Begay," was all that I could manage to whisper.

"Me too," Stella agreed, "but most of all I'd rather be Stella Presley."

My mouth fell open and I had to clamp it shut not to say how ridiculous I thought that admission to be.

"I always knew in my heart Father was at least part Navajo. And that's why it came out of him when he got angry up on the First Mesa and spoke to the Hopi in Navajo."

"Yes," Stella said. "It explains so much."

"But why would he try to hide that from us?"

"I don't know. Maybe…." She shook her head, voice trailing off into silence.

"Maybe what?"

"Maybe we'll find out in this diary, Charlie. That's the only way it will happen because Grandmother will never tell us."

I knew this was true. "Go on," I urged, "read a few more pages and we'll probably have our answers."

*Ruben Begay has many horses and lives down on the desert, but he comes up here to visit. I watched him walk past my little rock house one day and I could not help but note that he moves like a big, sensuous cat. When I asked Molly about this handsome man she warned that I should stay away from him because he has known many bad and loose women. Once, Ruben even had a young Hopi wife but she threw him out when she learned of all the women he was seeing when he was off to ride in the rodeos. Up here the men and women do not go through our torturous legal divorce where a white man and woman are almost guaranteed to wind up hating each other. When a Hopi husband or wife wishes to end a marriage…and that is usually the woman because she owns almost everything…they just separate. When this happens these people understand that the bond between those two has ended and there is no anger. Isn't that far, far more gentle and civilized than what we have in our white society? Molly has warned me that Ruben has a terrible temper and that he is a rogue. I must not think of him so much now that Phillip seems to have fallen in love with me.*

*June 18, 1946*
    *Dear Diary, This was one of the saddest and upsetting days I have had since coming here. An old woman who lives close by saw Phillip leave me late one night. She shook her finger and called me names that I was glad I did not understand. I was in tears! I had done nothing wrong but now these people are shunning me. Molly says that they have decided I should not live among them. How sad! When I first came here I hoped that these people would embrace me as one who was a seeker of their ancient knowledge of how to live in peace and harmony. Today I feel anger toward the old woman and many of those who called me names and also shook their fingers in my face.*
    *Molly told me that the Hopi are not as peaceful as I thought and she blamed this on the Tribal Council which is now the authority here instead of each of the clan leaders. Some of the Hopi support the Tribal Council because they have family members on it, but those that do not are very angry. They are called "traditionalists" for wanting to get rid of the council and resisting change in all things. She says that the traditionalists oppose change because they believe it is brought on by the white society. They even resist teaching their children English. The "progressives" however, embrace change. They want government housing, electricity and running water. They like cars, washing machines, radios and nice pickup trucks. I can see truths on both sides and it saddens me to know that the Hopi are split like that and often at war with each other.*

    Stella closed the diary. "That is enough of Mother's diary for tonight. I can't stand to learn more and I think it'll have a bad ending."
    "So maybe we should burn it."
    "No. I would wonder about it all the rest of my life. Wouldn't you?"
    I had to admit that I surely would.

# *Chapter 7*

After what we'd learned from the diary that night, Stella and I didn't talk about Elvis or our parents for a long time. That winter turned out to be one of the most severe on record and we lost many of our older cows. It froze hard almost every night, but the wind was the worst. Many a day and night we huddled in our little house and felt it shiver and shake under those icy blasts. Stella was depressed and near impossible to live with and every day she wrote Elvis a long love letter. Whenever the weather was good enough to drive to Winslow, which was not often, Stella would be so excited about getting a letter from Elvis that the night before she couldn't sleep.

And Elvis *did* write, but not directly to my lovesick sister. He wrote to our *family* and that hurt Stella. I even got to wishing that he would just write to Stella, but Elvis never did. From what I could tell from his letters he was constantly on tour. Sometimes when we got a newspaper there would be some news about "The King" as many writers now called him.

Elvis even visited President Nixon in the White House and another article was how he gave a poor woman a Cadillac for Christmas and made her promise not to tell anyone of his kindness, but the woman told the press anyway with tears of gratitude streaming down her cheeks. She couldn't possibly have kept such a secret…how could anyone living in a shanty have explained a new Cadillac? Elvis also sent presents to our family, a necklace for Stella that was gold and pearls, a set of earrings and some kitchen things for grandmother and for me a new Martin guitar and songbook.

The guitar almost played itself and had the sweetest and most wonderful sound of anything I'd ever heard. I loved that new Martin and I could barely keep my hands off it. Almost overnight my guitar playing became respectable and I worked hard to learn every chord in the new book.

Stella was often on horseback checking the cattle in the bitterly cold wind. She lost weight and looked hollow-eyed. Grandmother took to fussing over her all the time, trying to get her to stay inside more, but Stella seemed driven by sweet memories of Elvis and I figured she was out riding and reliving every word they'd said and maybe even having sex on a saddle blanket.

Many was the evening that Grandmother and I had to nearly pry Stella out of the saddle and carry her in by the stove to thaw. My sister didn't winter well and by the time spring finally did come she was thin and haggard.

"I'm going to take a town job in Winslow," she announced one morning when the sun was warming and the snow melting into mud. "We've got taxes and bills to pay. Charlie, if you weren't always playing that guitar you'd know that we haven't had much of any income since Father died. To make matters worse, you remember that our pickup truck broke down so we had to call out a mechanic. Remember how it cost us four hundred dollars?"

I had been trying not to think of money, but Stella and Grandmother were counting every penny and we ate just enough to keep our strength up against the cold. "Yeah, I remember. Do you really think you can find a job?"

"Yes, and you might have to do the same."

"I was hoping to make money with my music. I've really been working hard at it."

Stella shook her head as if I were a dolt. "And where exactly did you think you'd sing, Charlie? At the Junction Bar & Grill? Or the Frontier Saloon?" Stella became even more sarcastic. "And gee, if on a Saturday night and everyone hasn't already spent their weekly ten dollars on beer yet, maybe they'll pass the hat around for you and that would bring in another two or three dollars."

I was getting hot and I might have said something nasty if Grandmother hadn't stepped in between us. "That is enough! We are a family."

"Maybe so," I said angrily, "but I'm fed up with Stella telling me I'm a fool and a dreamer for wanting to make money singing and playing my guitar."

"Stella, enough of that talk. But Charlie, don't you forget how hard your sister worked all winter when you were recovering warm and dry. You never even once said thanks to her."

Grandmother was right and I suddenly felt selfish. "Stella, I'm sorry and you did carry us all winter."

"Forget it," Stella said. "I'll find a job, maybe even at some saloon where I can watch you sing."

After that I made it a point to saddle a horse every day and go out to check on the cattle. I didn't chase any and I rode slow and easy. It helped my body and my mind and I recalled the old saying that Father had always loved and repeated, *There's nothing so good for the inside of a man than the outside of a horse.*

We didn't have a television, but we did have a radio and it was powered by a generator like most everything else at the ranch. Elvis had told me to listen to all kinds of music, not just country and western, but classical, gospel, rock and roll…all of it can give you something. But you have to concentrate and feel the music way down deep. Pay particular attention how singers use inflections in their voices. No two singers ever do the same song exactly alike. You have to develop your own style early or you'll never find success. I tried to take Elvis' advice to heart.

One day Stella fixed up and left the house in a huff. I watched her wildly fish-tail our truck through the mud and I thought she was going to lose control and then we'd be in a real pickle.

"Grandmother, what is wrong with her? She drives like she's angry at the whole world…or crazy."

"She's mad because she has to look for a job."

"Oh, I see." And I *did* see because I remember that Father had also gotten prickly every time he'd had to leave Coyote Ranch and go off to town job hunting with his hat in his hand.

The day was raw and windy and I stayed inside and practiced on my guitar until my fingertips were red and painful. I wrote a new song and called it "The Town Job Blues" and it started like this:

*Oh I went to town a'lookin' for a job*
*but I found no work today.*
*So I went back home to tell my gal,*
*that I wasn't gonna bring home no pay.*

*And she says to me,*
*you gotta find some work*
*because the baby's sick*
*and the money is gone*
*and I feel so low today.*

*So I went around and found a job*
*and no more will I play.*
*There was a time when I thought I'd sing*
*and be a big recording star,*
*but now I'll just sit around*
*and drink homemade brew from an old fruit jar.*

I was so pleased with the lyrics that I put them to music before noon. I was still feeling proud of myself when Stella rolled in that evening to announce that she had a job in Winslow.

"Where?" Grandmother asked.

"At the Frontier Saloon, working nights."

"No," Grandmother snapped.

Stella headed for her bedroom shouting over her shoulder, "I can make more in one night off tips than I can make in a week as a stock clerk or cashier at some crummy gas station or liquor store!"

"I worry about your sister," Grandmother fretted.

"So what's new?"

Minutes later, Stella swept past us and jumped into the truck. She revved the engine and took off so I knew she was starting work at the Frontier Saloon right away.

Grandmother went into her room and quietly shut the door. But it was a cheap door and I heard her softly crying. She almost never cried and I knew she was worried almost sick about Stella so I knocked. "Grandmother, don't worry so much. It's all going to be fine."

"I don't know. Stella is in love with Elvis and he isn't going to love her back."

"We don't know that."

"He's famous. Women all over the place are after him. He's not going to fall in love with your sister. I know that, but Stella doesn't."

"Maybe Elvis won't come ever back, but Stella is strong. She'll do alright."

Grandmother wiped away her tears. "And what if she gets drunk or crazy in town and does something to mess up her life?"

I didn't have an answer.

Grandmother heaved herself to her feet. "I will make corn meal and other Hopi offerings and prayers for Stella."

"It's too cold and windy out there. And it's almost dark."

"Then I will make them in our barn," Grandmother said stubbornly. "You go to bed, Charlie, I'll be fine."

She lit a lantern and pulled on her coat. I watched her trudge out to the barn and then she hauled open the door but it wasn't easy for her. Grandmother didn't weigh more than a hundred pounds. I started to go help, but she slipped inside. I could see splinters of light between the boards as she moved about making her prayer preparations. When I was very young she had tried to teach me and Stella some of her prayers, but we hadn't been interested and she'd quickly given up the effort. I knew she was still hurt that neither one of us had taken up her Hopi ways, but we just weren't interested. Maybe someday...but now that we'd read the diary and knew some of the secrets of our family...I felt even less inclined to go Hopi...and then there was that awful, scarring memory of what had happened to us when we'd taken the old Chevy truck up to First Mesa so long ago.

For the next few months Stella didn't say much and she never got home before two o'clock in the morning. Grandmother always waited up for her, but I didn't. A couple of times though I did hear our truck lurch across gravel into our yard and I knew that when Stella came home she didn't talk to Grandmother and went right to bed. Then one moonlit Saturday night Stella didn't come home at all. I was asleep when Grandmother woke me up saying, "Your sister is in terrible trouble, Charlie! I know it in my heart."

It was four in the morning. "There's nothing we can do right now. She'll be home before long."

About eight o'clock Stella weaved the truck into the yard, almost running over a couple of our laying hens. When she slammed on the brakes and turned off the engine, she waved with a silly grin and then opened the door and fell on the ground. She jumped up, steadied herself against the truck and tried to comb her long, tangled hair. I could smell the liquor from fifteen feet. Her clothes were a mess and I'd never seen my sister so drunk.

"Well, well if it isn't the Coyote welcoming committee! What a fine thing for you to come out and greet me on this beautiful Sunday morning!"

"You're drunk," Grandmother shouted, gripping the porch railing so hard that her knuckles were white. "Come inside and have some breakfast and coffee."

"Not hungry. I'm going to bed, if you don't mind."

"I *do* mind," Grandmother snapped. "What else have you done besides getting drunk?"

Stella squared her shoulders, squinted one eye and said, "Grandmother I have found myself a *real* boyfriend. One that loves me right back."

"Who is he?"

"Never you mind." Stella winked at me. "We don't want to tell Grandmother all of our little secrets, now do we Charlie-boy?" She headed back out the door and I knew she was headed for town so I snatched the keys out of her hand.

"You're not driving," I told my sister. "I don't know how you made it home from Winslow, but you got lucky."

"I'm going to work tonight."

"I'm going with you," I said. "I'm going to see if they'll let me sing and play."

"They'll laugh you off the stage, Charlie! You're not ready."

"Maybe not, but judging from the way things are with you, I'm going to have to step right in and see if I can take up the slack."

Stella stared right through my eyes. "If they laugh at you, I'm going to have to kill a cowboy tonight and that'll for sure get me fired."

I grinned. "We'll make some coffee."

"I need sleep before the coffee."

I thought that was a good idea, but as I watched Stella struggle up the stairs onto the porch and disappear inside, Grandmother took hold of my arm and squeezed it tight. "I don't want you to go to work at the saloon. Bad things happen in saloons and you can already see the darkness working inside your sister."

"Grandmother, we need more money."

"They fight all the time at the Frontier Saloon."

"How would you know that?"

"I hear things," she told me. "So if you have to go there and a fight starts, you must promise you'll duck behind the bar or under a table or just run out the door. If you got hit with a bottle, it might dent that piece of tin protecting your brain."

"Yeah, I can see where it might," I agreed. "And if there's trouble, I'll grab Stella and run away."

"Don't wait to grab your sister, she can stand up and fight. She's tough and hard...like me."

I didn't know if I'd been insulted or not but I could see that Grandmother was very serious about this so I headed inside to practice on my guitar and then take a nap so I'd be fresh for the night ahead. I wasn't even sure they'd let me get up on the stage tonight, but even so I could feel the butterflies in my belly.

# *Chapter 8*

When I woke up, it was dark. I jumped off the bed, climbed down from my loft and there was Grandmother sitting at the table just looking at the walls.

"Where's Stella!"

"She left an hour ago."

"But she was supposed to take me into town so I could sing."

"You were sleeping so peacefully we decided you ought to stay here."

I couldn't believe my ears! Stella and Grandmother had conspired to keep me from what I hoped might become the beginning of a great musical career.

"I'll take the tractor into town."

"The tractor's clutch is out," Grandmother said with what seemed to me a lot of satisfaction. "Stay home."

"Then I'll…I'll saddle my horse and ride into town! If I cut across country, it won't be more than ten miles and Buster could use the exercise."

Grandmother shook her head. "You'll freeze to death and ruin that fancy guitar Elvis sent you."

"No I won't. But I think you're right about the guitar. I'll try to borrow one from one of the band members and leave the Martin here where it'll be safe."

"Be careful, Charlie."

I shrugged into my sheepskin lined coat and reached for my battered Stetson. "I will."

Buster wasn't too happy about being saddled at sundown, but I didn't much care. He made me chase him around in the corral, but when I got my catch rope he knew the game was up and let me jam the bit between his teeth. He tried to nip me in the back, but I knew better than to punch him in the jaw because a horse's jaw is harder than a blacksmith's anvil. I knee punched him in the gut and he deflated so I could tighten the cinch.

"Buster, I haven't got the time or the patience to play games with you tonight. We're in for a long ride and I don't want any foolishness."

Buster was a disagreeable ten-year-old buckskin gelding that Father had won in a card game in Tuba City. He would have gotten rid of the horse years ago except that Buster was an exceptional cow pony. He would also pack deer and he'd climb into any kind of trailer. Buster was what Father called an "honest horse" in that he took his cattle work serious and would not quit on you no matter how mean the country or how big a steer you roped. Buster was also sure footed and Father had always told me that was about as important a quality as a man could want in this tough country. You could have the fastest and quickest Quarter Horse in the world, but if it didn't pay attention to its footing, then it was worthless out here in Northern Arizona. I swung up into the saddle and my dog Rip jumped out from under the porch to go along as he always did when I rode.

"No," I said to the dog, "not tonight."

Rip continued to wag his tail hopefully.

"Stay!"

The dog slunk back under the porch, thoroughly crushed.

I loped across the yard and field then into the heavy sagebrush. By the time it was fully dark, I could see the lights of cars and trucks off to the north on Route 66. I didn't try to rein Buster because he could see his way in the dark far better than I could and weaved back and forth through the sage and dry washes. Where possible I kept him at a steady trot, but that was hard on me and I had to stand up in my stirrups and keep my weight on the balls of my feet.

Off to the east a couple of coyotes were howling up a storm, but I hardly noticed. I was worrying about if I could get a guitar and if I did could I play it. *And what if my voice broke on stage?* The very thought of that disaster nearly made me turn back to the ranch. If I made a fool out of myself on stage my friends would tease me unmercifully…and forever.

Winslow wasn't a big town like Flagstaff, but at night from a distance it had a lot of lights. As I grew nearer I got even more nervous and Buster could feel it and began to throw his head and act up. I had forgotten my spurs so I bumped him with my boot heels and said, "Behave yourself. We're almost there."

He either didn't understand or didn't care. I headed for the Frontier Saloon and pushed the horse into a gallop. By the time we arrived, Buster was puffing and sweating and I figured it was almost midnight. I slowed him to a walk and reined him through the maze of mud-caked and dented pickup trucks. I could hear amplified music and wild whoops. From the number of trucks I figured there must be a big crowd inside.

I rode up to a dead tree in the back of the saloon and dismounted. I tied the horse up so that there wasn't any chance of him getting run into by a drunk cowboy. I dusted off my Levi's and buffed my boots on them, then removed my hat to comb my hair. My knees felt a little weak like they'd been at the rodeo just before I'd gotten down on Buzzard. I took a few deep breaths in the cold night air and remembered that even Elvis had admitted to being nervous before he sang. He'd told me to just remember that, if you had the talent… which he said I did…those things would turn out just fine.

I wasn't a stranger to the Frontier Saloon. They had a good family breakfast and we'd been there a few times, Father and me. But after ten o'clock in the evening they shut the restaurant down and ask the families to leave and then the saloon took on a night life style. Townspeople arrived as did railroad workers and cowboys looking to hear some good country music and maybe find a woman to dance with and take home.

A local group called The Shadow Riders was playing every night and Stella said that they were gawd-awful but that they had so many friends and family coming in that it didn't matter. I had heard them play once in our Chevrolet dealer's parking lot during a big car and truck sale. The Shadow Riders would lounge around sitting on bales of straw dressed in their finest cowboy outfits sipping cheap whiskey when they thought that management wasn't watching. Whenever anyone showed up, they'd grin and pump the customer's hands and then pick up their instruments. Then they'd try to hawk a five dollar cassette of their songs that they said they'd recorded in Nashville, but probably recorded in their garage.

Tonight I wished that I'd showed them some attention so that they'd remember me and let me use a guitar and do my songs. But I trusted that Stella could do that much for me since all the money I made from my singing career would go to keeping us on Coyote Ranch. *Who knows, I thought, maybe I can make enough money so that Stella wouldn't have to suffer the "Town Job Blues".*

I figured I had a better chance of getting inside by using the back door, but no sooner had I pulled it open and hurried through the kitchen than a big man with a huge belly, grabbed my arm. "What do you think you're doin' in here?"

"Oh," I said, trying to sound casual, "I just thought I'd come in and enjoy the music."

"Uh-uh," he said, eyeing my closely. "You're not twenty-one and I can't let you inside."

"I'm man-sized and I just turned twenty-one."

"Show me some identification…like a driver's license."

"Damn, I forgot to bring it."

He shook his head. "Listen, if you really want to listen to the music…and I can't understand why any sober soul would want to punish themselves by doing that…then you can sit by this door."

"But I need to go inside to see my sister."

"What's her name?" he asked suspiciously, still holding onto my sleeve as if he thought I'd bolt and race past him into the saloon.

"Stella Coyote."

"How come your sister didn't tell you that you needed to be twenty-one to come inside after ten o'clock?"

"I have no earthly idea."

"Idea or not, Kid, you still have to be twenty-one. I'm not trying to be a red-ass, but that's the law. We've been shut down before for letting underage fellas come inside with the drinking."

"I'm not here to drink."

"Then you must be here to chase older women and while that ain't against the law and you're handsome enough to do it…it ain't a good idea."

"I come to play music," I told the big man. "I don't want to drink."

"Sure, you don't!" he said, finally cracking a smile. "That's what all you young fellas say. Hell, it's what I said when I wanted to drink underage."

I wasn't doing too well so in desperation I blurted, "I rode my horse over ten miles to come and see my sister."

His expression grew serious. "You got some emergency?"

"Well…."

"Did someone die or get hurt out at your place?"

He looked genuinely concerned. "Well, sorta," I hedged.

"In that case come on in!" He grabbed my upper arm so hard I nearly yelped.

Thank heavens! I spotted Stella in the crowd serving drinks. "There's my sister!" I could hardly see her through the thick layer of cigarette smoke and the Shadow Riders had their amplifiers turned up to full volume so I knew she'd never hear me call her name, but I tried anyway. "Stella!"

When the big man turned, he momentarily released my arm and I dashed into the saloon and lunged toward Stella. Some asshole cowboy stuck out his boot and tripped me. I flew into my sister and an entire tray of beers tumbled off her tray; glass shattered across the floor. Stella cussed and her eyes blazed as she shoved me into a tableful of cowboys who threw me back in her direction.

"What the hell are you doing in here!"

"I didn't mean to make you spill all that beer," I shouted, trying to be heard over the band. "I…I just come to say hello and play a few songs."

Stella shook her head as if she was having a really bad dream. Even the Shadow Riders stopped playing to listen and they were all grinning like this was going to be a huge joke.

When the place fell silent, I said, "It's time I tried."

After a moment of silence, my sister forced one of her most beautiful smiles and loudly announced, "Everyone, this is my kid brother, Charlie, who has this crazy idea that he wants to be a musician and so he's come to play and sing you a song. Would that be alright?"

Most of the customers couldn't have cared less who played music so long as it was loud. Some hooted, but most clapped. One drunk that I recognized gave me the finger. Through the smoke, they all looked pretty wasted.

Stella turned to the four men on the bandstand. The lead singer was a tall, skinny fella with a two-day growth of scraggly beard and a wooden splint taped to his nose telling me that someone had broken it recently.

Stella jumped up on stage and put her arm around the lead singer. "George, would you mind giving my brother your guitar?"

"Hell no," George said, ducking out of his guitar strap. "Here you go, Hotshot! But don't drop and break it."

I stared at the *electric* guitar and looked into George's bloodshot eyes. "I don't know how to play an electric guitar. Never touched one before."

"So you play an acoustic, man?"

"No, it's a hollow wood one."

"This is the only kind of guitar that is loud enough to be heard in this saloon. An acoustic would never work." He pushed the weird looking guitar at me. "So it's this one or nothing. Go ahead, Kid. Giver 'er a lick!"

George was grinning smugly and so were the other members of his band. They were probably sick of playing and eager for any diversion. Or maybe they were just hoping that I was even worse than they were and would become the butt of a longstanding joke.

"Come on, Kid! Play if you're gonna!" one of the cowboys in the crowd shouted. "What the hell you waitin' for, a formal introduction...do you think you're George Jones or Buck Owens!"

Everyone started hooting and whistling. I wasn't afraid of them but I sure wasn't gaining confidence, either. Cowboys were mostly real good guys, but when they got drunk they could be serious trouble.

Then something completely unexpected happened. Stella hurled her empty tray at the nearest cowboy who was giving me a hard time, put her fingers to her teeth and let out a shrill whistle that brought immediate silence.

"This is my kid brother, Cowboy Charlie! Gawdammit, he's a helluva hand and horse trainer and he deserves a chance so all of you just shut up and let him sing and play a song. Is that really too much to ask!"

There was a silence and even grumbling. Stella leaned in close and whispered, "Here's your chance, Charlie. I told you not to come but you had to do it so just do your best!"

George tapped my arm and leaned close. His breath was foul and so was his body odor. "Kid, do you want my band to play a little backup…maybe loud enough to cover your performance?"

"I guess so."

He gave me a plastic pick and pulled me up on the bare plywood stage. "Go to 'er!"

I hit the strings with the plastic pick and the guitar let out an ear-piercing screech that set everyone back on their heels. Before anyone could say anything, I took a deep breath and stroked the strings a lot softer in the chord of A. And without another moment of hesitation, I launched into my song. But the guitar was way too loud and it drowned out my voice and the clever lyrics that I had hoped would launch my stage career. Launch it just as surely as "Blue Moon of Kentucky" and "That's Alright, Momma" had done for Elvis at a Memphis radio station WHBQ back in 1954.

But that was not to be. My fingers hit the wrongs strings and the sound was like the cry of a jungle parrot. And the harder I hit the strings and the louder I sang the worse it got. Cowboys bent over double laughing and even the cowgirls laughed so hard they cried. George was on his knees howling and the rest of the band was seized by various stages of apoplexy. The only ones in the Frontier Saloon not laughing were me and my sister. In fact, I saw her face turn white and the pinpoints in her eyes dilate with rage. She tore George's electric guitar out of my hands and the strap pulled off my hat. Then, she did something dramatic even for her…she raised the guitar overhead and smashed it against the edge of the plywood stage.

George yanked what was left of his cheap electric guitar out of Stella's hands. "What the hell are you doin'!" he cried in horror.

"How dare you all make fun of my kid brother! You know Elvis stayed at our ranch and he said Charlie has a damned good voice…better by far than your sorry, whiny voice, George!"

To make her point even stronger Stella grabbed a full pitcher of beer and slung it at the Shadow Riders who hit the floor and went crabbing away like frightened cockroaches.

A cowboy more drunk than most jumped up from his table and charged my sister. But I tackled him and he hit the edge of the stage hard enough to be knocked out cold. Stella grabbed me before anyone else could attack and propelled me toward the back door.

She shoved me in our truck, jumped in and gassed it, sending a spray of dirt and gravel across the parking lot at the cowboy trucks.

"Gawdamn you, Charlie," she grated as we hit the highway and gathered speed out of town. "You cost me my job and you almost got yourself killed!"

"I'm sorry."

"Sorry isn't going to pay our bills!"

I knew better than to say another word until I finally remembered Buster. "I left my horse tied to a tree in back of the saloon!"

Her foot eased off the accelerator, but then jammed it to the floorboards again. "Nobody is going to steal that ornery animal. And if they try, Buster will most likely kick the shit out of them or bite 'em in the ass."

"Yeah, but they might want to steal Father's prized rodeo saddle."

"You brought his *best* saddle?"

"Yeah."

Stella slammed on the brakes right in the middle of the highway, yanking the steering wheel hard to the right. She spun the truck around, stomped the gas pedal and drove me to the saloon while killing the headlights.

"Where!" she snarled.

"See that big old dead cottonwood?"

A lot of cowboys were leaving, but either they were too drunk to recognize us or they didn't care. Stella drove our truck over toward the tree and hit the brakes. "Get out and ride home!"

I was more than glad to get out, given the way she was feeling toward me. I slammed the door shut and marched over to my horse. Buster laid his ears back, but didn't try to bite. I tightened my cinch and swung into the saddle. Stella hadn't driven away so I rode off and she followed me all the way to the highway.

"Charlie," she said, after rolling down her window. "I could just strangle you!"

"I know. I'm sorry."

"Aw hell," Stella said, "it wasn't your fault and you can sing a lot better than George and his freak show band. You just didn't know how to play his cheap electric guitar and I should have warned you it would sound a lot different from the Martin."

I nudged Buster with my boot heels. A truck full of cowboys roared past shouting and yelling at us. I just wanted to get home and get this long, disastrous night far behind. Stella and our Chevy matched my pace though I couldn't imagine why she didn't just drive off and leave me as we crept down Route 66.

"Stella," I said, when we were a half mile from the saloon. "Are you going to tell Grandmother what I did and how I got you fired?"

"Hell no!"

"Thanks." I was eager to slip into the high desert darkness and when I came to the first gate in the barbed wire fence that kept livestock off the highway, I rode through it, dismounted and fixed the gate back in place.

Buster was in a hurry to get back to Coyote Ranch and so was I. The moon was up and to the north I saw the Big Dipper and Polaris. But I was headed south and I decided that there had to be an easier way to make some money than being a saloon singer.

# Chapter 9

Stella was fired the next day and the owner of the Frontier Saloon was so angry he wouldn't fork over her last paycheck. The jerk claimed the damages we Coyotes had caused was more money than Stella was owed, especially after he said he felt obligated to replace George's electric guitar.

"That guitar wasn't worth anything!" Stella raged, grabbing up her coat. "I'm going to go have a talk with him."

"No," Grandmother said. "I'm glad you got fired. It was a bad place for you, Stella! And Charlie should never have been there."

"But I was making good money! Grandmother, we have taxes due this spring and we're broke."

"Then you and Charlie have to find better jobs and I will start making pottery to sell at the stores and gas station gift shops."

Stella sighed with exasperation. "You already have pottery all over this house, but you won't part with any of it."

She was right and I struggled to keep from smiling. Grandmother just loved her own pottery and she hoarded in boxes what she couldn't find places to openly display.

"Maybe today I'll take a few boxes to the trading post and a few stores."

Stella rolled her eyes at the ceiling and then stomped out the door. I watched her march out to the barn and I figured she would saddle one of the horses and go for a long ride. That seemed to be the only way she could burn off her anger these days.

Grandmother was serious. She had me carry boxes of carefully packed pottery pieces and put them in the truck. I could see how difficult this was for her. She had always saved her best work saying our families would appreciate it and her memory. Her pottery was red with intricately painted black designs including corn, water waves and lightning. Some had coyotes painted on them sitting back on their haunches howling up at the moon and they were my favorites. Other pots were quite large and as a boy I'd helped collect special clay and then watched her muddy hands and fingers lovingly shape the vessels. No two were exactly alike. Back then they had been a source of wonder and I remember Grandmother had even allowed me to make a few pieces and I'd loved the work. She'd shown me how to work the clay, slowly adding water until it was perfect and then how to etch in little designs. Afterward, we carried our soft clay pots into the yard where Grandmother was very particular about building her fire from dry sheep shit carefully placed on a piece of tin about the size of a large pizza pan. She'd pull up a little stool and then sit all afternoon fanning the fire and adding more sheep shit as needed to keep her firing at exactly the right temperature. The sheep shit would burn slowly to a fine, white ash and Grandmother knew exactly how long it took to fire her pottery to a beautiful finish.

As the number of pots had accumulated over those years, we'd packed them in cardboard boxes and when the boxes started filling every empty space, Grandmother decided that she needed to make something easier to store so she began to make beautiful woven plaques out of vegetable and plant dyed yucca shoots. These plaques were also decorated with Hopi designs and were considered to be traditional gifts offered at ceremonies and rites of passage. But since we'd been run off the Hopi mesas years before, she had no occasions to give these plaques to any of her people. So they had also accumulated over the years.

"Bring those boxes of plaques, too," Grandmother instructed.

"Grandmother," I said, going back inside. "I'm not sure this is a good idea. You won't make that much on the pottery…and you love it."

"I love Coyote Ranch even more."

"These are all beautiful," I said, meaning it, "but where can we sell them for more than a few cents?"

"We can sell them in Winslow, Holbrook and even Flagstaff. People traveling by car like to buy *real* Indian things…not that junk from Japan you see all the time in gift shops."

I didn't want to argue, but I was a whole lot less confident of any sales. Most of the tourists I'd seen at the gas stations and little gift shops were just hurrying across the country headed for towns like Los Angeles, Phoenix, Albuquerque and Santa Fe. In truth, I couldn't recall ever seeing any tourists in Winslow just wandering around downtown shopping for local Indian-made souvenirs. But I wasn't about to argue with Grandmother, especially given what a mess I'd made of things the night before. So I loaded the back of our old pickup and then waved at Stella as she galloped off in a cloud of dust like she was a Pony Express rider. Rip shot out after her and I hoped our dog didn't run his poor self to death trying to keep up.

Grandmother came out of the house wearing a shawl, a long, black dress of thick velvet and her finest turquoise and silver jewelry. I figured she wanted to look like a genuine Indian artist when she went into places hoping to sell her work.

"You drive, Charlie. But slow so we don't break all my pots."

I eased up the hill and we headed up out of our valley. Grandmother had carefully packed her beloved pottery in corn husks; I slowed for every ripple and pothole in the road silently praying that none of her prized pieces would be destroyed.

Grandmother was silent for a few miles and finally she turned to me. "I guess you didn't play so well last night, huh?"

"That's the understatement of all time. They gave me an electric guitar and I couldn't do a thing with it except make awful noise. I was worse than awful."

"No, Charlie, the *guitar* was awful. Maybe you should have taken the guitar Elvis gave you."

"I doubt it would have made any difference. I'm sure that everyone within a hundred miles of Winslow will be talking about how that fool Charlie Coyote howled last night. To be honest, I'm ashamed to leave the ranch."

"There's no reason to be ashamed. You sing good!"

"Well, I've sung my last song in public. You can't imagine how embarrassed I was last night. I was my own worst nightmare up on that stage."

"You'll sing again."

"Only to myself and to my horses."

Grandmother almost smiled and folded her arms. She didn't say anything more until we got to the highway. "To Winslow or to Flagstaff?"

"Go to Winslow so we save gas."

I nodded and eased the truck onto the highway. It didn't sound good but since it had well over a hundred thousand miles of bad roads on it, I figured everything on the Chevy was shot...especially the shocks.

"There," Grandmother said, after we'd driven a few miles. "Stop at that gas station and I'll talk to Mr. Garwood about carrying my pottery and woven plaques."

I wanted to object because Harvey Garwood was so disagreeable and his gas so expensive that none of the locals bought there unless they were running on fumes. But I could sense that Grandmother was determined to make a sale.

"I don't think he'll buy anything ," I said.

"Then maybe he'll trade a few pieces for gallons of his gas."

"I think the chances of that are about as good as this truck sprouting wings and flying us to Graceland."

"Just do what I say, Charlie."

"Yes, Ma'am."

I pulled up to a pump and turned off the engine. The old man himself came hobbling out to meet us. He was stooped and looked like he had bitten into a fiery chili pepper. He had round, thick spectacles on a big, hooked nose and wore a dirty baseball cap that read, SHIT HAPPENS.

Grandmother gave me three dollars for gas and climbed out and moved around to the back of the truck. She pried open a box and dug out a couple of her yucca stem plaques. She marched over to Mr. Garwood who was already starting to pump gas. "Mister Garwood, do you like these?"

He just glanced at them then turned his attention back to his work. "Sure, they're kinda pretty."

"I want to sell them to you."

"How much?"

"Twenty dollars."

"For the box."

"No," Grandmother said, her sharp chin jutting out. "For each."

"Ha!" he laughed. "I can't make any money if I pay you more than I can sell them for! Not interested."

Grandmother repacked the plaques and opened a box of her pottery. She brought out one that was small, but quite beautiful with its Hopi design.

"How much will you pay me for this?"

"Let me have a closer look," Garwood said, leaving his nozzle in our tank, but turning the pump off. He studied the piece carefully, noting Grandmother's coyote sign and signature. "Huumph," he huffed with a nod of appreciation. "This is mighty fine work, but I can't buy any of it. I'd have to take it on consignment."

"What does that mean?" Grandmother asked.

"Means when I sell it, you get half the money it brings and I take half for carrying it in my gift shop."

"No," Grandmother said, plucking the piece from his big, dirty hand and replacing it in the box and then surrounding it with corn husks.

"You sure are a difficult Indian to deal with, Lucy."

"We need money now."

He sighed as if this were the biggest and most painful deal of his entire life. I hated him for that, but he finally hemmed and hawed and said, "I'll give you ten dollars for the pottery you showed me and five dollars for the plaque."

"And breakfast for free."

Garwood actually laughed. "You are a tough old gal to deal with. But okay. Deal!"

To my surprise, the $1.29 breakfast special that Harvey Garwood's tired-looking old waitress served us was good and plentiful. I ate my fill. Before we left, the owner showed Grandmother a few of the other Indian gifts that he sold. Some of it was genuine, but most was fake including some awful looking kachina dolls made from wood that looked like pine. I heard him tell her that it was the cheap stuff that sold, mostly, but that some people really were looking for authentic goods and would pay extra. He asked her if she wanted to leave some more of her things on consignment and Grandmother finally agreed. We carried a box inside and Garwood and Grandmother took nearly an hour writing up an inventory on the price of each item. I was bored stiff and sat in the truck watching the occasional car or truck pass.

"Where do we go next?" I asked Grandmother. "I think you should have left more stuff back there."

"If Mr. Garwood can sell for his high prices, maybe he will make us some good money."

"Half isn't much."

"It is more than nothing, Charlie."

Grandmother seemed buoyed by our small success and she had made up her mind not to bother with the gift shops downtown, but instead to concentrate on gas stations and cafes. I thought it was a poor idea until we went inside some of them and I saw that they all had glass display cases with lots of expensive Navajo, Hopi and Zuni jewelry. And as the afternoon passed and the owners saw the high quality of Grandmother's pottery and yucca plaques and how each thought it would be a unique and valuable addition to their shops, they talked business in hard dollars. We took cash when we could get it and reluctantly accepted receipts when we had to leave pieces on consignment.

To the east of Winslow and long before we got to Holbrook, there was a gift shop where there were several cars parked outside two tall teepees. The teepees had buffalo heads and bows and arrows painted in red on their cheap canvas sides. They had always been a source of both disgust and amusement by the Navajo, Hopi and Zuni because there wasn't a tribe in all of Arizona that had ever lived in teepees for the simple reason that there were no native buffalo. But the tourists didn't either know or care about this fact and there were always cars parked in front of the self described "AUTHENTIC INDIAN TRADING POST".

When we entered the place I was surprised to see that every square inch of the "trading post" was stuffed with cheap "Indian" goods. The owner came right over to us and introduced himself. He seemed like a nice enough fellow, but I couldn't imagine why he wouldn't be ashamed of how most all of his merchandise was made in Japan, China or a place called Malaysia.

"People are always looking to get something for cheap," the owner proclaimed. "I don't see many of you real Indians in here but I always am happy you come. As you can see, my prices are the lowest and the quality is respectable."

I almost laughed out loud. My eyes landed on a box of arrowheads, each perfectly shaped and marked 40 cents each, 3 for $1.00. "Are these *real?*" I asked, picking up a handful and thinking I might buy one.

"Why of course! I found them on Humphreys Peak, spirit home of the Hopi."

Grandmother plucked the arrowhead out of my hand, studied it closely and then tossed it back into the box. "Let's go, Charlie. This man is a liar and a crook!"

"A crook! Why you stupid old squaw, I...."

Whatever else he was going to spew out of his mouth was stopped by my fist. He crashed over a table laden with phony peace pipes and rubber-topped tom toms decorated with dyed chicken feathers. It all went flying.

The man started to curse, but when I stepped in with my fists clenched he stayed down while blood dripped from his split lips. "You...you attacked me!"

Grandmother and I left, but we didn't hurry. We climbed in the truck and I started the engine then glanced back through the rear view mirror. "Grandmother, he's got a gun!"

"Stomp it, Charlie!"

The Chevy's nearly bald back tires spun gravel; it squealed and even left a little rubber mark when we hit the pavement. I could see the man standing in his parking lot waving his gun.

"That ugly tom-tom was probably made in Japan," Grandmother said calmly. "Slow down, there's a big truck stop and diner just up the road."

The truck stop and diner had tall neon signs that could be seen in both directions and read, CHEAP GAS AND GOOD FOOD! The sign blinked over and over and the letters changed colors from green to bright red. There were a lot of trucks and cars in the dirt parking lot.

We pulled in and got out. "Well, it's the biggest stop yet."

Grandmother nodded. By now we had gotten a pretty good idea of what we could make, both on cash sales to the owners or putting things on consignment. I was still having some problem with the fifty percent thing, but that was the standard...take it or leave it so having more pottery and plaques than cold cash, we agreed to the terms.

I was feeling irritable about us getting only fifty percent and when I voiced my displeasure, Grandmother surprised me by saying, "We're *redskins*, Charlie, so we always get screwed by the whites."

My jaw dropped and I swung my head to look at her to see if I'd heard right. Grandmother was trying not to laugh. Her comment was so ridiculous, but true, that it somehow seemed hilarious.

We both started laughing.

The truck stop owner was found and introduced to us. When he saw a couple of my grandmother's beautiful pots and plaques, he beamed. "I sell a lot of junk here, that's true. But I could use some authentic Indian gifts and I like what you're doing. How much do you need for these on consignment?"

By now Grandmother had a good idea so she gave him a price and he said, "I think I can sell $400 a week. So you'd get $200. How does that sound?"

I was so surprised by the huge figure that I was speechless and so was Grandmother, but she recovered quickly and said, "I have several boxes you can look at in our truck."

"Well go ahead, bring them in and I'll pick what to leave. We'll write an inventory and I think you'll be happy working with us. And since we are talking about you leaving so much merchandise initially, I'll advance you $200.00 today. Fair enough?"

"Fair enough."

"Cowboy Charlie," the truck stop owner said, "do you help your grandmother make pottery and these plaques?"

"She does the designing; I dig the clay and gather sheep shit to fire the pottery."

"That's good," he said. "I expect we are going to sell a lot of her work and she's going to need help. I don't want her overworking herself."

"Me neither. I'll help all that I can."

"You do that," he said.

We all shook hands and then I lugged the boxes into the truck stop. We priced things, wrote out the inventory and left. Grandmother's pottery would vary in price in his gift shop from $25.00 to $65.00 and the woven yucca plaques would earn her $12.50 each.

When we finally left the truck stop, Grandmother and I sat in the Chevy and stared at all the trucks and cars coming and going; most just stopped for gas, but a lot of them headed inside.

"I can't believe those figures," I finally said, as much to myself as to Grandmother. "The man thinks we can make $200.00 a week! Why, that would pay the loan, do a lot of repairs on the ranch and put gas in our tank and food on our table."

"It sure would," she said, grinning. "Charlie, stop at the grocery store. I want to buy us porterhouse steaks for a celebration tonight."

I grinned like a cat chewing up a cricket then burst into one of my favorite Elvis tunes, *"Well have you heard the news, there's good rockin' tonight!"*

# *Chapter 10*

For the next six months, Grandmother, Stella and I worked from sunup to sundown keeping the ranch going and making new pottery and plaques for the big truck stop managed by Mr. Todd and Mr. Garwood's smaller gas station and gift shop. It seemed like overnight we'd happily gone from nearly broke to actually being able to save money.

I missed Father a great deal and spent a lot of time riding the hills and sagebrush-covered flats looking for pottery clay and yucca fibers. The yucca fibers were the hardest to find and as demand for the plaques stayed steady, we began to buy them from the Navajo up by Tuba City. Sometimes I took the truck and drove for miles and Stella often came along. At first she just seemed to want to talk about Elvis, but as time passed, his name came up less frequently.

By October, I was sick of working with clay and thought that weaving plaques was about the most tedious thing I'd ever imagined. Then we learned that Mr. Todd had been replaced as manager of the truck stop by a man named Mr. Peterson who had his own ideas about fair play with his suppliers.

"Ma'am, I'm afraid we're going to have to renegotiate your agreement on these Indian goods," he informed Grandmother one afternoon after we finished delivering a large consignment. "Unfortunately, our costs per foot of merchandising area keep rising and we just can't afford to give you fifty percent of retail price anymore."

Grandmother stiffened and before she could get angry, I asked, "How much are you talking about now?"

"I can give you forty percent."

Grandmother said, "No!"

"Ma'am, no offense, but there are Indians trooping in here every day wanting to leave their crafts on consignment. Some have even offered to take just thirty percent…but since you've done well for us in the past, I'm being generous even giving you forty percent."

"You mean you'd replace us?"

"I'm sorry, but my job is to maximize profits for the company, not the suppliers. I'm sure you understand. To be honest, some of the customers who travel regularly thorough here and stop to buy have said that it would be nice to have some new things to buy from Indians. And I happen to agree."

"Charlie, let's get those empty boxes out of the truck and pack up everything this man has left."

The manager suddenly threw up his hands. "Now wait a minute! There's no need to do that. I'll still pay the fifty percent on what's on our shelves and even for what you brought in today. But after that...."

Grandmother's expression was fixed, her eyes hard and I knew she wanted to get her goods back and never see this man again. But I also knew that we needed the money so I pleaded with her to leave what was in the store and what we'd brought today...and I hoped I could come back by myself and strike some kind of compromise.

"I'll get the boxes we brought for today," I said, taking Grandmother by the elbow and practically dragging her back to the truck. She sat as still as a stone while I unloaded, got a receipt and returned to the truck. We drove away in silence toward home.

Finally, I asked, "Grandmother, what are we going to do now?"

"Mr. Garwood is an honest man and he will keep taking our goods at fifty percent."

"But his shop alone is not enough to pay our expenses."

"Charlie, you need to find town work. Stella and I will keep making plaques and pottery. Maybe we will drive farther away and find another big truck stop."

"I don't think there's another big one for fifty miles...maybe even as far as Gallup."

"We can go there someday."

"Sure," I said, trying to sound at least a little hopeful knowing we were entering the slow winter tourist season. *This could*, I thought, *prove to be another hungry winter after all.*

When we got home and told Stella about the latest setback, she stunned us by clapping her hands together and shouting, "Hallelujah, I couldn't have made another pot or woven another stupid Hopi plaque even if my life depended upon it!"

I stared at my sister. I'd known she was unhappy staying out at the ranch all the time but not *that* unhappy. "Well," I said, trying to curb my temper, "this means we're almost back to square one and in danger of losing the ranch when taxes come up again."

"Then we lose it!" she shouted. "I'm sick and tired of worrying about it. And you don't have to look for a winter job because I'll find one and live in Winslow. It's too hard to drive back and forth on our road during winter."

Grandmother said, "You can *both* find winter jobs and ride back and forth into town together. Maybe you can work at the same place."

Stella and I both thought that was a terrible idea, but we didn't say anything. Stella left and headed for the barn and I knew she was going for another one of her long, soul-searching rides.

I climbed up in the loft and brooded for awhile and then I picked up the Martin and worked on some songs that I'd written. They were good, but after the disaster that night at the Frontier Saloon, I sure wasn't eager to give public singing another try very soon. No sir. I would pick and sing for Grandmother when she asked but that was all.

When I came down for supper Grandmother said, "You could still make some money with your singing. You are really good! You sing like a bird."

"Like a bird?" I asked, almost laughing.

"Yes, you keep writing songs and someday you'll make good money."

"Fat chance," I replied. "Elvis hasn't even bothered to write or stop by in a long time. I read that his headline shows in Las Vegas are selling out every performance. I sure wish I had the money to go see and talk to him."

"But we *don't* have the money," Grandmother said gently. "So you'll have to keep singing and playing and getting better."

I didn't sleep well that night because I was worried about money. Winter was always hard and we had to buy hay and I needed to start cutting firewood from the pinyon and juniper which burned hot and gave off a lot of heat from our potbellied stove. Since those trees were everywhere around us, there was an inexhaustible supply but it was hard, dirty work and we went through ten or twelve cords before the snows melted in the spring. And how would I manage to do that if I had to take a town job for cash?

Another growing concern was that our old Chevy truck was about to quit. We'd run the tires bald all summer making pottery and plaque deliveries and the long, potholed dirt road between Route 66 and our house that had torn the muffler off Elvis' limousine was also finishing off our pickup.

So the next morning when Stella put on the coffee I told her that we had to find jobs and save some money to put down on a newer truck.

"I'm happy to do that and I think we ought to go to town and start looking today. But I'll tell you right off that it won't be worth it if we get lousy cashier's jobs or something that pays just a couple dollars an hour. We can do better."

"All I know is that we can't let go of Coyote Ranch," I said stubbornly

"I know, but staying here isn't going to do us any good if we have to starve every day!"

I threw up my hands in exasperation. "Stella, I don't understand you."

"That's *your* problem little brother, not mine! Since Father died trying to save your hide in the rodeo arena and Elvis abandoned us I'm beginning to think that we're...we're jinxed!"

I had nothing to say about that. I knew that Stella thought she could make a better life off the ranch, but I had my doubts. Since I'd been old enough to listen to serious talk from my friends, I'd learned that single Indian girls in towns very often ended up dead, on the streets or in prisons. Stella was hard on the outside but fragile as flowers on the inside...and she had her dreams... maybe that's all she had now that Elvis had seemingly forgotten her.

So I said nothing and refilled her coffee cup. Then I looked out the window to see Grandmother out by Father's grave, sprinkling corn pollen and saying her morning prayers. The wind was blowing strong and sunlight hit the pollen and it look like flakes of gold dust. I sipped my coffee and watched Grandmother, taking solace in her daily morning routine and steadfastness. Sure, Stella had shocked me about her wanting to leave Coyote Ranch, but I sure didn't want to leave this place.

A few hours later, Stella and I cleaned up and drove into Winslow and bought a newspaper to look at the help wanted ads. We bought donuts and headed over to Holbrook, the Chevy belching smoke and pistons thumping.

We bought another newspaper but there weren't any job openings we qualified for there, either.

"Charlie, what are we going to do now?"

I slumped down in the torn seat of our truck and finally said, "I just don't know. But we can't face Grandmother tonight if we don't give this our best try, can we?"

"No, we can't," my sister quietly agreed. "Did you know that Travis Lane is opening a livestock auction barn and feed store east of town?"

"No."

"Well it says so in the paper. I remember that Travis went belly up in the feedlot business about six years ago. He was the handsomest man! They say he ran off with the feedlot owner's wife. And that feedlot is where we bought that bald-faced roan gelding for sixty dollars some years ago."

"Ah yes," I said. "That horse broke a leg when Father was on him chasing at old cow we called Gertrude. We had to shoot the horse and Father was laid up for a couple of weeks from the spill."

"Maybe he needs help. I remember that Travis had a lot of family money. I recall that Travis's father was into oil down in Texas and I suppose that Travis inherited a lot of money when his father died."

"If he has so much money why would he come back to Winslow?"

"Let's drive over to the feedlot and see Travis. He reminded me of Paul Newman."

"Look, Stella, we're looking for work…not a wealthy boyfriend for you."

"Don't be silly! Travis might be hiring."

"Alright," I agreed. "But you can ask about jobs. I never much cared for the man."

"Why not?"

"He had a reputation for liking women…single or married and young."

Stella made a face. "What kind of a sister do you think I am!"

I didn't care to answer that question so I started the truck and we drove off. My sister had a lot of fine qualities, but no one would ever confuse her with Mother Teresa. I thought about Travis Lane and remembered him as being a kind of "hell on wheels" fella. He talked fast, slapped everyone's back and played the role of a "good ole boy" but he was a brawler when drinking. Travis was a big man…and he liked to fight almost as much as he liked to drink and romance women. I didn't think I would have much use for the man and I knew that, if Father had been with us, he'd have warned us away from Travis Lane.

When we pulled up at the auction barn I saw a couple of men hard at work hammering and repairing the old, broken down livestock pens. There were beer cans, trash and junk in the yard and I didn't see any cattle, but I did see a pen with some horses.

When we got out of the Chevy I noticed that the barn door was open and I could hear a radio blasting Buck Owens singing, *They're gonna put me in the movies…."*

I tuned the song out because it reminded me that a long string of bad movies like *Clam Bake*, and *Harem Scarum* that had been bombs. All those awful movies had nearly done Elvis in and had left him richer, but bitter because of the lack of critical acclaim.

"Come on, Charlie, let's go inside."

I headed for the two story barn noting that it had been repainted. Inside, I saw the sale floor surrounded by rows of seats rising up nearly to the ceiling. The sale floor itself was small and might hold a dozen wild-eyed cattle. On the right side was a gate where a wrangler drove stock onto the sale floor and on the left side was another gate where they were driven out again when they were either sold or passed on if the final bid was too low. If you climbed up about ten rows you'd be on the same level as the auctioneer who had an assistant that kept a running tally of sale prices corresponding to the numbers painted on the livestock except for horses which were just given a short description. A large man in work clothes was up on the top row of seats painting them gunmetal gray. I was shocked to see that it was none other than Travis Lane.

"Travis?" Stella asked.

"That's me, alright. And who might you be, pretty girl?"

"I'm Stella Coyote and this is my kid brother, Cowboy Charlie." She gave him that killer smile that almost never failed with men. "We were just kids when you left town so you probably don't remember us."

Travis carefully laid his paintbrush across the top of the paint can and gave us a wide grin. He had a mustache, the whitest front teeth I'd ever seen on a human and a square jaw.

*Yep,* I thought, *this old hound dog is some longer in the tooth, but I'll bet he still likes to go sniffin' bottoms.*

"Coyote, huh? Well, I don't recall you two, but I sure do remember your mother and father."

I couldn't help but blurt. "You remember my mother when she was still alive?"

Lane's smile got lost. "I knew her right well before she died."

I didn't like the sound of that even a little bit.

"She was a fine woman," Lane quickly added. "How is your father these days?"

Stella shook her head. "He was killed by a rodeo bull trying to save Charlie."

Travis Lane clucked his tongue. "Sorry to hear that. He was one hell of a cowboy. I tried to hire him at the auction but he wasn't interested. So I hired a lesser man instead. What can I do for you?"

"We're both looking for work."

"Have you asked around?"

"We did but no luck so far." Stella gave him that smile again. "We were hoping that you might need some help."

"My boys outside aren't happy repairing fences and gates so they're quittin'."

And right then the pair of cowboys walked through the barn door. "Mr. Lane, we're finished, but we might be willin' to come back and work with the stock when you get the auction goin'. You see, we're cowboys, not carpenters."

I saw something change on Travis Lane's rugged face and knew that he was fighting his temper. He suddenly stood up, reached into his pocket and pulled out a wad of bills big enough to choke a mule. He peeled off some money and tossed it into the air. The bills fluttered down toward the sale pen and I saw that they were all twenties.

"Don't either one of you come back asking me to hire you again. You're leaving me in a fix!"

"But, Mr. Lane, we...."

"Git your money and git off my property," Lane growled.

When the two men had gathered their money and left, Stella said, "Charlie and I can fix gates and fences. We've had lots of practice out at our place. Can we have their jobs?"

"You're a girl. No, I stand corrected. You're a beautiful young woman and I don't think you are cut out to do carpentry work."

"*This* woman can do carpentry and a whole lot of other things," Stella said quickly, putting her hands on her hips and staring up at the big man.

They locked eyeballs and I suddenly felt uneasy. There seemed to be something going on that I didn't understand and didn't like. But I kept my silence because we really needed the work.

"Alright," Lane said, "follow those boys to their truck and make sure that they don't walk off with my carpentry tools. Then go to work doin' whatever they were doin' when they quit. I pay four dollars an hour."

"Thanks!" Stella said. "You won't be sorry you hired us."

"I believe you," Lane said.

Stella and I hurried outside. The cowboys who had just quit didn't take any tools. I picked up a hammer and nails and walked toward the corrals. There seemed to be enough work for six men and that made me happy. Several minutes later, as I was nailing up a rail to a post, Stella emerged from the barn with a smile on her face.

"What are you grinning about?" I asked.

"He still reminds me of a big Paul Newman."

"Who cares," I muttered. "Help me hold up this rail and let's get busy."

She reached for a hammer and some nails. Stella was a hard worker and she knew how to fix fencing. "Charlie?"

"Yeah?"

"You don't seem happy about us both finding good work."

"I'm happy," I grudgingly admitted. "But I don't like the way that Travis Lane was eyeballing you."

"No crime in a man looking."

"As long as that's all he ever does."

Stella kissed my cheek. "You're a good, sweet kid brother."

"Shut up and let's fix some fence," I growled. "That man is old enough to be your father."

"He doesn't look at me like he thinks he's that old."

"I know," I said, hammering furiously. "And that's the thing that most bothers me."

"I can handle him."

"You'd better," I warned. "Or I'll…use this hammer on his head."

"Men," Stella said as she stuck a couple of nails between her lips and started working, "you're all really just children."

I didn't have a thing to say about that. I would earn my pay, but I sure didn't care for Travis Lane…to my mind he was as full of foul wind as a burro in a bean field.

# *Chapter 11*

Even after a few weeks of working for Travis Lane, I still didn't like him much. But he left Stella and me alone to do our work and at the end of the day he paid us both with cash. We worked hard, six days a week from eight until five repairing pens and loading chutes, cleaning up trash, hauling in tons of hay and patching water troughs. We got fifty head of cattle. And finally, we painted the entire barn red and put the words, TRAVIS LANE, LIVESTOCK AUCTION along with his phone number in big, bold white letters.

You could even read it out on the highway.

"People can read that for a mile in either direction," Travis crowed. "You did a fine job on the lettering, Cowboy Charlie!"

"Thanks."

I had come to accept the man for what he was and I was loyal to him for paying us fairly and on time. But now and then I caught him eyeballing Stella hungrily when he thought neither of us was looking and I didn't like that in the least…but what really frosted me was when I caught my sister flirting with him either with her words, her swaying hips or her eyes. It made me uncomfortable and every evening when we got back to our mailbox I was praying for a letter from Elvis…but it never came.

The one thing that did give me comfort was that Travis seemed to have a lot of women he was messing with…sometimes even disappearing with them in the daytime. I learned that he had bought an old ranch house south of town and I came to recognize some of the regular women's cars and trucks.

Stella recognized them too. And when she did she usually said something insulting. I had my eyes on a girl that I'd gone to school with named Loretta Hickey. Trouble was, she was dating a guy named Fred who had a beautiful '58 Chevy Impala and a football letterman's jacket. But in the weeks ahead while Stella and I worked at the sale barn, Loretta often stopped by to ask how I was doing.

Whenever this happened, if Stella was around, she made it clear that she didn't like Loretta and once even told me that the girl was homelier than a hound which was not true. I think Stella disliked Loretta because her father was a successful real estate broker and her mother also sold real estate and was big in the town's clubs and charities. The Hickey family was far better off than the Coyote family with a big house; I figured envy was a big part of Stella's problem.

Loretta was short, buxom and bubbly. She had blonde hair and blue eyes and she filled out a pair of Levis every bit as nicely as my sister. Loretta had a great sense of humor and she treated me well even though I was darker. One afternoon when I was taking a short break from fixing some feed troughs, Loretta drove up and we started talking about this and that. Finally, I asked her if she was serious about the guy who still wore his letterman's jacket several years after graduation and was so proud of it that he even wore it in warm weather.

"Fred wants to get married and he has a good job at his uncle's tire shop, but I want to go to the Northern Arizona University in Flagstaff. Did you ever think of going to college?"

I shook my head. I'd been a fair student…mostly one that was happy to just get by with average grades. "I don't think that's in the cards for me."

"Why not?"

"Well, for starters I don't have the time or the money. We're struggling to hang onto our ranch and we'd lose it for certain if I went off to college."

"I see." She smiled a little sadly and changed the subject. "Charlie, I heard about what happened when you tried to play and sing at the Frontier Saloon. Everyone knows that Elvis is your friend and that he gave you a very expensive guitar. But I didn't know you had a beautiful voice."

"Compared to Elvis, I can't really sing a lick."

"I heard you were awfully good. Charlie, would you bring that guitar to town someday and play a song for me?"

"What?" I wasn't sure I'd heard right.

"It would mean a lot."

I shrugged. "Where would I sing? In a parking lot or in the sale barn?"

"Well, we could drive out of town a ways and you could do it in your truck."

I couldn't help myself and I grinned. "Do *what?*"

She caught my drift and her cheeks turned pink. "Charlie! You know what I'm talking about. Don't act like a horny boy."

"That's about what I am, Loretta."

She blushed even deeper. "Fred and a couple of his friends formed a small band, but not one of them can sing worth spit. So, Cowboy Charlie, are you ever going to play and sing a song just for me?"

*Why not!*

"Alright, I'll bring my guitar on Saturday. Travis Lane takes my sister to lunch every Saturday so I could sing you a song in the sale barn and no one else would be around. But if you start laughing…."

She reached up and touched my cheek. "I'd never laugh at you. That would be cruel and anyway, you're way too big and handsome to make fun of."

Before I could say another word, she kissed me quick on the lips and ran to her Volkswagen beetle that probably ran fifty miles on a gallon of gas.

A short time later when I was fixing a gate, Stella showed up and I must have been grinning because she asked, "Mind letting me in on your joke?"

"Nope."

"I saw Miss Bust-Out-Britches drive away."

"Just don't you bother yourself about Loretta Hickey."

"She's *not* interested in you, Charlie, and she never will be. Loretta is a town girl who has far bigger plans in mind. She lets everyone know that she intends to go off to college."

I knew that Stella was right and she was just trying to keep me from getting hurt like Elvis had hurt her, so I clammed up and kept working. But that evening, I practiced on my guitar until Grandmother and Stella yelled at me to quit and let them sleep. I decided that I'd play one of Elvis' hits, "Love Me Tender". It was a slow love song and easy enough to play. I figured I might win Loretta's heart with it so I meant to put my all into the effort. My real concern was what Stella would say when I brought my guitar to work in the morning.

When we headed off to work the next morning, I had my guitar. I was feeling as irritable as a tomcat walking in mud.

"What's the guitar for, Charlie?"

"Never you mind."

Stopping beside the truck, Stella grinned. "Let me guess. You're bringing the guitar so you can sing to Miss Bust-Out-Britches!"

"If you start ragging on me about Loretta, I might get mad enough to bust your britches!"

She climbed into the truck. "No, you'd never do that."

Stella knew me very well. And when I started the truck, I was thinking how odd it was that Stella didn't like Loretta any more than I liked Travis Lane. I just didn't trust him around my sister and, if I thought he was…well, doing something that he shouldn't do, I was prepared to try and knock his bright white teeth out. And while Travis was a big man and had the reputation of being a hard fighter, I wasn't too concerned because I stood now six-foot-three and weighed just over two hundred pounds…all of it muscle and bone.

That morning at work I expected that Stella would tell Travis about the guitar and what my intentions were concerning Loretta. I figured they might even start ribbing me, but thankfully that never happened. And when noon rolled around and they headed off to lunch, I sighed with relief.

I had a sandwich and a banana and climbed up to the top row of seats. I was too nervous to be hungry so I lifted the Martin out of its case and began to pick a little and hum my love song in the sale barn.

"Hello, Charlie."

Just the sight of Loretta made my heart beat faster. She wore a red ribbon in her hair and she had on a flashy cowgirl shirt with fake pearl buttons…the top two or three unbuttoned. I'd never seen her look so good.

Then, she swayed up the steps to sit just below me. She leaned back with her breasts straining against her blouse and I swallowed hard, my mouth as dry as an Arizona rain barrel.

"Go ahead and sing me a song, Charlie."

I cleared my throat, looked up at the dusty rafters and played her "Love Me Tender," and I did it like Elvis did it…slow, a little breathy and sexy with lots of emotion.

I was good and when I finished the song her eyes were misty and wide with what I hoped was love and lust. I laid my guitar down and she threw herself into my arms almost pushing me over backward.

She was all over me! Next thing I knew, we were ripping off our shirts and most everything else and although there wasn't much room between the seat rows, we made enough to make wild, frantic love. I remember the exact moment that it happened because, in our frenzy, my watch was ripped off my wrist and it fell through the cracks of the bleachers to land and break on the concrete far below.

All I knew was that the gray paint wasn't as dry as I'd thought when it was hard rubbed and that there were some splinters in Loretta's butt that had to be removed later that afternoon along with paint.

We were still grunting and grinding when I heard Travis Long's truck honk. Thank God we had some warning! We jumped up and struggled into our clothes. It was a good deal hotter up near the tin roof than it was down lower in the stands and we were both drenched with sweat and trying to catch our breath when my sister and boss poked their heads into the sale barn.

"Everything clear up there!" Stella shouted.

Loretta and I exchanged quick, panicky looks and both nodded. My pants were still unbuttoned and her blouse was all twisted up and her bra was undone but we knew there was no time for finishing touches.

"Yes we are!" I yelled, picking up my guitar and running through a chord progression. "How was your lunch?"

"Not nearly as good as yours, obviously" Travis Lane said with a laugh.

"Charlie was just playing me a song," Loretta managed to squeak.

"Yeah, I'm sure," Stella said, giving us both a wink.

"I'd sure like to hear Cowboy Charlie play," Travis offered. "Since you and Elvis are friends, why don't you do one of his songs…how about "Love Me Tender?"

Then, before I could recover, Travis and my sister burst out with guffaws. I wanted to jump down there and strangle them both. Instead, I glanced over at Loretta and she looked as if she was about to cry.

Right then and there I did something that I never thought I'd have the courage to do. I laid my guitar down and scooted over to Loretta and laid my arm across her shoulders. In a low voice I vowed, "Don't you worry, this won't get around."

"Charlie, I…."

I knew that she was scared that her family and friends would hear about how we'd been caught making love in broad daylight up in the bleachers of the sale barn. I knew that her reputation would be ruined in Winslow for the rest of her life.

"Stella, I'm asking you and Mr. Lane to give me your words that nothing will be said about us."

A moment that seemed like a lifetime passed before Travis said, "I give you my word of honor. I swear it on my dead mother's grave."

He looked sideways at Stella who said, "And I swear on our mother's grave wherever that might be. Charlie, nothing will ever be said about this to anyone."

"Thank you," Loretta sobbed. "Thank you!"

"Yeah," I added, "thanks."

"Looks like you might need a few minutes alone to…straighten up and say goodbye," Travis told my girl. He glanced at his watch, one far nicer than my busted one laying far below on the concrete floor. "It's half past one, and those chutes sure aren't going to be fixing themselves."

"I know."

They ducked out and Loretta and I quickly put ourselves back together. She looked pale and nervous and when I tried to kiss her goodbye, she stood up and hurried down the row of bleachers to the bottom. I thought she might just leave without a word but she stopped and the door and said, "I'm sorry, Charlie."

"I'm not."

"I really loved your singing and playing."

"You can hear more any old time you want, Loretta. I'll play my songs just for you."

Our eyes held for a moment before she rushed outside and I figured the next time I saw her Loretta she would be cruising Winslow with Fred in his cool '58 Chevy Impala with tuck and roll seats and fancy damn spinner hubcaps.

# Chapter 12

I didn't see Loretta for awhile, but then she started showing up and we began to spend time again.

"What about Fred?" I asked.

"Oh, he's going to a trade school for auto mechanics," she told me. "I think he'll do real well at it but…."

"But what?"

"Well, I never wanted to marry a guy with grease under his fingernails."

Loretta said it with a laugh and it made me wonder what she thought of a man with dirt and horseshit always under his fingernails, but I decided it was better not to ask. As for my sister, Travis was seeing her off the job far more than I liked. He bought her presents such as new western clothes, turquoise and silver jewelry. And what really upset me was that he gave her a beautiful Quarter Horse she named Sun Dancer because the mare was a flashy palomino. Travis told everyone that the mare had an impressive racing bloodline and it was obvious that she had cost a bundle of money.

When Stella brought the mare to our ranch Grandmother wasn't a bit happy. "Stella," she demanded to know, "why is Mr. Lane giving you such expensive presents?"

"The horse was on the race track and pulled up lame. She's just going to stay with us and I'll work on getting her sound again. Right now, she's too high spirited to be a good ranch or trail riding horse. My intention is to train her to become a barrel racing horse and then I can go to rodeos and win us lots of money."

Grandmother just shook her head. "It's too much, Stella. That man is not going to be good for you and neither is that horse."

Stella walked away and Grandmother pointed at me saying, "And neither is Loretta good for you!"

I hadn't wanted to talk about Loretta to my family. One reason was that her family wasn't a bit pleased that their college-bound daughter was seeing a half-breed cowboy. Her father had even asked me what my intentions were about going to college. When I didn't come up with the right answer he told me I ought to stay clear of his daughter.

Work was going fine. When Travis Lane's corrals, sale barn and chutes were in good shape, he bought six unbroken mustangs out of Utah. They were the best looking mustangs I'd ever seen, with straight legs and decent size and conformation. I was impressed enough to ask, "What are you going to do with them?"

"Well, Cowboy Charlie, I'd like you to break and put some rein on 'em," he told me. "Everyone says you're the best at that sort of thing…better'n riding bulls for certain."

I flushed with embarrassment at the not so subtle reference about my sad experience with Buzzard. "Stella and I drive here and back every day and it doesn't leave me with any extra time to break those mustangs."

"I'll give you an hour a day on my dollar to work with them."

"I'll think about it."

"I only paid a hundred each for them and if you put a good rein and stop on 'em I can probably get six hundred each. Five hundred bucks profit per horse…and I'll give you two hundred for each sale. I'll pay the feed and any vet bills. Be a lot of money in your pocket and some in mine."

"Are you in a big rush?"

"No, but feed costs do mount up so I'd expect you to have them ready to ride and sell in…oh, two months."

I thought about the money and my time and said, "That works for me."

"Good, then do we have a deal?" He stuck out his big hand and I shook it.

An extra twelve hundred dollars sure would make it worth my time in the saddle. But when I told Grandmother that evening about the deal she was less than enthusiastic.

"You could get bucked off onto your head and bend the tin plate, Charlie. Remember the doctors said no more rough stock?"

"I'll take it slow and easy. Those mustangs probably won't do more than suck up their bellies and hop around a little when I first ride."

"You don't know that for sure," Stella said. "If Travis would have told me about this plan I'd have objected."

But I held my ground. "I can make twelve hundred dollars. That money would go a long ways toward trading in what's left of our truck on a better one. I need to do it."

"Are you sure about this?" Grandmother asked.

"I am."

"Be careful."

The very next day I began working with the six Utah horses. Two were mares and the other four had been gelded. I'd always loved horses and I thought these were good animals. I watched them closely for a day, moving in and out among them in the corral. I didn't see any viciousness…just nervousness which was expected. Mustangs are often trapped, sometimes in box canyons and sometimes they're run down and roped. Whichever way it happens it isn't easy on the wild horse and of course they're scared witless. Then they're often blindfolded, sometimes hobbled and taken to a distant ranch corral or maybe straight to a livestock auction via a truck. It didn't take a lot of imagination to understand how terrifying it would be for an animal that had never even been touched to be trucked down a highway with the roar of traffic and the whining of heavy tires and creaking of steel filling its cramped space.

I thought about all of that as I moved among them, slow and quiet. To these horses, man was the enemy. The second day I brought out my rope and began to twirl it around and around the horses and then I roped a mare and let her run while I sort of dug in my heels not to pull her around, but just to get her accustomed to the rope. When she calmed down I shook my rope loose and did the same with each of the other horses. It took all week to get to the point that they didn't go crazy with the feel of the rope and the next week I took to using a halter on each horse. The whole idea was not to just ear them down and toss a saddle on their backs while they were fighting.

It took patience and understanding to break a horse correctly and I knew that there were plenty of different opinions on how to get the job done in the right way. Father had taught me his way and I found it to be the best. I'd say that the first two weeks of working with the mustangs, my biggest annoyance was when Travis and Stella stood by the big round corral giving me their opinions on just how I should proceed. Travis, of course, putting feed into their bellies, wanted me to progress faster. And Stella, knowing that if you rushed an animal and pushed it into fear that it might buck or even rear over backward, wanted me to take even more time and go slower. And finally, Loretta took to coming around and since she was also good with horses, I had to listen to her nickel's worth of advice. Danged if I didn't want to take those horses out to our ranch where only Grandmother would be watching and approving my every move. I just wished everyone would both tend to their own business and let me tend to mine.

"We aren't going to make them kiddies' ponies, Charlie!" Travis called from outside the corral. "Or rent horses or dude ranch horses. These animals just need to be broke to ride and rein. When are you going to stop the ground work and get into the saddle?"

Just out of stubbornness, I suppose, I took a few days longer than necessary and then when no one was around, I saddled each animal and led it around the corral awhile then mounted. All of them shuddered and seemed to falter a little when I made them walk, but not a single one panicked and started bucking… well, except for the sorrel gelding which I'd already decided was the most obstinate and independent.

"Easy," I crooned, keeping a short rein. "No need to make this hard for either one of us."

Just then Travis and Stella appeared and that made me mad. The last thing I wanted was for them to be yelling at me about how I should handle this sorrel.

There were some bronc busters who liked to take their first ride in deep sand, the obvious reason being that if they got tossed, it would be a soft landing. Also the bronc couldn't pitch nearly as hard. I'd even heard of a few that liked to take the first ride in a pond or shallow lake for the same reasons. But Father had held firm to his belief that, if you bucked them out in sand or water, you might do fine the first time, but when you got onto to the hard ground, the green-broke horse was going to get even.

That made one hell of a lot of sense to me.

"Cowboy Charlie," Travis said, "I really think you ought to lead that one down to the dry riverbed and buck him out in the sand."

I ignored both Travis and my sister. I was angry that they'd showed up and I jerked the sorrel's head around and swung on board. The sorrel ducked his head and jumped straight off the ground, grunting and snorting his outrage. When he came down he landed on locked knees and the jolt was so severe my head snapped forward like the popper on a bullwhip. I almost lost my right stirrup and while I was trying to get my boot back in place, the sorrel ducked his head low and got even busier. Next thing I knew I was sailing over his ears. I hit the bottom rail of the corral fence and rolled under it in a daze.

Stella was the first one to reach me. "Are you hurt?"

I spat dirt and blinked a few times to focus. "Only my pride," I managed to moan, pulling myself up on the rails.

Travis came up to me and blustered, "I know you're running a risk here so I'll have a go at that sonofabitch!"

"No, Sir, you hired me to do this job and I'm going to do 'er."

I think Travis was putting on some bravado to impress both Stella and Loretta who had suddenly appeared in her Volkswagen and was looking awfully worried. Travis wanted to impress the girls bad enough to say, "Are you forgetting that the sorrel is my horse, Cowboy Charlie?"

"No, I'm not forgetting, but it's my job to break them, remember? We have an agreement, don't we?"

When he didn't say anything right away I screwed my Stetson down tight and climbed through the rails. I caught up the rope and swung back on top of the sorrel so quick he didn't have time to slide away. I should have been wearing spurs, but I didn't. With dull spurs' rowels you can still administer punishment to match what you are receiving. But the sorrel and I were quickly at each other and I was grabbing leather when I needed to because this wasn't a rodeo ride and I couldn't be disqualified. The sorrel was a hard and determined bucker. but I was just as hard and determined. Our fight lasted maybe two minutes and it passed in a blur. When the bucking started to get easier, I knew that the sorrel was getting tired and feeling defeated. I let him get his last bucks in, but they weren't much…hell, the last couple were just crow hops.

That horse and I made our peace. He was huffing and puffing and I made him jog fast around and around the corral just nudging him with my boot heels and talking friendly into his ears.

"Cowboy Charlie," Travis called, "that was a helluva fine second ride! You're a natural on a horse and you ought to think about riding rodeo broncs."

Stella gave our boss a hard shove. "Are you kidding! You know that Charlie's got a tin plate in his head! What the hell are you talking about?"

Travis Lane was not used to be spoken to that way and he bristled. "I was just complimenting your brother, dammit! You don't have to go hysterical."

"Well don't give out any more idiotic advice to Charlie."

Those two faced off and then Travis spun on his heel and headed back to the sale barn with Stella in his wake. They were yelling and cussing and I sure hoped there wasn't going to be a regular fist fight in the barn.

I unsaddled the sorrel and turned him loose knowing that I'd ride him every day for a half hour and then he'd be good to sell.

"Charlie," Loretta asked, "you wouldn't ever take up bronc riding would you?"

"No."

"Why'd you go and buck that sorrel out when you could have worked him some more on the ground and it all would have gone easier?"

I had no answer. Maybe it was because of Stella and Travis jawing at me from the sidelines and making me angry and impatient. Then again, maybe it was just because I wanted to see if I still could ride a bucker. "I don't exactly know what I was thinking, Loretta."

"You weren't thinking," she said. "But you sure can ride!"

I winked. "You'd be the best one to know."

Loretta turned beet red and then she stomped off to her little German car and drove away in a hurry. I didn't know if she was mad or not, but I figured she'd get over it if she was.

* * * *

Our auction barn finally opened and after we sold the Utah horses for exactly what Travis had predicted, I took the twelve hundred dollars and purchased a red, 1975 Chevy half ton pickup with a "four on the floor" and good rubber all around. It was in almost mint condition and I bought it at a used car dealer in Flagstaff making sure it was a town vehicle and not a ranch truck all of which have been beat to death on dirt roads, pastures and fields. I really liked my truck...it had a big V-8 and it was set up to pull a stock trailer full of horses or cattle. It had a cassette tape under the dash and speakers in the door panels. When I first took Loretta for a ride I had some Elvis tapes and we sang along with his music just cruising down Route 66 like we owned the whole damned world.

"You know, with a truck like this I sure won't be ashamed to drive to Flagstaff and pick you up at your dorm on Saturday nights. But first I'd drive to one of those car washes and then this truck would look like a million dollars and your friends would all be green with envy. Yep, when we drive around up there we'll look just like those kids with big futures and lots of money."

"You know that I don't give a damn about what other people think. I like you just the way that you are."

"I wonder if that will change after you meet all those college guys."

Her eyes turned misty blue. "I'll always love you, Charlie Coyote."

"Then why didn't you insist that I be the one who helped you move into your dormitory instead of your parents?"

"They're paying all my college bills. What choice did I have?"

"None, I guess."

That night we stayed out late and when I took her home the lights in her house were ablaze. Her father stormed out on the front porch and when Loretta jumped out to leave, he yelled at me, "It's over, Charlie! Find yourself some... some waitress or clerk to squire around. Loretta deserves better than you!"

I couldn't believe what I'd just heard...but then I should not have been surprised. I had been getting unspoken messages from Loretta's parents for months that they disapproved of our dating. But the "waitress or clerk" thing just sort of tipped me over the edge.

"Fuck you!" I shouted just before I stomped the gas pedal and spun my Chevy around in a complete circle in his driveway. I knew that he was shot-gunned by flying rocks and I thought I heard glass shatter on his front porch, but the truck was as angry as I was and when I straightened it out I flattened his mailbox and my tires squealed rubber as I hit the highway.

I loved Loretta, but there had always been something inside that had warned me this day would come sooner rather than later. And maybe Loretta's old man was right and I just wasn't much of a marriage prospect and never would be up to snuff.

I didn't care right then and I decided to get a bottle of Old Crow and drive out into the sage and howl with the other coyotes.

The next day Stella and Grandmother both knew I was heartbroken and that afternoon when I was loading some salt blocks into the back of the Chevy, Stella rode Sun Dancer over to say, "Charlie, I'm sorry about you and Loretta. I know you must feel awful about her going off to college while you're stuck here working from sunup to sundown."

It was all that I could do to nod my aching head.

"You need to find a nice ranch girl...someone who...who would love living out in the country."

"I could say the exact same thing for you and your feelings for Elvis."

"Yeah," Stella said quietly, "I guess you could."

"Why are you messing around with Travis Lane?" I asked bluntly. "He's too old for you and has a terrible reputation with women."

"I know that. But he...he's fun and he genuinely adores me."

*"Adores?"* I asked with a grin.

"Kind of, yes."

"We're both all screwed up," I told my sister as I went to work replacing a rotted fence post.

"You haven't been practicing with your guitar or writing any new songs lately. You ought to get back to both."

I nodded because I'd been thinking exactly the same thing. So that evening I did take the Martin out of its case and found that the tips of my fingers were tender again. The pain when I pushed down the steel strings was what I needed to take my mind off Loretta and I played until I couldn't bear to press down another string. Then I went into the house, climbed up into my loft and with the help of a flashlight started writing songs again...sad ones...but songs still and yet. This next one I titled, "A Sad Cowboy Song".

*When a cowboy loves a cowgirl he's got nothin'*
 *but smiles for the whole wide world.*
*He'll give her his best horse...and even his saddle of course*
 *'cause he's happier than anyone ever has a right to be.*
*But if she leaves him...oh if she leaves him...*

93

*he's a sad sack for certain and deep in misery.*
*He'll wonder why and start down the lonely drinkin' road*
*feelin' lower than a stomped horny toad.*

The first time Stella heard my new song of sorrow she cracked up. but I didn't care. I knew it wasn't the best song in the world, but I liked it anyway and it made me feel better so I sang the song over and over, changing the chords and the phrasing…changing it all as my feelings bubbled up and down in my throat.

And then, wouldn't you know it… Stella and I showed up at the ranch after work and there Elvis was sitting on the front porch drinking lemonade with Grandmother!

"Oh look what we have here!" Stella cried, jumping out of my truck before it even rolled to a stop.

I was every bit as happy to see Elvis again, but I had been wondering how Stella would greet him after he'd ignored her many letters and she'd taken up with Travis Lane.

Well, it didn't take me long to find out.

Stella bounded up on the porch, threw her arms around Elvis and kissed him right on the lips in front of Grandmother. Elvis finally broke the lip lock and leaned back to smile at all of us.

"I've been away too long," he announced. "I came back to breathe some fresh air, ride the range and maybe hear a few Indian stories. Cowboy Charlie, how the hell are you?"

"I'm real good," I said, meaning every word of it. I looked around and then asked, "How you'd get way out here? You didn't walk, did you?"

"Of course not. Mark brought me out here and I sent him back to Nashville." He sized me up and said, "How tall are you…six-foot-four?"

"Just a little shy of that."

"Well, you look great!"

"So do you," I lied, because The King didn't look good at all. He was as pale as any man I'd ever seen…any woman either. And there were dark circles around his eyes. He looked a lot heavier, too. I knew that he never exercised, had a sweet tooth and I'd read that he ate a pound of crisply fried bacon every morning which was a lot of grease clogging the veins.

"I hear you broke some mustangs recently."

"Six out of Utah."

Elvis frowned with concern. "I don't understand that, Charlie. Why would you risk your health…no, even your life…by getting thrown off onto your head for a few lousy dollars?"

"Well, they weren't so few to me. We needed a new truck…well, a good truck and that's what we just drove up in." I was hoping he'd compliment my red Chevy, but I was disappointed.

"I understand that it didn't go so good for you when you played at the Frontier Saloon."

"No, it didn't. But I wrote you all about that a long time ago and you never answered."

"I'm sorry. Same to you, Stella. I get so many fan letters every day that I just don't get around to reading most of them, let alone answer them. If I tried, I'd never get anything else done although I love my fans and admirers with all my heart."

I had it on the tip of my tongue to say that I thought we were all a lot more than just "fans" or "admirers" but I bit that off deciding that it would sound small…even petty. So instead, I just shrugged and said, "I guess I wasn't meant to be a performer…even a mediocre one."

"Well of course you were, Charlie! If you really want to sing and play before people, then you can!"

Stella slipped her arm around Elvis, but he didn't seem to notice.

"The thing of it is," I said, "you didn't see me up on that stage that night. I was terrible. Worse than terrible."

Elvis started to say something but Stella interrupted. "Never mind about that. I'm sure that Elvis isn't interested in our little disaster at the Frontier Saloon."

"Oh, but you're wrong! Charlie, tell me all about it."

"Now?"

"Yeah."

I took a deep breath. This was not something I cared to revisit. I told Elvis about not wanting to take the Martin to town on a horse and then about getting up on stage and being handed an electric guitar and making a huge fool of myself. I ended up by saying, "We got into a fight and Stella lost her job, but we got lucky and found better ones at an auction and sale barn right here in Winslow."

"That sure sounds like a bad opening night," Elvis said. "But I'll tell you something. Starting out as an unknown is really hard. When I started, I first got a six month contract playing in bars and dives in Texas and Louisiana. I was billed as "The Hillbilly Cat" and there were plenty of nights that I had to fight like a wildcat just to get out of those rough honky-tonks with my head still on my shoulders."

"Is that right?"

"It sure is. I played and sang anywhere I could make a dollar. I didn't eat right and I often slept in my car with other band members. We were always broke; we washed up and shaved in gas stations and counted the miles and the pennies every day. So don't tell me that just one bad night is going to make you give up on the music business."

"I want to play and sing, but I have this ranch to help keep up. And anyway, Stella and I have those steady jobs."

"Make a lot of money there, do you?"

I glanced at Stella and it was plain she was uncomfortable with the question, but Elvis was expecting an answer so I scratched the back of my neck and said, "Well, not a lot…but the paychecks never bounce."

"How much an hour?"

"Four dollars," I said quietly.

"And we get taken to lunch sometimes," Stella quickly added, careful not to say that she also accepted nice gifts.

"And I made over a thousand dollars on those Utah horses," I quickly added, trying to put a better spin on it.

"I don't mean to offend you and I know what it means to take home an honest day's pay for an honest day's work, but that isn't much money. And, Cowboy Charlie, even in a small town saloon, you ought to be able to make fifty dollars a night."

"Yeah, I know."

"I want to work with you on the guitar," Elvis said. "And as for that electric one, well, it takes a whole different way of playing and strumming so it's not surprising to me at all that you were bad, having never used one before."

"Thanks."

Later that afternoon after we'd visited awhile, Elvis asked me to go get the Martin and when I returned to the porch, I said, "I'd sure rather listen to you play."

"Maybe so," Elvis said, smiling, "but you're the one that needs the work right now. So let's see what you've learned from all those song books I sent."

I hesitated, pretty sure that Elvis would be disappointed in my lack of progress. But Grandmother said, "Go on, Charlie! Play us something. You're a lot better than the last time Elvis was here."

I thought about doing the song I'd played for Loretta up in the bleachers, but changed my mind and said, "I'll try a Johnny Cash hit."

"I like all his work," Elvis said with real meaning in his voice. "He's got a style that can't be duplicated. Which of his songs are you going to play and sing?"

"Sunday Morning Coming Down."

It wasn't too hard to chord and I played it slow and mournful. I didn't get far before Stella cried, "That's awful!"

I quit playing. Stella glared at me like I was pissing on a kid's birthday cake. "It's how I feel about things right now," I told her.

"Then you should play it sad," Elvis urged.

So that's what I did. I sang about how the guy 'wished that he was stoned because he felt so all alone on a Sunday morning sidewalk.'

"That is so beautiful and sad," Elvis said, "that it's poetry."

So we sang it together, again...and again.

Finally, Stella had had more than enough. "Why don't you both go into the kitchen, get a couple of knives and end it all if you feel that low down!"

"Sorry," Elvis said. "And I guess you're right." He had brought his own guitar and he picked it up. "Charlie, do you know the words and chords to "Blue Moon of Kentucky?"

I'd always thought that was one of Elvis' best. "I know the words but not the chords."

"Then just sing along and watch my hands."

He launched into the song and I didn't even try to follow his fingers and playing. I did manage to harmonize, though, and we were having fun. We started doing a lot of his old hits, me just quietly strumming, Elvis really getting after it with his guitar. They were Elvis songs that I loved, like "That's All Right Momma" and "There's Good Rockin' Tonight" and one of my very favorites, "Jailhouse Rock. "

I'd never seen Elvis so happy. And as he played he'd tell me how you could do the same song, but use vocal changes and inflections to make the song almost new and quite different.

"If you do the same songs over and over, night after night, you've got to juice 'em up a little with changes or you'll get bored."

"How could you get bored with a thousand girls screaming at you?" I asked with a laugh.

"Good point," he said. "But I'm talking about you and people who are starting out in the business. You're in a bar or saloon or maybe just sitting on a curb playing for people passing by. When you start out you have to realize that a lot of people in front of you want to talk more than listen. So you change things and just please yourself with your music. If you do that, you'll keep playing no matter how bad the audience."

I was thinking that Elvis Presley could massage words and tones just as beautifully as Grandmother could subtly massage and contour her pottery clay.

We played until way after dark and I could have played and sang with Elvis all night.

But at last Grandmother and Stella called us to the supper table so we went to eat. On the way to the food, Elvis laid his arm across my shoulder and said, "I swear that there are successful recording artists working the studios in Nashville that would die for your voice."

"Are you serious?"

"I wouldn't lie to a friend like you," Elvis promised. "All you need to do is work on that guitar and gain some live stage experience. If you do that, you'll become a professional and you'll make a success of it."

"Trouble is," I told him, "there aren't many places to play around here other than the Frontier Saloon and they sure won't give me a second chance."

He winked. "You want to bet on that?"

"What are you saying?"

"I'm saying that after supper we'll take a run over there and this time you'll have this Martin in your hands and I'll play as your backup."

I protested as hard as I could. The idea of Elvis being anyone's backup was outrageous. But his mind was made up about it and after a few minutes, it was clear that we were going to do it.

"Don't worry, it'll be fun," he vowed. "I'm lookin' forward to it!"

"I am too," Stella said, "I wouldn't miss this for the world!"

"Grandmother, I sure hope you don't want to come."

"No, but I wish you well."

We put our guitars in their cases and headed for my truck. Stella had on her best cowgirl clothes and hat and her tightest Levi's so she looked pretty fine.

We didn't talk too much on the way out to the highway and I think even Elvis was feeling my nerves. When we pulled into the parking lot, it was crowded and you could hear George and his Shadow Riders trying to drown out the usual boisterous crowd.

When we got out of the truck and gathered our guitars, Elvis said, "What happened the last time...it won't matter tonight. Everything changes right here and now. You go in with your head held high and act like you're doing them a favor by playing and singing tonight."

"Is that how you think of it?" Stella asked.

"Not really," Elvis said. "I've never gotten over being grateful to my audience...no matter what the setting...how big or how small the room or how rich or poor the people."

"If I don't get tossed out on my ear again," I said, "that's the way I'm going to feel about it, too."

Elvis and my sister seemed to think that was pretty funny, but I was so nervous I thought I might toss my supper as we headed for the saloon.

I entered the Frontier with Stella at my side and Elvis close behind. The muscular bouncer started to put a hand on my shoulder to turn me around, but when he saw Elvis, his jaw dropped half way to his knees.

Just as I remembered, the big saloon was dim and smoke-filled; none of the patrons even recognized us until we stepped up on the stage and had a quiet word or two with George and his band. The drummer nearly fell off his stool before Elvis grabbed the mike.

"My name is Elvis Presley."

The roar of laughter and shouting that had been going on died off like an amplifier whose plug had suddenly been pulled.

A young woman close to the stage looked up, stared and passed out cold.

"Folks, this is my good friend, Cowboy Charlie Coyote," Elvis said just as friendly as if he was a regular every night. "And I understand that some time ago when he tried to play and sing things didn't go too well. But no matter, this young man has a bright future in the music business and we're all privileged to hear him again. So mind your manners like the good folks I know you are." Elvis turned to me. "Go ahead, Cowboy Charlie!"

I nodded and hit a chord or two. Then I began to play and sing. My finger-tips were sore from all the playing we'd done earlier, but danged if I didn't sound good! The audience began to smile; people grabbed their glasses and beer bottles and leaned back clearly enjoying my music. I knew they were being especially nice hoping that Elvis would play soon…and he did after I stepped down off the stage with a thunderous roar of approval.

"See, what did I tell you?" Elvis asked as he strapped on his guitar. "You're going to be a big success and this is just the beginning."

I took a deep breath of that smoke-polluted air and it actually tasted sweet.

Elvis let out a holler and starting singing "Proud Mary." He was banging on his guitar and gyrating and those cowgirls started to go crazy and even some of the tough cowboys lost their usual cool. He did another fast one and then he chilled the audience down with, *You're so young and beautiful…and I love you so.*

I saw tears rolling down Stella's cheeks; the song was so moving that even I felt a lump in my throat. Elvis could bring that kind of powerful emotion out, any time or any place .

Then Elvis and I played and sang a few songs together like we'd been doing at Coyote Ranch. It was easy and fun and after about an hour, Elvis leaned close and said, "Let's do one more and call it a night."

"Are you sure? They really like us."

"I'm sure," Elvis said. "Try to leave your audience begging for more. Never stay on too long and…well, I'm awfully tired."

I suddenly felt ashamed of myself. Elvis had probably come a long way today and he did look worn out. "What would you like to play?"

"Let's do, "Love Me Tender"."

I knew that one well and when we sang it together there were more tears running down my sister's cheeks and some of the women in the crowd were trying to stifle their soft sobbing.

Then we were on our feet, putting our guitars away and shaking hands as we headed for the door with Stella on Elvis' arm. Cowboys and cowgirls and everyone else was just trying to touch Elvis and I followed along in his wake. I don't think my boots were even touching the sawdust covered floor.

On the way home, Elvis seemed quiet, deflated even and I was worried about him and told myself that it was just weariness. Stella, however, was over the moon with excitement. She talked about Sun Dancer and how she was going to start going to bigger rodeos and making a lot of money on that horse and how I was going to sing at rodeos and other places and make even more money. Maybe we'd even sell the Coyote Ranch and buy a bigger one.

"I'd be happy to hang on to what we've got," I told her. "And maybe buy that land adjoining ours."

Elvis said he thought the ranch was just fine the way it was, but having more land was always a good idea. And although he seemed bone-tired, I could tell as he gazed out at the stars on our long, dirt road that he was content and happy. I couldn't imagine he'd be any happier than I was…tonight had maybe been the best of my entire life. No more teasing from people around Winslow about how I'd choked at the Frontier Saloon and couldn't even handle an electric guitar. No sir! Now all that they'd be talking about was how Elvis and *their* very own Cowboy Charlie had sung together one magical evening in Winslow, Arizona, at *their* small town saloon.

# *Chapter 13*

Stella and I were so excited about Elvis that we completely forgot about our jobs at the auction barn. We all slept late the next morning until Grandmother shouted, "Charlie! Stella! Wake up, because here comes big bad trouble!"

I was dreaming of being on-stage again, only this time I was in a huge Las Vegas showroom. It was plush with immense, glittering chandeliers and the crowd filled every seat while anxiously waiting for my performance. Elvis slapped me on the back and said, "Give 'em your best, Charlie!"

"I sure will!"

Elvis stepped out first and the applause was deafening. Then he motioned me to come join him on the stage and the applause stayed wild and strong. Elvis told everyone that they were privileged to be the first to hear what was certain to be a chart-busting country love song that I'd wrote called, "When a Cowboy Loves A Cowgirl."

Oh, that was a sweet dream that I didn't want to end.

But Grandmother's shouting became louder and more strident. "Charlie! Get dressed and come down out of that loft! Stella, you better get out here quick, Travis Lane is coming and he's haulin' ass!"

Travis drove his fancy pickup truck fast into our yard and then slammed on the brakes sending chickens flying. He leaned on his horn and when I jumped to the window, I could see his face twisted in rage. No doubt the man had heard all about how Stella had arrived at the Frontier Saloon with Elvis Presley and had left on his arm. It didn't take a lot of guesswork to realize he was crazy jealous.

Grandmother gave us a few extra moments when she grabbed up her broom and confronted Travis on our front porch. If she hadn't done that, I honestly think the man would have burst inside ranting and raving.

"What do *you* want!" Grandmother demanded. She had never liked Travis Lane and I wouldn't have put it past her to take a swing at him with the broom.

"My employees on the job! Three hours ago!"

"You wait right here," Grandmother said. "I'll get them."

"And I heard what they did last night at the Frontier Saloon with that gawdamn 'Elvis the Pelvis'!"

I figured I'd better try to simmer Travis down or there could be trouble. So I didn't take the time to stuff my shirttails into my pants before I burst outside. Travis was waiting, hands balled into fists.

Before I could say a word, he shouted in my face, "It's pushing noon! Are you and Stella still working for me...or not!"

"Sure."

"No, you're *fired*, Charlie. Where is Stella!"

My sister came out the door. She had taken the time to tuck her shirt into her tight Levis and although she looked composed, I could tell by the way her eyes were slightly squinted that she was spitting mad. "Travis, you need to calm down. Have you had breakfast?"

"Hours ago! And do you know what I heard at the café?"

"Are cattle prices down again?" Stella asked with her rare, but wicked expression of ignorance and innocence.

"C....c...cattle prices! Is that what you said! Hell no! Everyone in the place was talking about you and Elvis at the saloon last night. Stella, you made me look like a fool."

Stella raised her hands palms up as if completely confused. "Why, Travis, we just had a good time. How do you think I made a fool of you?"

I thought the big man was going to explode. I'd never seen anyone madder. His face was bright red and his eyes bugged.

"Everyone was talking about you and Elvis and how I'd need to be finding a new sweet-punch."

Stella's smile froze on her face like ice on winter windows. "I guess maybe you do, but then you've always had a few back-up punches, haven't you, Travis?"

It was a well known fact around town that Travis was seeing at least three women at the same time...even thought it did seem to most that my sister was his current favorite.

Travis swallowed hard and his voice fell to a hiss, "Stella, get in my truck! We're goin' to lunch and you're going to be hanging all over me today in public."

"Never again," she said, taking a back step.

I stepped between the pair. "I think it's time you left, Travis."

His big head swung around. "Unless you want to swallow your teeth, you'd better keep your mouth shut!"

"Mister," Elvis said, standing just inside the screen door, "you've been asked to leave."

"Well, well," Travis said, lips forming a sneer, "if it isn't the famous King

Elvis & Cowboy Charlie

of Rock and Roll…or is it the Demerol King of Memphis? Are you going to come out and sign my autograph this morning?"

Elvis opened the screen door and stepped out on the porch. He wasn't nearly as tall as me, but there was something about him that would have demanded respect even if he hadn't been world famous. He was dressed in heavy pajamas and barefooted. His hair was mussed and his eyelids drooped. I almost expected Elvis to yawn, but he didn't.

Travis Lane sized him up with contempt. "Is this a man or a fairy prince dressed in cotton pajamas?"

There was little doubt in my mind that Travis intended to lay a severe whipping on the smaller Elvis and then brag about it all over town. There was also no doubt in my mind that I could never allow that to happen.

I was about to throw a punch when Grandmother's broom slashed down and struck Travis across the side of his beefy face. "You git out of here!" she cried. "Never come back!"

If anyone else on our porch had touched Travis, there would have been one hell of a brawl, but even Travis couldn't stomach attacking an old Indian woman so after he ran his finger over his cheek to see if there was any blood, he said, "I'll go, but the next time I see you in town, Stella, I'll set things right."

Elvis crouched just slightly and his hands came up, fingers straight and tight together. "I don't tolerate men threatening women."

Travis stared at Elvis. He outweighed The King buy at least fifty pounds… most all of it muscle. "Why don't you and your white pajamas step out in the yard with me and let's see what happens?"

I knew that Elvis would follow the man down the stairs and I understood that he had studied karate and was a good fighter. But I also knew that Travis was a vicious monster in a brawl. He would hurt Elvis and do everything in his power to ruin the famous man's face…*permanently.*

I couldn't let that happen. Just as Travis was taking a back step down off the porch, I launched off the balls of my feet and sent a powerful uppercut to the man's jaw. I felt that punch run like an electrical jolt from my bare knuckles up through my wrist and into my shoulder. It hurt every inch of the way, but it was a beautiful punch and I had the satisfaction of watching Travis land at the foot of our porch stairs.

Travis struggled up and before he could attack, I threw myself at the man, dragging him back down with a choke hold around his thick neck. We rolled over and over and I knew that I was no match for his weight, experience or power so I held on tight while choking that big sucker. Travis was pounding at my body with his fists and elbows, but he couldn't get any distance between us so his punches were hard, but not devastating. I could hear him wheezing for air as I squeezed his neck tighter and tighter. He kept trying to get his thumbs into my eyes or nose and I knew that if he did I'd be finished.

"Ahhh!" Travis grunted, again and again in pain.

I looked up to see both Grandmother and Stella kicking the hell out of Travis. A few of their kicks hit me and they hurt worse than any of the big man's punches. I figured that I'd be lucky if one of their kicks didn't bust my ribs.

"Cowboy Charlie," Elvis yelled, "turn him loose!"

I glanced up and there was Elvis, circling us in a crouch, hands out, fingers stiff and quivering with power. Travis must have seen him too, because he screeched, "Let me up and I'll whip you both!"

I was remembering a line from a Buck Owens' song about *"having a tiger by the tail"* and that's what I had trying to keep Travis on the ground and under control. And just when I thought I felt the big man starting to lose consciousness, Stella accidentally landed a kick right in my own throat. I nearly lost consciousness and my choke hold was broken. Travis staggered to his feet, me still on the ground spitting dust and fighting to breathe.

I turned my head up and saw Elvis attack. He leapt forward with his right hand chopping down like an axe. It struck Travis's neck and the big man staggered. Elvis did a round-house kick that caught Travis at the side of his knee bringing him down hard. Travis bellowed while trying to grab what I was sure was a broken or at least dislocated knee.

That was end of the fight. I'd started it...but Elvis had finished it and I couldn't have felt more relieved. I was struggling to breathe with tears in my eyes, but I could see well enough to have the satisfaction of watching Grandmother, Stella and Elvis drag the big man to his truck and shove him inside.

"I'm going to sue you, Elvis! Sue you for a million dollars!"

Stella yelled, "Oh, yeah! And who are you going to use as witnesses to the fight, asshole!"

"I want my palomino mare back," Travis raged. "I'll have some men come and get her this afternoon and don't you dare try to stop them!"

Stella's eyes widened and I knew this was devastating news. She'd been working on the barrels every day and the horse was obviously going to be a money winner.

Elvis saw the look on my sister's face and strode forward. "How much for the golden mare?"

"What?"

"Name me a price for Sun Dancer."

Travis laughed scornfully. "Tell you what...I'll drop the lawsuit if...."

"You have no lawsuit," Elvis said flatly. "And I can buy Stella a proven winner on barrels for a few thousand dollars. So once again, what's your price on that palomino mare?"

I knew that nothing caught Travis Lane's attention more than money.

"Five thousand."

"I'll pay three."

"Four thousand and we have a deal," Travis said, starting his truck.

Elvis glanced back over his shoulder at my sister. "Alright, but we'll want a bill of sale."

"Sure, when the four thousand arrives, I'll sign one and hand it over. But don't keep me waiting." He looked at Stella and me standing on the porch with Grandmother and shouted, "Oh, in case you two are too stupid to figure it out...you're *both* fired!"

"Fuck you!" Stella yelled back.

Elvis walked up to the porch. "Are you alright, Charlie?"

"Sure." Which wasn't exactly true.

"He outweighed you fifty pounds and you still got the best of him," Elvis said, helping me into a rocking chair. "You ought to feel proud of yourself."

"If you hadn't stepped in he'd have kicked the hell out of me."

"I'm not so sure of that. Grandmother, breakfast time is long past. You got something to make sandwiches with? I'm kinda hungry."

She took his arm and led Elvis inside and I heard her say, "You should change out of those pajamas before we eat."

"I'll do that." He stopped and turned. "But just so you know...these aren't pajamas. They're what I wear when I do karate. I should have put on my black belt, but I was too rushed."

Later that afternoon, Stella saddled up Sun Dancer and Elvis rode Buster out of our ranch yard. They were smiling and laughing; it was a beautiful day with high, pillow-clouds towering up into a deep blue sky.

"We'll be back by supper!" Stella shouted to Grandmother and me on the porch. "But if we aren't, don't wait up on eating."

We nodded and then Grandmother said, "Stella worries me. She was so happy before and then Elvis was gone for a few years and she went dark inside and now she's happy again. I'm afraid that she'll go dark the minute he leaves. Do you know what she almost did when she came out of her bedroom?"

"No."

"She had a gun and was going to shoot Travis Lane dead!"

"You're probably right about that," I agreed. "But what worries me even more is that we both lost our jobs. We need an income and your pots and plaques aren't selling well these days."

Grandmother snorted. "Too many other old Indian women are bringing their pottery and plaques to the stores and selling them cheap."

I knew this was true, but that didn't help our finances.

Elvis and Stella didn't return until after dark that evening, but we heard them laughing. The next day Elvis decided I needed to work harder on the guitar and learn at least twelve or fifteen songs to play professionally. So we spent a lot of time working on songs. Elvis had a memory for music that just amazed me. He could remember chord progressions and notes to hundreds of songs while I could barely remember a dozen.

One afternoon, Stella said she wasn't feeling all that good so she suggested that Elvis and I should go riding together. I saddled Buster and a bay gelding we called Shorty, though he was a tall, handsome animal with a little age on him. Elvis looked good on Shorty and it was clear he had done a lot of riding. We jogged our horses out of the yard and across the valley. I picked a cattle trail up through the sagebrush to the top of a ridge because it was the best view on the ranch.

We stopped with the wind in our faces and gazed back into our valley. Elvis finally broke the silence by saying, "Charlie, you and your family have something very special here."

"I know that," I replied, wondering if we'd still own it a year from now or if the bank was going to take it over.

"I own a ranch," Elvis said, eyes drifting across the huge expanse. "It's called the Circle G and it's only a few miles from Graceland. I bought it, stocked it with Santa Gertrudis cattle. Do you know anything about that breed?"

"I can't say as I do."

"They originated on the famous King Ranch down in Texas and are America's first beef breed born of Brahman bulls and Shorthorn cows. We also have a lake on the property with a big white cross in the pasture."

I could not imagine why in the world anyone would put a white cross in the middle of a cattle pasture, but I thought it better not to ask.

Elvis had a slight smile on his lips. "The pastures are deep with grass and on it sits a hundred-year-old ranch house."

"If it's that old it must be in mighty poor shape. Maybe you'll tear the old thing down and build a nice, new house on your ranch some day."

Elvis laughed. "It's already a nice house, but I'm having it constantly renovated. I like to take my Memphis Mafia buddies there sometimes. I bought 'em some house trailers and put 'em near the house."

"How many?"

"Oh, six or seven. And I bought some horses, saddles and tack so we could all ride together."

"Must have cost you plenty."

"Oh, it did. I have a palomino stud named Rising Sun and I'll bet if we bred him to Sun Dancer we'd get beautiful foals." He frowned. "Do you think that palomino of Stella's will ever be good enough to win money on barrel racing?"

"I sure do. Sun Dancer is fast, smart and cat-like on her feet. And Stella knows what she's doing. I think someday they'll be riding at the Cow Palace or the National Rodeo Finals."

"Then your sister would be famous?"

"Oh, I don't know about that. But she'd make quite a name for herself."

"Fame is a double-edged sword," Elvis said heavily. "Most people will never understand that, but it's true."

"You look like you handle fame pretty well."

"I try, Charlie. But I struggle and I'll be honest with you when I say that there are a lot of times when I'm sitting in some fancy Las Vegas hotel that I stare out the window and wish I was just like you."

"Me! Aw, come on!"

"I'm dead serious," Elvis said, very seriously. "You know, the more you have, the more you have to worry about."

"I'm not sure I understand."

"Well think about it," Elvis continued. "If you own about everything you desire...what's left to desire? And then you have to worry about keeping what you have and it becomes an endless worry cycle that never stops. And I can't go out in public...you don't know how much I'd like to just ride around in my cars or on a Harley and talk to ordinary folks. So I mostly have to sneak out of Graceland at night. Hire a movie theater or a restaurant. I even hire doubles, guys that look enough like me that they can jump into one of my limousines and sail out through my gates taking the crowds and reporters along with 'em."

"You have big gates at your driveway?"

"Sure! Charlie, you have no idea what it's like. I love my fans...I honestly do. Every time I step on stage I offer a little prayer to God that I'll be worthy of the price they paid to hear me. I want to make them happy. Some of those people have saved for a year to travel to a plush resort or casino, book a hotel room and then buy an expensive ticket just to hear and see me. It's a burden that wears heavily on me. I *never* want to give them a bad performance…but more and more I find my heart just isn't in it."

"I can't even imagine how it must feel to play to big crowds," I told him.

"I've played to huge crowds at places like Madison Square Garden and the Houston Astrodome. On stage, the lights blind you and the air is dead still and hot. You can't see faces out there…it's all mostly just a blur except for those right at your feet. But you hear them screaming your name…and a few times I've felt like I was a small animal standing before a huge beast. It can be overwhelming…but when you're finished and you know you've done your best and they love you…well, it makes it all worthwhile. It's the greatest feeling in the world. Me and my backup boys have worked together for quite some time and I've kind of felt like I was the commander of a combat unit and that our job is to capture the hearts and minds of the crowds."

"I never thought of it *that* way, Elvis."

"It's all teamwork, Cowboy Charlie. Colonel Tom Parker and the people that setup a big stage show work together closely. There isn't much left to chance when the production begins. There is way too much money at stake to take chances. Do you know that last year I played almost two hundred concerts?"

"No, I sure didn't."

"It got to be a hard grind. When I show up in Las Vegas I go into my hotel through the back entrance and I'm never allowed to mix with the waiting crowds. My people reserve three or four entire hotel floors in advance. One for me, another for my close friends and immediate assistants and still another for the band and backup singers. And still another for Colonel Parker and his staff. My routine before a show doesn't change. I eat about six o'clock in my hotel room then we head for the arena or stadium or the hotel's main showroom."

"Do you still get stage fright?"

"I sure do! That's why it was so fun the other night playing to those cowboys and cowgirls right here in little old Winslow. I just didn't worry any about either one of us disappointing those folks…partly because a lot of them were drunk…or close to it. After we played at the Frontier, I rode back with you and your sister and slept like the dead. But at the big shows, when I finish I'm so keyed up that when I go back to my room I can't sleep at all. So I take sleeping pills or downers and I finally fall asleep a few hours after the sun rises. But I can't even sleep well then because I have to get moving or ready for another show. So every day the whole thing starts all over again. Charley, did you ever get one of those glass balls at Christmas…the kind you shake and the snow falls on a little town so peaceful and nice?"

"No, but I've seen them in the stores and I've shaken them."

"That's kind of like I am sometimes. I get shaken up and then parts of me fall and I have to be shaken all over again…and again. A glass ball isn't worth looking at if the snow isn't falling."

"Then why not cut back?"

"I know that probably doesn't make sense to a cowboy, but at the same time that I'm burning out, the crowds and excitement keep me on a high that I don't get anyplace or any other way. It's really hard to explain…but there are people in show business who understand and are just as addicted to that high as I am. I could give you names…but I'd rather not."

"I never thought of the bad side of being famous."

"Well, now you've heard it," Elvis said. "I'm telling you all this so that if you become rich and famous…you won't be able to say that you weren't warned."

I wanted to lighten the mood. It was a fine Arizona day and Elvis seemed to be sinking into despair so I jokingly said, "Maybe I'll just try to be a little bit famous."

"You can't do that. When you go into it, you have to give your music your all or you won't get anywhere. There's too much competition out there for being average…it's an all or nothing sort of a deal."

"How big is your ranch in Tennessee?" I asked, still wanting to change the subject.

"One hundred and sixty acres." Elvis stood up in his stirrups and gazed around. "Lots of grass and water back there in Tennessee. Big trees and wildflowers everywhere…magnolias, dogwood….it's something to behold. But this place of yours is every bit as beautiful in its own way. I guess after being out here in the West I kind of feel silly calling one hundred and sixty acres a 'ranch'. This is a *real* ranch, Cowboy Charlie."

"It is," I agreed. "Grass and water are on the scarce side, but it's for sure a working ranch."

"I need more space in my life," Elvis said quietly. "I was wondering if you and Stella could sort of ask around and see if there are any ranches for sale in this part of Arizona."

"Are you serious?"

"I sure am! This high country makes me feel and sleep better than I have in years."

"But you don't need to buy a ranch out in this country," I argued. "You can come and stay at Coyote Ranch just as long as you like…whenever you like."

Elvis didn't seem to be listening. He pointed to the south, where the land stretched forever it seemed. "I suppose that's all government land?"

"I wish it was and then we could try to buy the government grazing rights," I told him. "But it's owned by a huge copper mining company. Copper is a big deal in Arizona."

Elvis shook his head. "How do they extract it?"

"They dig huge open pit mines."

"That's what they do in parts of Appalachia," Elvis said. "They use monster trucks to haul out the coal, instead of always digging it in the mines. Would they open a pit mine out there?"

"If they started operating I suppose they would...day and night."

"That would kill the silence," Elvis quietly mused.

"Grandmother constantly worries about that," I admitted. "But we can't do a thing if it happens. Let's ride a little more."

I guided Buster over the ridge and down into a wash. I was looking for arrowheads and ancient pottery which could often be found in this country.

"Elvis, they say that people called Sinagua and Anasazi lived here many centuries ago."

"This is hard country so they must have been on the skinny side."

"They were hunters and gatherers," I explained. "Not like the Hopi who plant corn."

"I wish I could go back in time and see those people. Simple, honest lives are what they led...and I wonder if they prayed like we do."

"I'm sure they did," I said.

We were both silent for a few minutes thinking about the "Ancient Ones" as they were called in these parts.

"Charlie, how come you and Stella never speak of your mother?"

"What?"

"Don't make me repeat myself. You heard me. I asked Stella the same question and your grandmother, too. But I haven't been able to get any answers. It's none of my business, but I'd like to know...didn't you love her?"

"I never knew her," I confided. "Stella remembers her a little."

"Is she buried here?"

"No."

"Why not?"

I took a deep breath. "My mother was a rich girl from the east named Ellen Allen. She was quite beautiful and high minded, so my Father told us. But she had some problems. Serious ones."

"Drugs or alcohol?"

"No. More complicated. When she arrived in Arizona she heard about the Hopi and when she went up on the mesas to visit them she decided that they had all the answers to life."

"Nobody has *all* the answers. Not the Pope or even the Dalai Lama," Elvis said.

"Well, my mother thought the Hopi did. Grandmother said she had a darkness that Stella might have inherited. Maybe my mother thought the Hopi would save her because they're a very spiritual people."

"I've heard that about most Indians."

"But the Hopi squabble and fight just like all peoples do and that must have been deeply disturbing to my mother."

"So what happened to Ellen Allen?"

"She fell in love with a Hopi man and from what little I know she was going to marry him, but then along came my father and she went off with him to get married. They lived on this ranch and had Stella and then me. Grandmother says that my mother was never happy out here...that she missed the Hopi people, but there were hard feelings toward her among them. So not long after I was born, she left and was never seen nor heard from again. We figure she was either murdered or died out in the country. She loved to walk in the canyons and far places. I like to think she died happy...but some say she was maybe murdered."

"By who?"

I just shrugged. "No one can say."

"Or *won't* say," Elvis replied. "Would you really like to know the answer to what happened to her?"

"More than just about anything," I admitted. "I go crazy sometimes thinking that her bones might be bleaching out in the wild. I'd like to bring her back and bury her here on the ranch. Stella feels the same way."

"What if she just ran off with another man? Have you thought about that?"

I was quiet for a few minutes then managed to reply, "We try not to think of that, either."

"Maybe you should go back to the Hopi Mesas and start asking questions."

"I don't think that would be a good idea. They wouldn't talk to me or Stella and it would just open up old wounds."

"But you need to know what happened to your mother," Elvis insisted. "I could hire investigators to help and...."

"No!" I said much too sharply. I picked my reins up and bumped my heels against Buster's ribs. "It's time we rode on."

"Okay, I get it. For now we'll just not talk about it. But you need to understand that I also have very strong feelings for mothers. My mother was named Gladys and I...I loved her so and miss her every day of my life."

"I wish I'd known mine," I managed to say as I let Buster pick his way through the rocks and brush.

"Look, Cowboy Charlie, I didn't mean to bring up something bad in your past and I'm sorry."

"Forget about it."

"Alright, but don't you and Stella forget to keep your eyes open for a ranch nearby. And don't tell anyone that Elvis Presley is interested in buying or they'll raise the land prices. I want it to be big and I'd build a ranch house…a modest one…and put in a pond."

"What's the pond for?"

"I'd stock it with fish…bass mostly. I'd have it nice for ducks and geese to float around in."

I had to laugh and it felt good given the dark mood that I'd been falling into. "Elvis, I hate to tell you this, but coyotes would gobble up your ducks and geese in no time if they didn't fly away first."

"No kiddin'?"

"I'm afraid so. How about a big stock pond instead?"

"You mean…a pond for cattle and horses instead of water troughs?"

"That's right."

"Well, a stock pond would be just fine. But I'd still stock it with fish… bass, crappie, bluegill and maybe some catfish. We'd go out together with cane fishing poles and catch us a bunch of fish then fry them up special like my mommy used to do when I was a boy. Yes, sir, I sure would like to spend some time on my own ranch near here. So keep me in mind."

"I will," I promised, not quite able to picture Elvis living out in this hard, lonesome land, but hoping just the same that he would do exactly that someday. "Come on, Elvis. I'll show you an old ruin where the Indians lived long ago."

"Then let's ride," he said, grinning like a cat under a milking stool.

Two days later, his driver appeared in the limousine and Elvis hugged us and was gone again, promising to return sooner next time.

Stella went into her room and cried for hours. I saddled Buster and went riding. But there was no joy in any of us that day. Despite his obvious and growing health problems, Elvis carried a shining inner light and when he was absent, it seemed the world became a little bit dim.

# *Chapter 14*

We loved Elvis'rare visits, but felt a huge letdown after he departed trying to get back into the routine of everyday living. Elvis must have stopped on his way out of Winslow to pay Travis Lane for Sun Dancer, because we didn't see the auction owner come around anymore. And when Stella and I drove into town, all that people wanted to talk about was Elvis, but we kept our silence. He was our friend and we weren't about to compromise his trust for a little attention. Elvis had told us right from the start that he didn't want to talk much about his career or his personal life, both of which were constantly in the news and we accepted that.

I threw myself into fixing up Coyote Ranch. Stella and I had saved a lot of our paychecks and we used the money to repair the corrals and fences. I bought two gallons of white and painted the stock trailer, but I also replaced the tires and floor boards. They were so rotted that I marveled that they hadn't collapsed under the weight of a horse long ago.

I wanted to do most anything to put Elvis in the past for awhile and stop missing him so much. That proved impossible because my sister talked constantly about Elvis and she had pictures of him tacked all over her bedroom and was always listening to his records. Stella had never revealed if they'd made love…and of course I'd never ask…but I thought they might have a few times on those horseback rides. It wasn't an event I cared to consider.

Grandmother kept me busy digging clay and cutting yucca strands. When we had restored our low inventory, I drove us all to Albuquerque where we tried to get her goods into gift shops. But we were always turned away because over there they wanted Zuni and Navajo souvenirs to sell, not traditional Hopi. The truth was we had to dump some of her beautiful pots at rock bottom prices just to pay our travel expenses…my newer Chevy proved to be a thirsty beast.

"There's an All-Indian Rodeo in Holbrook next month," Stella announced out of the blue and as we crossed the state line heading back into Arizona. "I plan to enter the barrel racing and I'm sure I can win."

"A belt buckle," I said, knowing those were small rodeos with very little prize money.

"It's just a start. Sun Dancer is ready. After I win, we can move up to bigger rodeos."

Grandmother had made it clear that she wanted us to stay away from rodeos. "They're no good for either of you," she warned. "They killed your father."

"No," Stella corrected, "a bull named Buzzard killed Father."

"Grandmother," I said, "we need to make some money and I could enter a few bronc riding events. They're not nearly as dangerous as bull riding."

"No!"

"But I'm really good on a bucking horse! I could win and we could split our expenses and have two chances to make money at every rodeo."

Lucy Yoyetewa shook her head. "That tin plate might come loose if you land on it and it would slice your brain like cheese."

I knew from long experience that you couldn't argue with Grandmother or ever change her mind, so I just ground my teeth, shot a glance at Stella and kept driving west on Route 66. There were a lot of Indians on this stretch of highway and most of them drove dusty pickups like mine. They had dogs in the truck beds and some had banners on their antennas touting "Indian Power"... whatever that meant. It seemed to me that the sad fact was that most Indians were powerless. On the reservations in Arizona Indians usually lived in shacks without running water or electricity and I'd heard it was that way all over the country. The majority of Navajo never registered to vote and crafted silver and turquoise jewelry or wool to make the rugs that brought high prices and were sought after by collectors. However, the work was so time consuming that if they figured their earnings per hour, it would be pitiful. I felt that Indians probably had less power than anyone in America and I doubted if that would change in my lifetime.

The next day I watched Stella as she ran the barrels on her Quarter Horse mare. She and that palomino were poetry in motion. They were fast and their turns around each barrel were razor-thin close. And after the final turn, Sun Dancer would dig in her heels and race toward the finish line as if her tail were on fire. I had no doubt that they would become winners...maybe even world champions before the dust settled.

"You're ready!" I yelled.

Stella rode her mare over and dismounted. "I've been thinking about you."

"Me and not Elvis? How could that be?"

"I'm serious. I think Grandmother is right about you staying off the rough stock. It's too dangerous."

I felt a stab of anger...or maybe relief. "So what would I do at the rodeos while you were winning cash? Feed your horse and keep it brushed? Keep your saddle and tack clean? What?"

"Don't be a smartass. I was thinking that you ought to buy a few calves and steers and work on roping. You're already good at it...but you could be much better."

"Stella, the ones winning calf and steer roping have been doing it since they were in diapers. They spend hours a day practicing and have expensive horses. Buster is a great cow pony but he sure isn't fast enough for rodeo. Maybe I could become a steer wrestler."

"Not a good idea."

"If roping, steer wrestling and riding the bulls are out, that only leaves bronc riding."

"Grandmother would have a fit."

"We don't have to let her know. She doesn't often leave the ranch house and go to town so I think it would be easy enough to get away with it."

"You're wrong, Charlie. Grandmother misses *nothing.*"

"Look, I love and respect her, but if I can't rodeo then all I can do is try to make money in the music business."

Stella rode off yelling over her shoulder, "No one will hold their breaths on that, Cowboy Charlie!"

Two weeks later it was time to rodeo. I was edgy and anxious as we hitched up the trailer and loaded the mare; even more so when Grandmother marched out wearing a long, velvet dress and her nicest pieces of jewelry.

Stella and I had not expected her to come along, but she climbed right into my truck and fixed her eyes ahead. I knew that it would be useless to try and talk her into staying at the ranch.

I could still remember all the details of Father's death in the rodeo arena as I drove out of our yard. Most vivid were the memories of getting on the bull in the bucking chute and of Father and Homer's words of advice. After the chute swung open, I didn't remember much of anything which was a blessing.

I hadn't visited the rodeo grounds since that terrible day...but now it all came back to me. The deep-in-your-gut excitement. There were cowboys all over the place and plenty of cowgirls, too. Lots of horses tied to stock trailers, saddles hanging off tailgates, bales of hay broken and water buckets tipped over. Laughter and talk and an undercurrent of danger, fear and anticipation. Some of the cowboys waved at us and when we stopped to unload Stella's mare, a number of them came over to say hello and wish us well. They liked to eyeball my sister and I caught some of them watching me with a curious look on their faces…like they couldn't understand why I'd come back given what had happened to me on Buzzard years earlier.

"Charlie," one of my old friends asked, "you ain't ridin' today, are you?"

"Not sure."

"Watch out for Travis. He's told everyone he's going to whip you to a nubbin'."

"He can try," I said, feeling my heart start to pound faster. "I won't be hiding."

"If he comes at you, Charlie, we'll be around and take care of his big white ass. Don't you worry. Travis doesn't have a friend here, but you Coyotes do. If Travis causes trouble, we'll stomp him and brand him."

"Brand him?"

My friend, Joe, laughed. "Oh, you know. Carve an arrowhead on his butt-cheek or something."

"Have you already been drinking?"

"I've had a beer or two. I entered three events and it cost me ten dollars."

"I intend to ride broncs," I said. "Could I use your rigging and borrow your spurs?"

"Hell yes!" Joe watched some Indians and said, "Those are Apache from San Carlos. They're wild bastards, but damn good riders. None of 'em rope worth a shit, but I expect they'll try. I got some whiskey in my truck."

"No thanks."

"Maybe I'll offer some to the Apaches. Get 'em a little drunk so they fall off quick and foul up their roping."

I chuckled but didn't think that Joe would do such a thing…there just wasn't a devious bone in his body.

After I was sure that Grandmother was taken care of and Stella was mounted and riding around, I headed to the rodeo office deciding to pay my entry fees. Grandmother would have a fit, but she wouldn't try to stop me.

"Charlie," the man who took my money and wrote down my entry number said, "good to see you back."

"Thanks. Good to be back."

"You're riding bareback bronc out of chute number four."

"What's the bronc's name?"

"FamilyWrecker. Saddle bronc riding will be the next event I'll put you riding toward the last on a horse called Slippery Sally. She's the best bucker of the lot so you'll have your hands full. Ride 'er to the buzzer and you'll win some money for certain."

"Sounds good."

"To be honest, Charlie, we miss your father and we missed you. Never expected you to ride here again. But I'm glad that you're riding horses and not the bulls anymore. Buzzard surprised us all. I heard he was sent to the killer after he gored some other rider in Nevada. He just got meaner and crazier as he got older; sometimes that happens with Brahma."

"Yeah."

I took my entry numbers and left, not wanting to talk about Father and what had happened. I need my mind focused on *today*, not back when Father died and Elvis saved my life.

"Hold up there, Charlie!"

I recognized the voice and spun on my boot heel expecting a punch, but Travis Lane surprised me. "Charlie, I want to apologize. I feel real bad about what happened and I guess I deserved the punishment you and Elvis gave me out at your ranch."

"Huh?"

He stuck out his big fist. I hesitated wondering if this was a trick and once he had me he'd try to crush my hand…but people were watching so I shook his hand and his grip was firm, but not punishing.

"No hard feelings?"

"Not from me."

"Elvis was as good as his word. He came over to my auction barn and paid me for the mare. I should have brought the bill of sale out to your ranch, but I just couldn't bring myself to do it. Too many bad memories, I guess. The paperwork is in the glove compartment of my truck."

"Then you should get it and hand it over to my sister."

"Alright," Travis said, "I will. And Charlie, I see that you've entered the bronc riding and I know you've got the talent to win. What you did with those six Utah mustangs was…."

"Thanks," I said, cutting him off and walking away. I didn't hate Travis… never had. Hating is like drinking battery acid…it just corrodes your guts. I was, however, worried that Stella might throw a punch at Travis. But I pushed that worry aside and focused on my first riding event.

When I got to the chutes I saw that Family Wrecker was a bald-faced buckskin with one white eye and the other blue. He was in the chute and none else than Homer Yazzie had already done me the favor of putting Joe's rigging on the bronc.

"Thanks, Homer."

"Glad to do it. You need spurs, gloves and a rosin bag, Charlie. Take mine."

He must have seen me coming because they were already in his hand. I cinched the spurs down tight, pulled on the gloves and worked the rope and leather hard. I suddenly had a fluttery feeling in my belly that I hadn't felt in a very long time.

"Family Wrecker is a good horse, Charlie. Make sure you get him right out of the chute and spur hard. He usually takes a couple of big jumps and if you're still up there he'll duck back and spin to the right."

I got my riding hand set tight, my other hand up and nodded to the cowboys. The gate swung open and Family Wrecker burst out into the arena bucking like crazy. Three jumps and then he ducked back and spun. When I was still on top he took off running and jumping which was easy to handle and I used Joe's dull spurs on his neck and shoulders until the buzzer sounded.

The crowd must have liked my ride because they sure applauded. Other riders didn't do as well and I was thrilled to see that my score of sixty-eight held up making me the winner of forty-six dollars.

I knew that Slippery Sally was going to be a lot harder to ride even with a saddle…and I wasn't disappointed. She wasn't a big mare, but she knew how to come down on stiff legs and to twist her spine like a snake. She was all over the place and I was hard pressed to make it to the buzzer, much less do anything with the spurs. When the buzzer sounded, the mare quit. Just stopped like she'd been quick-frozen.

She was a professional and I had to grin as I made a showy dismount, landing just as nice and easy as if I'd stepped off a train rather than have the pick-up rider haul me off behind his saddle.

"Hell of a nice ride!" he said. "Welcome back!"

"Thanks." I whipped off my black Stetson and waved to the crowd. Stella waved back, but Grandmother just stared. I hoped she was proud of me, I knew that Father and Elvis would have been.

A few minutes later, the announcer said, "Ladies and gentlemen, Charlie Coyote has just scored a seventy-six! Give him a big hand and welcome him back to rodeo!"

I won again and felt like a celebrity. Fifty-three dollars and a nickel-plated belt buckle which I soon sold for five dollars. It had been a fine, fine day!

The rest of the morning and early afternoon was spent talking and laughing with cowboys. Stella's barrel riding event was the last of the day and I knew she was too nervous to make small talk. Grandmother was in and out of the stands talking and eating a lot of fry bread. She smiled at me a time or two and I felt relieved that I'd not have to listen to her scolding all the way back to our ranch.

The first four barrel riders were good and no barrels were overturned, but they were not in Stella's and Sun Dancer's class. Their times were respectable...27.0 seconds up to 30 seconds. When Stella rode out on her beautiful mare, there was applause and then she crossed the finish line and headed for the first barrel, too fast it seemed to make a tight turn.

But she did!

Sun Dancer slid neatly around the first barrel and clawed out of the hole racing for the next barrel. That mare was so pretty and fast that the audience fell silent and watched her run. When she rounded the second barrel and headed for the far one, people began to cheer and shout. Stella could have almost walked the mare to the last barrel, but that wasn't her style and she paid for her mistake when the palomino's shoulder knocked the last barrel over.

The crowd gave a collective groan of disappointment as Stella raced back across the finish line and out of the arena.

The announcer said, "As you know, Stella Coyote will have a five second penalty."

There were two timers and they came together and bent close staring at the stop watches and whispering. Then one of them hurried over to the announcer where they had a hurried conference.

"Ladies and gentlemen," the announcer shouted, "this is unbelievable! Even adding the five seconds, Stella has posted a remarkable 29.4 seconds!"

The crowd gave her a huge round of applause. My sister had won second place and probably about fifteen dollars. I hurried over to congratulate her and she seemed more pissed off about not winning than getting second place even with a barrel down.

She managed a smile as she unsaddled and began to brush the mare. "Charlie, I'm wrung out. Let's get our money and go home." She turned to Grandmother. "Did you have a good time?"

"I ate too much fry bread and tacos. But it was fun. Charlie?"

"Yeah."

"You did us proud."

I smiled. No better words could she have said to me right then. Stella winked and we all went to get paid our prize money.

"Oh," Stella said, "Travis gave me the bill of sale for Sun Dancer and apologized. He also said we could go back to work for him any time."

"That's nice," I said, deciding not to relate how we'd had that conversation before I rode.

We loaded up and headed out driving slowly through the rodeo grounds because we didn't want to raise dust or run over any ranch dogs. Stella said,

"Charlie, this is just the beginning! We're going to make some real money between us this season and…."

Stella's voice died as Travis and a voluptuous young blonde walked across our path. They had their arms wrapped around each other and were laughing. I glanced sideways at my sister knowing I could not begin to understand what was on her mind. But her mood had changed and it was suddenly dark as midnight under a frying pan….and yes, maybe even dangerous.

I figured that Travis Lane was a wise man for giving her an apology and that bill of sale. I wouldn't have wanted my sister for my worst enemy and maybe he understood that he didn't either. Nobody had ever accused the big man of being stupid…except when it came to fast and pretty young women.

# *Chapter 15*

Rodeo was all that Stella and I talked about that next week. We'd had a small taste of success, but we thought we could quickly move up in the competitions and earn serious prize money. Grandmother didn't say a word, but I could tell that she was worried about our high and mighty aspirations. She worked on her crafts and kept to herself. That bothered me because, in the past, Grandmother had always been a part of our discussions and plans. Even when Father was alive we never made a move without Grandmother's approval. However, with rodeo fever gripping us, Stella and I forged ahead on our own.

"We have to find out where and when the upcoming professional rodeos are so we can enter and earn some big prize money," Stella said. "There might even be one held not too far away next weekend."

"Where are we going to get the rodeo entry fees?" I asked. "Bigger rodeos pay more prize money, but the entry fees are a lot higher."

We both glanced across the kitchen at Grandmother's cookie jar where she kept her pottery and plaque money…but we doubted that Grandmother would be willing to front us given her disapproval of rodeo. I wasn't discouraged because I believe in the old adage that "if there is a will, there will always be a way."

Early the next morning I drove to town to see our friend Homer who worked at the Chevron station pumping gas and changing tires and oil.

He was happy to see me and because things were slow we talked about rodeo. The more I learned, the more excited I became. Homer had been quite a drinker in his early days, but those times were past. He was too old to be a competitor anymore, but it was clear that he'd once been a top-notch rodeo cowboy.

"It's an exciting life, but you're on the road all the time, eating poor food and sleeping in flea-bag hotels…*if* you are in the money. If not, you sleep in the bed of your truck. You're faced with many temptations from women, drugs and alcohol. If you want to be at the top of that game, you have to eat right and exercise. Get as much rest as you can and avoid all those temptations."

"I see."

"I doubt that you do see," Homer told me. "You ain't thinking of riding any more bulls, are you?"

"No," I promised. "Just broncs."

That seemed to satisfy him. "I wouldn't be any help to you if you wanted to ride bulls again. You know, it was partly my fault about what happened to you and your father when we got you on Buzzard."

"Why is that?"

"I think I messed up and put your hand down too hard."

"At the last minute, I loosed the grip just a mite."

Homer grinned. "You did?"

"Yep." When I told him that, which wasn't quite the truth, I could see something in him change and I liked to think that it was a ton of guilt slipping off his big shoulders.

Homer expelled a deep breath. "I sure appreciate you telling me that, Cowboy Charlie. You don't know how much better I feel."

"I should have told you after I got out of the hospital."

Homer wanted to shift the conversation. "I saw you ride those broncs this past weekend and you're a natural. And it ain't often you get stomped or hung up in your rope on broncs. You might do a somersault and land on your head, but it isn't likely. Still, rodeo has been the ruin of many a good cowboy."

"I expect so. Father said the same thing and he was pretty good in his day."

"He was better than 'pretty good'," Homer said. "He was damned good, but he made the same mistakes I did and it cost us both. If I'd have been sober and sensible, I'd probably be sitting in a rocking chair today on my own land watching my own livestock instead of pumping gas, changing oil and fixing flats. But I didn't have anyone to warn me of the temptations and pitfalls. That's why I'm telling you these important things."

"I appreciate it very much. Is there a rodeo this coming weekend? One where Stella and I can make some real money and not just belt buckles or Stetsons?"

"There's one in Williams, west of Flagstaff. I could take the weekend off, probably...would Stella and her barrel horse be going too?"

"We're in this together."

"I'll make a few calls and get you both entered."

"How much will it cost?"

"Don't know. Maybe ten or fifteen dollars an event. But the prize money will be a lot bigger than it was for you last weekend. It's always a gamble, Charlie. You and Stella will have expenses. Gas, motel room and food. You'll need at least fifty or sixty dollars and that's if you take some canned food to eat."

"We can do it."

"Alright, then. I'll pay my own way. You'll pay yours."

When I told Stella about how much money we'd need, she surprised me by saying it was no problem. Then, before I could ask her why not, she headed out the door to work her horse on the barrels before the sun went down. I liked the way it settled on the distant San Francisco Peaks. Grandmother and most of the Indians around these parts believed those peaks were sacred…I just thought they were beautiful, especially when they were snow-capped.

I walked out onto the front porch and started working on a new song I'd decided to call, "The Rodeo Blues." Grandmother came to sit beside me and listen. I picked and sang and we just rocked for awhile and then she said, "You're getting real good, but that new song is kind of sad."

"Yeah," I agreed. "I might need to perk it up a bit. But those sad songs are popular nowadays."

Grandmother didn't like sad songs…actually I didn't either. We watched Stella practice on the barrels and she seemed fast to me. Grandmother must have thought so too because she said, "I heard you tell Stella about a rodeo in Williams this weekend."

"That's right." Not much got by the old gal; her eyesight might be dimming, but I swear she could hear a caterpillar crawl across our backyard.

"How are you going to get the money to enter and for gas and food?" she asked.

"Stella says she has it."

"She socked some away while you were working," Grandmother said, not making a judgment as to whether this was right or wrong. "But I was thinking that you could play your music at the rodeo and make some money."

That was a pretty good idea. "So does that mean that you're no longer against me competing?"

She rocked for a few minutes in silence. "You have to protect your sister."

I felt that Stella was more than capable of taking care of herself and that there wasn't much danger in barrel racing. Sometimes flying around a barrel a rider would bust their knee or the horse would lose its footing and fall, but it was rare and Stella and Sun Dancer were a perfect team. I began to work a faster tempo on my guitar and change words in my new song.

"You know, Charlie, Stella is exactly like her mother."

My fingers stilled on my guitar strings. "What do you mean?"

Grandmother's lips worked silently and she toyed with her favorite turquoise ring. Finally, when the sun had gone down, she said, "Stella has a darkness inside and it worries me. Your mother came to a crazy and bad end."

I froze, then asked, "What are you talking about?"

But Grandmother had said all that she was going to say and went inside leaving me alone.

Stella had finished her practices and the barn was illuminated with a lamp. I put my guitar in its case and sat on the porch waiting for her. When she left the barn and approached the porch, I stood up in the gloom and said, "How'd it go?"

"We're ready to win some cash in Williams."

"Good."

"What were you and Grandmother talking about?"

I shrugged, still unsettled by Grandmother's remark about our mother and her 'crazy and bad end'. "Nothing important."

"She's worried about us both at the rodeo," Stella said. "I tried to tell her we'd be fine. We'll have friends there and we'll have a good time."

"Maybe I'll take my guitar and sing."

"That's a great idea! They usually have a dance on Saturday nights. I'm sure you'd get your chance."

"We'll do well."

"You don't have to convince me of that," Stella said, "but don't let Grandmother's worries become your own."

"Not a chance."

Stella squeezed my arm and went inside. She looked so happy and confident that I dismissed Grandmother's dark words and decided to play a little longer by lamplight. I looked up at the first evening star and wondered if Elvis might also be outdoors and watching it. Probably not. Most likely he'd be in some fancy hotel room getting ready to put on another filled-to-capacity show. Too bad, it was going to be a full moon tonight over the sage and hills. Elvis would have enjoyed sitting, talking and playing songs on our old porch.

# *Chapter 16*

Things didn't go well on our way to the Williams Rodeo. Our old stock trailer blew a tire and nearly flipped on Route 66. Sun Dancer went crazy in the trailer and banged herself up. We had a hell of a time getting the horse out and then I had no choice but to hitch a ride into Flagstaff because we didn't have a spare. Using most of our money, I bought a spare tire mounted on a rim and returned three hours later. I got the blown tire replaced and we finally managed to coax Sun Dancer back into the trailer, but she was badly spooked.

"This isn't starting off too well, Charlie."

"No shit, Sherlock."

Stella blinked. "What'd you say?"

"I heard it somewhere. I don't even know who Sherlock is."

"He was a famous detective in London. I don't think Sherlock Holmes was a real person, though."

I didn't have anything to add to that so we got back in my truck and drove on toward Williams with both of us wondering where we were going to get some money for the entry fees now that we'd spent it all on the damned spare tire.

While I'd been waiting for the spare to be checked, I'd called Loretta Hickey at her dormitory. She hadn't been in so I'd left a message that I'd be riding in the rodeo the next day and hoped she could come watch. And maybe I'd be playing at the rodeo dance, too. The girl didn't seem too interested and I kind of doubted she'd even deliver the message, but it was all I could do so I hung the phone up. I was dirty from changing the tire and in too much of a hurry to try to find Loretta while dragging a horse and trailer through town.

"Miss Bust-Out-Britches busy today?"

"I wish you wouldn't call Loretta that."

"Well, it fits… or more accurately, her Levi's fit her like they were painted across her wide ass."

"Stella!" I warned.

"Sorry."

But I knew she wasn't. And lately, Loretta had been out a lot when I'd called. I was starting to wonder if she'd already found a college guy after deciding that I was just a hopeless cowboy looking for love and yearning for fame and fortune. Maybe Loretta didn't think my prospects of a successful future were very bright. The blowout and the spent money along with no word from Loretta all conspired to put me in a lousy mood.

That mood got worse the next day when I rode both bareback and saddle bronc and got bucked off in both events just before the buzzer. I don't know why I didn't ride better, but the broncs I drew were rank and they forcibly reminded me that I'd moved into a much higher level of competition and wasn't as great as I'd thought when I'd won in Winslow.

I found a place to hunker down behind the bucking chutes and consider what had gone wrong. An old cowboy saw me and came over. He squatted down beside me and rolled a cigarette with just one old, knobby hand. I was impressed.

He struck a match on his thumbnail and smoked. I glanced over at him and said, "Howdy."

"Howdy, Cowboy Charlie."

"How do you know my name?" I asked, certain we'd never met.

"Knew and liked your dad. Heard about what happened with Buzzard. Damned sorry to hear about it."

"Thanks."

"I been to the National Finals six times and won twice. Rode in all the big rodeos from Cheyenne to Denver."

I wasn't sure that I believed the man, but said, "Maybe you could give me some advice."

"Sure could. You ought to stop riding."

"Huh?"

"You're too big. You could be a bulldogger or steer roper, but you're too tall and heavy to ride the rough stock professionally. What are you, six-three?"

"That's about right."

"I was six-one and two hundred pounds when I was a steer wrestler. At first, I tried to ride bulls and broncs…but I learned the hard way that I wasn't built for those events. I became a steer wrestler and did real well at it for many years."

I looked at him more closely. He might have been that tall and heavy once, but that must have been a great many years ago. Still, you could see the width of his shoulders and easily imagine that he had once been a big, powerful man.

I nodded, not dismissing his advice. But the idea of racing after a steer and jumping off a fast horse wasn't my idea of a good time. In fact, I'd always thought steer wrestlers were a little light in the brain-pan. Sometimes both the steer and the man flipped over and I'd seen some bad wrecks. I saw a bulldogger in Tuba City get his neck broken and become paralyzed.

"What is your name?" I asked.

"What's it matter?" he asked, blowing a cloud of smoke. "Names don't mean anything. Especially when you get old and nobody cares who you are or once were long ago."

"I appreciate what you have to say, Sir. But despite what happened today I am good on a bucking horse."

"Oh, you ain't terrible or anything. But I'm just trying to steer you in the right direction so you don't waste a lot of time and money…and maybe more injury. But it don't matter to me what you do. I liked your dad…in fact we were friends…and that's why I am telling you what I know about the game."

He was smoking his hand-rolled cigarette down to a nub. I noticed his fingernails were white and the ones that held the cigarette were stained yellow and they trembled ever so slightly. I'd never heard anyone call rodeo a "game" but I was sure the old man was legitimate and I wasn't about to argue his point.

He blew twin vapors of smoke out of his nostrils and studied his cigarette as if it held all the answers to life. Then he stubbed it out on his boot heel, broke the paper and poured the last unburned shreds of tobacco into the little sack where it came from and tightened the draw strings then put it all into his pocket before drawling, "Yeah, Kid, you should be a *bulldogger*."

"I don't have the horse to make it happen even if I knew what to do and not to do in that event."

"That is a problem, fer sure. But you know, about forty years ago I had the same problem. But I listened to an old boy about the same ancient age that I am now and he convinced me that I didn't have any choice but to take up bulldogging because it is the only rodeo event where big, powerful fellas have an advantage over smaller men."

"What about the horse?" I asked, wondering if he'd ever get to the main point of why I couldn't try bulldogging.

He pushed his dirty straw hat back and squinted at me. His face was as brown as Grandmother's clay and he was missing most of his teeth. He wore a big, gold ring with a diamond the size of a pea; I figured it was just glass, though. He said, "An experienced horse is too expensive for a kid like you… so you have to find yourself a young horse…not too tall…that can run like a scalded-assed ape."

"Then why are we even talking about this?"

"I told you I liked your pa. My name is Twister McCabe."

He stuck out a bony hand and his grip was as hard as iron. "Twister's my nickname on account of when I got a hold of a steer I could always twist him down damn fast." The old cowboy pulled up his shirt tail and pointed to a big rodeo buckle. "I won this at the Calgary Stampede way back in 1939. My average time that week was 7.2 seconds and back then that was damn near unbelievable."

"Well it still is."

"Naw," Twister said, today's top 'doggers' are doing it a lot faster. Maybe not as an average of times, but if I was your age again I could match them. Or if I was your age and size."

I nodded, curious as to know where this conversation was headed.

"I've got an idea," Twister said, removing his tobacco and papers and rolling another of his skinny cigarettes. "Once in a while I take on a student."

I finally understood where he was going. "Mister, I...."

"Just hear me out, Cowboy Charlie. There are some bulldoggers here that are almost your size with the ability to become world champions. I could help them."

"Sure you could. At least they know the basics."

"The *wrong* basics. I want a fella who doesn't know beans about bull-dogging. I would teach him from the ground up to the horse and back down to the steer. I teach the little things that shave off seconds and I provide them with a horse they can grow and work with until they get into the bigger money."

"What's in it for you?"

Twister McCabe grinned and looked me straight in the eye. "I like the game and I can still be the best damn hazer in the arena. You see, when I'm in the game, I feel alive again...not just another spectator. So Cowboy Charlie, are you interested in a partnership? You're being offered private bulldogging lessons by an ex-world champion!"

I was so surprised that I hesitated in answering. "I...I don't know, Twister."

"Better figure it out quick. I'm real picky and don't offer twice. I expect a man's best and give him no less than my best."

"I...I got a ranch to work."

"Where at?"

"Just west and south of Winslow."

He smoked in silence for a minute, glanced at me a time or two and I knew he was trying to make up his mind about my chances. Finally, he drawled, "That's close enough. You can come to my place and we'll get started unless you have something better goin' on...which I seriously doubt."

The "seriously doubt' part irked me enough to say, "I aim to be a singing star."

He chuckled. "Well, you can't be both...at least not for awhile. I figure, if we team up right away, you can be earning money is six or eight months. You'll start earning big money in a year...maybe a little longer depending on how well matched you and your horse turn out to be. That's when we'll be going to rodeos all year round."

"That a fact?" I was getting excited.

"Yep. The real money is in the National Finals and to get there you have to have the points built up from the other rodeos." Twister reached into his shirt pocket and handed me a business card with his Flagstaff phone number and a post office box address. He rolled another cigarette and smoked a few minutes in silence. "I cover all of your first year expenses and take seventy-five percent of your earnings."

"Seems like an awfully big cut to me."

Twister shrugged. "It's not enough to cover my expenses let alone my time and the horse I'll pick for you. But to make this work you have to have enough money to cover your own personal needs."

"Like eating?"

"No. I pay the restaurant and motel bills. The second year I'll take sixty-percent of the winnings and I'll cut you free if you aren't doing good enough on the circuit. Third year fifty percent...and after that, twenty-five percent as long as you are using my horse and I'm your hazer. Either one of us can break this deal at any time."

"I need some time to think about it, Twister."

"You got a week. If we're a go...make sure you understand that learning to be the best isn't fun. It's hard work and you'll hit the dirt more often than you pull down a steer. You'll be covered in bumps and bruises and maybe even break a few bones...that's part of the education and you need to understand that up front with me. Oh, one last thing...you can't ride rough stock anymore."

"Anything else?" I asked. "What about my music?"

"If you don't break your fingers or your hand, play whatever you want as often as you want. Don't matter to me."

I nodded and waved his card. "I'll give it some good thought."

"One week, Cowboy Charlie."

I walked or rather limped away with my mind all a jumble about what I'd just heard and the surprising offer that had just come my way. When I reached our stock trailer, I found a bottle of aspirin and a nearly empty pint bottle of Old Crow. I gulped down four aspirin and looked back to see that Twister McCabe was gone.

The rodeo announcer called out that it was time for the last event of the day...barrel racing so I headed on over to the arena and found a seat to watch and see how Stella and Sun Dancer would make out. Since I'd been bucked off in both my events, she was our last and only hope for get-home gas money.

I looked around at the mountains. Williams is a pretty town and the altitude is high so you have the sweetest, cleanest air imaginable. Bill Williams Mountain is just off to the south and off to the north was the Grand Canyon. I liked this town a lot…it was small and had a lot of color and history. There were timber mills and logging operations, the railroad crews, the businesses that thrived on the people who passed along Route 66 and much more to offer. The Sultana Club was a wild, downtown saloon and that's where many of the cowboys would go tonight after the rodeo.

Most of the barrel racers were warming up their horses…but not my sister. She was hugging a handsome man in a shiny red silk shirt. I had never seen this particular cowboy, but from the looks of him, he was a phony. The working cowboys all around wore worn out Levi's and patched boots. This one looked like he'd just stepped off the page of a magazine advertisement for clothes running in *True West*. He was holding an expensive bottle of foreign beer and laughing. I didn't like him from the get go.

"Stella," I said, trying to keep the edge out of my voice, "don't you think you ought to be warming up your horse? You'll be up soon."

"Who is he?" the Hollywood cowboy asked, sneering at me.

"Lenny, he's my kid brother?"

"Oh yeah, I saw him get bucked off in both saddle and bareback bronc riding. I seem to remember he might have lasted all of three seconds."

Lenny extended his hand, a thick gold bracelet dangling from his wrist. "No offense meant, Kid."

I ignored the hand and said to my sister, "Do you want me to hop on Sun Dancer and warm her up?"

"No, everyone has seen enough of you on a horse for one day."

Lenny giggled like a girl. "Aw, don't be too hard on yourself, Kid. You just have to accept that you can't ride worth jack shit."

Something snapped inside of me. My right hand shot out and my long fingers wrapped around Lenny's throat while I kicked my leg out behind his and drove him onto a pile of fresh horseshit which pleased me greatly.

My fists were balled and I stood waiting for Lenny to jump up and try to have a go at me, but he just cleared his throat and looked over at my sister. "He always acted crazy like this? Is he alright in the head?"

Stella was caught by surprise. She didn't know if she should be furious with me or disgusted with Lenny, so she just shook her head and walked off toward her mare.

"Charlie!" I immediately forgot Lenny because there was my girl Loretta Hickey rushing toward me with outstretched arms. When we kissed, I felt like I'd won the bulldogging World Championship at the National Finals.

"Charlie, this is my roommate at school, Annie Foster."

Annie was cute with a bobbin nose and a beautiful tan. I could tell she was a city girl with family money. Her hair was short and dark and her clothes were nice, but certainly not meant for working around livestock. She was wearing a pair of boots, but they looked weird to me with high heels and tops that snugged up tightly against her legs almost to her knees. In addition to the boots she had chosen to wear a pink straw western hat, but it was shaped all wrong. I figured that she must have bought it in some high-toned gift shop in Sedona, Scottsdale or other such rich-people place.

Lenny jumped up and shoved off muttering curses at me under his breath.

We stood there grinning at each other and finally I broke the silence by asking, "Have you been roommates long?"

"Since I started at NAU," Loretta said. "Annie and I are sorority sisters."

"Well," I replied, not knowing or even caring what a sorority was and being pretty jaded by my own sister today, "that's real nice…being sisterly, I mean."

They thought that was funny for some reason.

"We might as well all go watch Stella ride the barrels," I said, taking Loretta's hand.

"Who was that dandy that Stella was with? The one whose throat you grabbed before you threw him down?" Annie asked.

"Just another hot-shot, dime-store cowboy who forgot his good sense and manners."

"He must have said something pretty awful to you the way you grabbed his throat and threw him in that pile of horseshit."

For some reason, I laughed and because I was feeling extra cowboyish and as pleased as a goat in a garbage can, I also took Annie's hand and paraded those two pretty girls up into the grandstands.

The barrel riders were already competing and Stella would be the last contestant. When it came time for Stella and Sun Dancer, the time to beat was 19.2 seconds run by a Utah cowgirl on a short, but quick sorrel mare. When Stella came into the arena she and Sun Dancer were running hard and fast. Her palomino mare slid around the first barrel and dug hard for the second. They took the second barrel in a hurry and the crowd began to cheer when they headed for the last and farthest barrel. With the mare's ears laid back flat, she hit the final barrel and I caught my breath sure that it was going over…but it didn't and Sun Dancer with her tail windmilling headed for the finish line. I saw both timers hit their stop watches and stare at them and knew that they were astounded.

"Ladies and gentlemen," the announcer said over the loudspeaker, "we have a new leader in this event at 25.8 seconds! We'll see who wins the overall at tomorrow's Sunday rodeo. Be sure and be here for more excitement!"

The Williams crowd clapped and hollered with boisterous approval. I just stood there watching my sister as she rode back on into the arena, yanked off her hat and waved to the crowd. Her black hair shone in the sun like a raven's wing and I couldn't have been prouder if I'd have won a championship belt buckle riding big, bad bucking broncs.

After the crowds thinned out, Stella said she and Lenny were going to be at the Sultana Club that night dancing and celebrating. Remembering my promise to look out for my sister to Grandmother, I knew I'd be there too. And besides, I wanted to see if they'd let me play a few songs at the club. I guess I'd have to say that that prospect was even more unnerving than riding bulls.

When I told everyone that I hoped to play a song or two, Loretta and Annie were excited, but Stella was not. "Are you sure that's such a good idea? I mean, it isn't like you've got Elvis to hold your hand tonight."

"No," I confessed, "but I have to give it a fair try."

The Sultana was old and dripped with cowboy atmosphere. It was right on the main drag and it had a long bar on the right when you walked inside, lots of tables and a little stage toward the back where musicians tried to sing louder than the laughter and shouting of the cowboys and tourists. It was a favorite hangout for bikers, loggers, cowboys and railroad workers...a tough place but one run with a bouncer or two always in sight and an eye for keeping the peace by tossing out any would be troublemakers. I'd heard of the Sultana for years, but never been inside and now, with my Martin guitar and a huge and rowdy rodeo crowd spilling out of the doorway, I was so scared I nearly turned around and walked away.

I weaved my way through the crowd toward the stage area and saw it was already set up and waiting for the first set. A skinny fella wearing a sea shell necklace and with his long, red hair tied in a ponytail was fiddling around with an amplifier and testing a microphone.

"Hi there," I offered, having to shout over the noise. "Mind if I play a song or two before your band comes on?"

The guy wasn't friendly. "This is our gig, Cowboy. Go ride off on a pony and sing something like Gene Autry or Roy Rogers."

"What's a 'gig'?"

He stared at me like I was from outer space. "Are you for real?"

"Yeah. And I...well, I was taught some songs and chords by none other than my friend, Elvis Presley."

He snorted with derision. "Yeah, and I'm the lost son of the coal miner's daughter!"

"Oh," a big cowboy who'd overhead the conversation from a nearby table shouted, "let the kid play! We're tired of waiting on you hippie freaks!"

The news of what I was asking seemed to shoot through the crowd of mostly cowboys and their lady friends and they took up a chorus in my behalf. They were boisterous and drinking beer by the pitchers. The ponytail guy disappeared, probably to hurry up his other ponytail friends so I grabbed the live mike, cleared my throat and said, "Good evening! My name is Cowboy Charlie Coyote and some of you might recognize me as the guy who got bucked off twice today faster than a country preacher taking up a collection."

They laughed at the comparison.

"Hell," I said, taking in a little confidence by their reaction, "I didn't last any longer than a grasshopper in a chicken pen!"

Now they *really* laughed and I had most of the saloon's attention. Some of the cowgirls were giving me catcalls and I hoped I wasn't blushing...or if I was they didn't notice. I had to give Elvis all the credit because he'd told me many times that the best way to warm up a crowd was make a few self-deprecatory jokes.

"I don't get along with electric guitars so I'm going to sing something real traditional in the cowboy way, strumming my acoustic guitar. My first song is one I hope you like and it was made popular by the Sons of the Pioneers called, "Tumbling Tumbleweeds."

They shouted and I took that as a sign of approval. I didn't dare wait to fine tune my guitar and I wished I had a beer to soothe my throat, but I started the song and finished it in what I thought was fine fashion. The crowd thought so too so I did another called old favorite named, "Cool Water."

"Hey, you handsome young dog, how about doin' something that rocks!" a thirtyish cowgirl shouted jumping up and throwing out both arms in what looked like an invitation to fully embrace her and all her physical charms.

I managed with great effort to tear my eyes away from her low-cut top and monstrous boom-booms and launched myself right into "Jailhouse Rock." I didn't know if they'd go for rock and roll music but they sure did! I didn't give them time to stop hollering for more and played "Suspicious Minds" and then changed things up with a song made famous by the Kingston Trio called "Greenback Dollar."

*They were lovin' my music!* I was feeling such an adrenalin high that I thought my heart might burst, but now they were dancing in between the tables and really into my songs. Elvis had told me to always quit when the audience was dying for more and the band behind me was tuning their guitars and making as much of a distraction as they possibly could so I decided to end my session with a Glen Campbell smash hit song I loved called, "Galveston." And just like that, the whole crowd grew quietly happy and they hung on my every word. I had changed everyone's mood just like magic and I was happier than a flea in a dog house. All my bad thoughts of getting bucked off those rodeo broncs vanished like campfire smoke in the wind.

When I bowed and thanked the crowd for their enthusiastic support, the big-busted gal ran up, hugged me near to being smothered and jammed money into my shirt whispering, "Later, honey!"

I didn't think I was even close to being ready for her and anyway there were a lot of other gals coming up to congratulate and thank me with more dollars and brazen invitations.

Was this ever wonderful! That's when I saw Loretta and Annie pushing forward. Annie looked thrilled with me…Loretta not at all. She was glaring at my new female admirers…eyes sharp like razor blades.

I left the Sultana with Loretta and Annie. We were laughing and having a fine old time. We found a café, ate and then parted company. I admit that I kissed both of the sorority sisters, but Loretta a lot longer and harder. Then I headed for the rodeo grounds because I needed to make sure that Stella was behaving.

They were gone!

I found someone who was camped close by and he said, "Charlie, your sister and that dandy left in his big car for Las Vegas."

"What!" I couldn't believe my ears. "But…but she's supposed to ride tomorrow!"

"I know. They said they'd be back in time and they were going to see Elvis Presley perform at the International Hotel."

"That's crazy!"

"I'm just telling you what they told me. They were drinking hard and the dude had a Cadillac convertible. They roared out of there with their radio blasting."

I didn't know what to do. Finally, I fed Sun Dancer and lay down on my cot under the stars fretting about my sister and feeling I'd failed my promise to Grandmother that I would closely look after and protect her.

Then I thought about my performance at the Sultana and that made me feel better. Boy, the women that I could have had tonight! But Loretta had been there and I didn't want to act like a jerk in front of her and her cute sorority sister. But the more I thought about Loretta, the more I came to believe that our romance was over. She was a college girl and I was just a wannabe rodeo cowboy. Then my mind drifted back to Stella and that phony Lenny guy and my blood nearly boiled.

*God help us all if they crash that Cadillac and kill themselves on their way to see Elvis Presley.*

# *Chapter 17*

Late into the evening I watched the stars and listened to people laughing and winding down. There were a zillion or more stars and I was thrilled about my performance in the Sultana, but depressed and worried about Stella. And I tried to understand just why I'd come to realize that Loretta Hickey and I weren't going to last any longer. Maybe we'd crossed the line the minute she'd gone off to college and since then we'd only been going through the motions. Whatever...we were done, love had died and I knew it.

I finally slept and the next morning I watered and fed Sun Dancer and had a big breakfast, still worrying about Stella. At noon I wandered over to where Twister McCabe was sitting and smoking his twisted little cigarettes. Today he had bulldoggers around him and Twister looked exactly as he had the day before with the same shirt, same battered and stained straw cowboy hat, same easy smile.

I stood off a ways listening and I and noticed that every one of the bulldoggers showed a lot of respect for that old man. They were big cowboys like me and I figured they were all looking for helpful advice. That quickly made me realize that being picked by Twister was a privilege and high honor… and maybe even a life changer.

When their event was close the bulldoggers hurried off to ready their horses. I hunkered down on my heels next to the former world champion. "Twister, I don't need a whole week to come to a decision. If your offer still stands, I'll take it."

"It stands. Why don't you stop by my place on the way home? You can meet my missus and we'll sign papers."

*Papers?*

Twister smiled reading my thoughts. "Cowboy Charlie, from long experience I've learned you need to have a written contract to avoid future misunderstandings. You don't have to sign anything today. You can take it home and show it to your family or an attorney. It's simple and straightforward. I don't work with anyone without a written agreement."

"Makes sense."

"Why it sure it does. Where's your sister today?"

"She took off with that fancy cowboy named Lenny for Las Vegas last night to see Elvis Presley in a casino showroom. I'm expecting them to roll in here at any moment."

Twister frowned. "She upped and left you and her horse?"

"Yep." I couldn't meet his eyes.

"I sure hope you don't do something that foolish when we're bulldoggin' as a team. If you did then I'd break our contract...and maybe your neck."

"I understand." I stood up. "I'd better get her horse ready."

Twister gave me directions to his place. I nodded and was gone, uneasy about Stella and wondering if I should ever tell Grandmother what she had done last night. *Probably best not*, I decided.

Noontime came and went and still no Stella. I could hear the announcer saying that the barrel racers needed to get ready. I bridled and saddled Sun Dancer and then swung into Stella's saddle not bothering to lengthen the stirrups. I wanted to warm the mare up a little in case Stella suddenly showed.

Just as the event was about to start, Stella and Lenny shot through the gates and onto the rodeo ground.

"Charlie, I'm sorry!" Stella yelled, standing up in the front seat.

"The barrel racing is just about to start, so get ready!"

Stella jumped out of the convertible and mounted her horse. "Wish me luck!" she yelled, galloping away.

I didn't get a good look at my sister, but maybe that was for the best because my quick impression was that she looked rough. Lenny hadn't bothered to even get out of his car. He just leaned back in the driver's seat with a wide grin on his handsome face.

"Charlie, you got all lathered up over nothin'," Lenny said. "You're too young to be such a worrier, but Stella says you are."

"Did you see Elvis last night?"

"Nope. We couldn't get tickets that we could afford and we couldn't get past the guards to the back stage for a private visit, either. I didn't give a damn, but your sister was sure pissed off. So we went drinkin' with some friends I discovered." He patted his steering wheel. "Had to drive over a hundred miles an hour in some stretches to make it here on time, but we did!"

One by one the barrel racers ran their event. I didn't bother to go watch because I was both angry and nervous. We needed the money and Stella had damned near blown our chance.

When Stella's turn came she blew a kiss back to Lenny and I lost sight of her. The announcer had already told the Sunday crowd that Stella had the fastest previous run so everyone was rooting for her to win. And damned if

Stella and Sun Dancer didn't win in just 19.0 seconds flat!

All my anger washed away. I was happy and proud to learn that Stella had earned just over $200.00! It wasn't a fortune, but it was desperately needed money and more than I'd ever earned at a rodeo.

Stella finally rejoined us by galloping her mare right up to the convertible then bailing off and giving Lenny a big hug and kiss while I took care of the horse. I knew that Sun Dancer was going to help us save the ranch.

"Charlie," Stella said as I was currying the palomino, "I'm sorry that I worried you so…but, well, we thought we could see and talk to Elvis and you know how much that means."

"Sure do," I said quietly.

I began to walk away, but she grabbed my arm. "There's something that I have to tell you and it can't wait."

"I'm listening."

Stella took a deep breath and let it out slowly. I could smell the heavy fumes of alcohol on her breath and saw that her eyes were bloodshot. "Charlie, when we couldn't even get to see Elvis I got real angry and drunk."

"Do you really need to tell me?"

"Yeah," she said quietly, "I do because I started to realize that I didn't mean a damn thing to Elvis. *You do*, but I've just been fooling myself that someone like him would ever be in love with someone like me. So…."

She choked and I saw that her eyes were starting to brim with tears.

"So what?" I asked, suddenly concerned.

"So Lenny and I went to the Chapel of Love and got married around midnight."

I just stood there dumbfounded. I didn't know what to say…it was like the world fell out from under my boots.

"I…I think I love him, Charlie. And…and he understands why you threw him down and choked him yesterday and he's forgiven you. Now you have to find it in you to forgive me."

"I can't believe this," I finally managed to whisper.

"Here," she said, pulling a Polaroid picture out of her Levi's. "This is a free snapshot they gave us. I ordered some better pictures for only $30.00 and they're sending them to the ranch."

I stared at the picture. Stella looked just about like she did right now and so did Lenny. Stella was clutching a tiny bouquet of wilted flowers. Standing next to the bride and groom and wearing a tired smile was some bald guy in a shiny blue robe holding what I knew was the Holy Bible.

"Jesus, Stella!"

"You're not happy," she said, scrubbing her eyes. "I just knew you wouldn't be."

I shook my head. "It was the wrong thing to do, for me, for Grandmother but most of all for yourself. You deserve a helluva lot better than him."

"Hey!" Lenny shouted. "That's no way to talk about your sister's husband! Stella loves me!"

I was so mad I was ready to kill. I wanted to drag him out of that fancy convertible and really kick his arrogant ass, but I didn't. Instead, I hissed, "My sister loves Elvis, you pompous jackass! You're too dumb to realize you got Stella on the rebound!"

"Charlie!" my sister cried. "You can't talk to him like that. Right now you're just angry because you got bucked off and can't see a future for yourself except for maybe playing for small change in some crappy bar or cowboy saloon."

Her cruel words rocked me back on my boot heels. "Is that what you really think?"

She looked away and said, "I don't know what to think. But I've got to find some happiness and Lenny is it. We're going to rodeos together as husband and wife. He's got a bumper hitch on this car and there's a good used horse trailer for sale here at the rodeo we can afford to buy. It'll work for us if we pull hard together."

I shook my head. "I don't know a thing about your new husband, Stella. But from what I've seen my guess is that he's never worked a hard day in his life. I think you've ruined everything."

She took a deep, shuddering breath. "Tell Grandmother we'll be around before long. Tell her that I love Lenny and we've got a future. And...I wish you all the best, Charlie. I just don't think that being a professional bronc rider is in the cards for you...ever."

I didn't feel like telling her about Twister's offer and all the possibilities I had in store. So I swallowed hard, gave my sister a bear hug and kiss on the cheek and walked away.

On my way home I'd stop at Twisters and sign that contract, no matter what it said. And then I faced a real tough decision...how was I going to tell Grandmother that we'd lost our Stella to a worthless jerk?

Twister hadn't gotten back to his place yet, so I turned off my truck's engine in his front yard wishing I could have a pint of something strong to drink, but knowing it was a good thing I did not. After a little while I walked around looking at his small, but nice house, his fencing and the half dozen or so good looking Quarter Horses. I wondered which one he'd start me on…and finally decided they all looked so fast and of such quality that it really didn't matter.

I was just about to go back to my truck when the front door opened and two Queensland Heelers burst outside and charged me. I jumped into my truck and slammed the door as they yelped and growled and jumped around. I'd never been a big fan of the breed, but they did make good cattle dogs.

A smallish woman came out onto the porch and studied me for a few minutes before she called, "Are you Charlie Coyote?"

"I am."

"Well come on inside and have a glass of lemonade! No point in just sitting in your truck out here in the yard because it could be hours before Twister shows."

I was feeling so low about Stella that I knew I'd not be fit company so I yelled out that I had to leave, but I'd be back in a day or two. The little woman yelled back, but I didn't hear what she said and I didn't make any effort to avoid running over the Heelers, either. I was in a dark and angry mood and I needed to gas up and get home.

Grandmother would be heartbroken when I told her about Stella getting married…but there was nothing I could say or do to change the truth. Sometimes, you just have to swallow the sadness and move on with your life…like my sister had done last night in a Las Vegas wedding chapel.

Grandmother took the news even harder than I'd expected. She cried and then she'd asked me a lot of questions that I couldn't answer about Lenny. *Where was he from? What did he do for a living? Was he a nice man? What was his last name? Did he have a family in Arizona? Any kids from a former marriage?*

"I don't know. I don't know. I don't know," I had to say over and over as she grew more and more exasperated by my ignorance.

*Are they coming by after the rodeo…maybe tonight or tomorrow?*

"I…I don't think so, Grandmother."

Her little fists knotted and I thought she was going to go after me…but instead she went into her kitchen, found a bottle of whiskey and poured a shot.

"I could use one of those, too," I said, sheepishly.

She glared at me as if it were all my fault, then she finally nodded. So we went out on the porch and rocked awhile as the sun dropped over the hills and the sky turned crimson and gold. The whiskey and the sundown soothed both of us and raised our spirits a bit.

"I sure am sorry, Grandmother. It happened so quickly and I never had a clue that she'd do such a thing."

"She loves Elvis and did it to spite him. Stella can be that way."

"I know."

"We need to work even harder without her."

"I know that too."

Then I told her about Twister and she seemed happier and asked me a few questions about the old ex-world champion. I answered as best I could and told her that I was through with Loretta Hickey.

"That's just as well," Grandmother said. "She was a nice girl, but not right for you."

"I guess not."

"You just liked the way she filled her pants."

"I'm ashamed to say that was a big part of it."

She rocked for awhile and then, right out of the blue, asked, "Did you ever get into them, Charlie?"

I was so shocked by the question that I almost dropped my glass. "Grandmother, for gosh sakes!"

I looked her in the eye and it seemed she was trying not to laugh. *Maybe,* I thought, *we'd be okay just the two of us out on Coyote Ranch.*

With my sister gone, I decided to give steer wrestling a good, honest try so I drove up to Flagstaff every Thursday and Friday. The best part of it was that I got to ride faster horses than I'd ever rode before and be around Twister and his wife. The worst part was that it was tough, hard and repetitive. I ran horse after horse and a bunch of steers into exhaustion trying to master the techniques. We started out on big, slow steers and by the end of each day I'd be getting tromped and stomped real bad.

"Cowboy Charlie, it's all about timing," Twister kept saying after every miserable attempt during which he was the hazer, "and technique. You just have to do it over and over again."

I gave him a lopsided and weary grin. "I think these steers have my number."

"They're nothing compared to the ones you'd see in the bigger rodeos. But the thing is that they may have the size and weight, but you've got the brainpower over 'em."

"I'm not even sure about that," I joked, climbing back onto one of his horses and taking a deep breath. "Let's do 'er again."

Each day we did maybe thirty steers and by the time I hauled my weary carcass into my truck and headed for Coyote Ranch, I was so beat up and tired I could barely speak. Grandmother made me take hot baths with Epsom Salt in them after each session, but I was always in a world of pain and just about the time I'd stop limping and gimping around, and away I'd go for more punishment.

"I wonder how Elvis is doing?" Grandmother asked one day just before Thanksgiving when the cottonwoods were shedding their brown leaves down near the seeps and dry washes.

"He's at the International Hotel in Las Vegas," I told her. "If I had money, I'd drive over there instead of to Twister's place and see him perform."

"Well, you don't have money and neither do I," she told me. "Why don't you write him?"

"I doubt he'd even get my letter and if he did it would be lost among all his fan mail."

"Write him anyway and tell him about Stella getting married. It would be better that way than him just finding out when he drops by the next time."

That made sense so I did write Elvis a letter c/o the International Hotel. And I told him about Lenny and asked how he was doing. I also told him that I was working with Twister McCabe and trying to learn bulldogging. I ended by saying, *Steer wrestling is really hard, but I'm slowly getting the hang of it. Sometimes the steer wins and stomps the bee-jeezus out of me, but sometimes I do it alright and down he goes in under ten seconds. The trick is to be consistent. Twister sure knows how to ride and handle cattle...I swear he can read their minds.*

*I am practicing my playing and listening carefully to the guitar work of Chet Atkins and Glen Campbell and I try to play along with them and with your music, too. Like with the steer wrestling, I'm getting better.*

*I have been keeping my eye open for ranchland around here, if you still are interested. The mining company that owns that big piece of land hasn't done anything with it yet. Grandmother is doing well, but is sad not having Stella around. The important thing is that we are holding our own and I hope you can visit next time you're passing through our part of the country.*

I signed off and sent the letter while I was in town, but that same day I saw a dusty truck and old beat up horse trailer coming down the hill into our valley. I wasn't sure who it was until it stopped in our yard and Stella climbed out.

"Hi, Charlie. Happy almost Thanksgiving!"

Stella didn't look good and neither did the truck and trailer. Lenny was behind the wheel and he didn't even get out to say hello. *What had happened to his Cadillac convertible?*

Something wasn't right and I struggled to muster up a happy smile. When I hugged Stella, I smelled whiskey and realized she was drunk. I wanted to tell her that Grandmother would not be pleased, but I was too late because she came out on the porch and just glared at the new arrivals.

Lenny finally got out. He belched and killed a can of beer then tossed it into the bed of the pickup along with a whole lot of others.

Stella glared right back at Grandmother. "Are you going to welcome us as family...or not?"

"Come on in," Grandmother said stiffly before she turned and went back inside.

"She's really pissed off, isn't she?"Stella said.

"Do you blame her?"

"No, I guess not."

"Are you even a little happy?" I blurted.

Stella smiled. "Hell yes! Me and Lenny are rodeoing full time now. Life couldn't be better."

I had my doubts about that. "Is Sun Dancer in that old trailer?"

"Yeah, but she's got a bowed front tendon. Barrel racing full time is really hard on a horse's legs."

I wanted to add that it appeared to be hard on my sister, too. But I kept my silence.

"Will you unload the mare, Charlie? Put her in the barn and see to her leg and give her a good feed. I'll see if I can make some peace with Grandmother."

"Good luck on that one," I said, plenty disgusted with Stella and her husband. "What else happened so wrong?"

Stella shrugged and failed at an attempt to smile. She leaned in and whispered, "Lenny's parents don't approve of me and they've cut off his money. They're even threatening to cut him out of their will. We've been fighting and having a helluva rough time, truth be known."

"I could see that in a glance." I loved Stella and she had always been on my side so I hugged her and whispered, "Go in and tell Grandmother that you're sorry for eloping and then not coming to visit sooner."

"I will." Stella took a deep breath, then another before she carefully walked over to the porch and up the stairs. She gave me a final over-the-shoulder look just as she went inside and she had the expression of someone stepping up on the gallows to face a hangman. I felt awful for her...and when I turned and saw Lenny reaching into the truck for another beer, I nearly stomped over and laid him low.

I knew that Grandmother would forgive Stella and so would I. But with Lenny it was an entirely different matter…and the idea of having him staying at our ranch awhile and sharing Thanksgiving with us in a few days was enough to make me lose my appetite.

Lenny said nothing as I unloaded Sun Dancer. When I got her out I was shocked by how bad the mare looked. Both of her front legs were wrapped in filthy bandages from fetlock to knee and she was dead lame and about two hundred pounds lighter than she'd been at the Williams rodeo. My blood started to boil and it was all I could do to hold my tongue.

"Bad luck has been hounding me and Stella lately," Lenny whined as I slowly led the mare to our barn.

Lenny followed me. "I wanted to visit a couple of months ago, but Stella couldn't swallow her pride and so we stayed away." The man was unshaven and his once fancy clothes were dirty. "You never did like me, Cowboy Charlie. I can see that hasn't changed."

I ignored him and took care of the mare. I unwrapped the bandages on her legs and was relieved to see that the damage wasn't as bad as it could have been. With rest and liniment and treatments, I thought she'd be fine…maybe by next spring.

I sure as hell hoped that Stella and the worthless piece of crap she married didn't intend to stay here until that happened. Because between now and next spring and across a long cold winter with damn little money coming in and no place much to escape there wasn't a doubt in my mind that I'd go crazy and end up killing them both.

# *Chapter 18*

Grandmother asked me to treat Lenny as family, but I just couldn't. And then one afternoon Stella saddled up a horse and rode out to where I was mending a fence with Rip by my side.

"You ought to slow down a little," she said, dismounting.

I didn't have anything to say to that so I slammed the heavy iron pike back into the ground which was hard and rocky. Posthole digging was about the least favorite of all my jobs, but it had to be done. Our fence posts were of cedar, and they lasted a long time, but not forever.

"You ought to have Lenny out here helping."

I scoffed. "Judging from what I've seen…about all that Lenny is good for is hoisting a can of Coors."

"That's a hard thing to say, Charlie."

"Well what do you expect me to say when you and that guy…."

"He's my *husband!*"

"Okay, but he's also the guy that you ran off with, hurting Grandmother. Then you show up at Coyote Ranch broke and with your mare in bad shape so excuse me if I'm not too happy about you or your husband. Stella, you've changed and not for the better. Grandmother used to worry about your dark side and I didn't understand…but I do now."

She started to turn away but then our ranch dog Rip whined and she said, "Charlie, I rode out here to tell you that I really need a friend. I need *you* to be that friend."

I looked into her eyes and had to nod my head. Stella and I had always butted up against each other, but at the same time we'd stood together through good times and bad…and these were bad times.

"Alright," I heard myself say.

Stella visibly brightened. "I hear that you're really working hard both at your music and bulldogging."

"I am. Twister thinks we can make good money."

"You've put on a lot of muscle since I last saw you and look great."

"Thanks." I wanted to tell her that she looked great too, but that was obviously untrue. She and Lenny both looked wrung out and defeated, yet they somehow drove into Winslow every now and then to buy a couple of cases of Coors. "Stella, I heard that a person can get an annulment and get out of a bad marriage. Maybe you should consider that…you and Lenny just aren't right and I doubt that you ever can be."

She chewed on that for a few minutes. I grew tired of waiting and grabbed the pike and returned to working at the posthole.

"Charlie?"

I stopped.

"We're leaving for California early tomorrow. Lenny wants to see if we can mend fences with his parents and…and get some money."

The thought occurred to me that Lenny's parents might be upset because Stella was obviously part Indian. But I held that opinion.

"Will you keep Sun Dancer and get her sound for me until I come back?"

"Sure. And, if you go bust, you know you can come back anytime."

She put her hands on her hips. "But *not* Lenny."

"I didn't say that."

Stella shook her head sadly. "You didn't need to. I can read you like a book. But thanks for helping with my horse."

"You be careful, big sister. And…and, if you get in trouble, I'll come running."

Stella swung onto her horse then rode away fast. Fifteen minutes earlier, I'd been sweating and pounding at the rocky ground, making some slow progress and with nothing particularly troubling on my mind. Now, I attacked the posthole and my mind was nothing short of a train wreck.

I didn't sleep well that night and when I finally got up early the next morning I saw a light on in the barn. I knew that Lenny definitely wasn't an early riser and that it had to be Stella saying goodbye to Sun Dancer. Suddenly, I wanted to say goodbye to my sister so I hurriedly dressed and went to see her.

When I swung open the barn door, I saw Stella had our mother's diary in her hand. She looked up at me and said, "I read just another page or two, Charlie."

"I haven't looked at it since the last time we were out here together. What else did you learn?"

"Our mother was…was in turmoil. She wrote things that don't exactly make sense and there is desperation in her words."

"I don't want to hear about it. I came out to say goodbye."

"I'm going to read something you need to hear."

I knew that I had to either leave…or listen, so I stood rooted.

*July 19,1946*

*Dear Diary, I am pregnant and I do not know how to tell Phillip that he is most likely the father. This is a complete catastrophe because since a child derives his clan from his mother and I being white have no clan which means my child can never be a Hopi and will forever be an outcast among these people. My mind is coming apart! I don't know what to do or say!*

Stella bent her head and I watched her shoulders shake as she began to sob. But then she threw back her head and said, "I can deal with this. It doesn't matter that our father wasn't really *my* father."

"Yes it does," I argued.

Stella returned to the pages.

*July 21, 1946*

*Dear Diary, Phillip has asked me if he is the father of the child I carry. He also wonders if I had been sleeping with Charles. He says if Charles is the father, he will kill him. God forgive me for I have brought anger and even hatred to this village instead of love and peace. What can I do now instead of bringing division and bloodshed?*

Stella looked up at me and her eyes held something I did not want to understand, but she said, "Here it is, Charlie. Here is why we were run off First Mesa as children and father was beaten. Are you ready for the truth?"

I managed to nod.

*July 28, 1946*

*Dear Diary, Phillip and Charles have fought nearly to the death. Some of the women have tried to stone me; children have set their dogs on me. My parents to whom I have begged forgiveness and understanding have sent money instead. Fifty thousand dollars is a lot of money but it is nothing compared to all the sadness I have brought to everyone who knows and once loved me. This money means that I have been disowned and banished. I loved my parents and now I have broken their hearts. I want to die!*

"Stella, I've heard enough."

"Charlie, that has to be the money that bought Coyote Ranch! Please just listen to a little more."

*August 23, 1946*

   *Dear Diary, Phillip refuses to even talk to me. Charles has taken me away because I lied and assured him that he is the father of the child I carry. What else could I do! Charles married me, but he loves rodeo far, far more than me. He often leaves me alone sick and heavy with Phillip's child. But there is one ray of sunshine in my life…I am going to give birth to a healthy baby and I have used the money my parents sent to buy an Arizona cattle ranch. I named it Coyote Ranch and living way out in the sagebrush means that I will be left in peace…if not happiness.*

   Stella looked up from the pages. "So you see, brother, I'm a half-breed who will never know for sure who is her real father. And the one I knew didn't really love our mother. He married her out of pity…and *for her money that bought our ranch.*"

   Stella put Mother's diary back in its hiding place. "We're got to read this all someday. We have to know what happened to her."

   I didn't think that was such a good idea. I didn't want to know any more of our mother's sorrow.

   Seeing my doubts, Stella said, "I have to know and I think you do too."

   She was probably right. Many had been the time since she'd left with Lenny that I'd felt a powerful urge to read that diary…but somehow I felt that it belonged to both Stella and myself and so it had to be read when we were together. Maybe that didn't make a lot of sense, but that was my feeling about it…along with a certain sense of dread.

   I almost wished our barn would burn to the ground and take Mother's dark past and shameful secrets with it.

# *Chapter 19*

Stella and Lenny left their horse trailer parked beside the barn when the sun was high in the sky. I had heard them arguing late into the night and I was damn glad that they were finally leaving. Grandmother and I waved from our front porch rocking chairs until they were gone and then she asked, "What do you think about that marriage?"

I didn't hesitate or mince my words. "They're pure poison for each other."

"I agree. Stella needed gas and food money for the trip to California. I gave her what she asked for."

"Good. We'll do alright."

"What will happen to your sister? She is lost in spiritual darkness."

My mother's diary was riding hard in my mind and so I had to ask, "Like her mother?"

Lucy Yoyetewa nodded.

"Grandmother, Stella wouldn't...wouldn't kill herself would she?"

"Stella is much harder than your mother was."

"Stella is tough, alright."

Grandmother rocked in silence for awhile watching her chickens scratch out in the yard. "Charlie, I want you to take me up to the Hopi Reservation to see a shaman."

"Haven't we got enough troubles already?" I asked, not one bit pleased at the idea. "And it's a long way up to the Hopi Mesas."

"If we don't do this and Stella dies, then how will we feel?"

I knew that Grandmother was right...Stella's spirit was being consumed by the darkness and maybe Hopi medicine could help...it sure couldn't hurt. "When do you want to leave?"

"Tomorrow morning at daybreak. We'll feed the stock heavy enough until we return."

Remembering that terrible visit long ago, I wondered to myself if we would be permitted to return.

We were up and on our way at sunrise. I didn't have a lick of faith in some nameless Hopi shaman and knew it would cost plenty...still, what else could we do but try?

Although the Hopi Reservation was less than a hundred miles from Coyote Ranch, it was like another ancient world that time had forgotten. We drove across the Navajo Reservation where we saw the round, mud-covered hogans and sweat houses. There were thousands of sheep being tended mostly by children riding runty horses with thin dogs at their sides. Finally, we entered the Hopi Reservation and Grandmother began to tell me about her people in a peculiar sing-song voice I couldn't ever remember hearing before. When a girl of about eleven waved and I waved back at her as she trotted through the sagebrush, I couldn't help but think that Grandmother might have been and looked exactly like that once.

"Charlie, my people have lived on this land for over a thousand years...far longer than the Navajo. We live up on the mesas and there are twelve villages, each with its own leader and clans." Her chin lifted and she breathed the high desert air with a smile. "The Hopi have always resisted change...especially from the white people who wanted to mold our beliefs and customs to fit their own thinking. And even today the white scientists come to tell us how to raise more and better corn. But their seeds die in our dry ground and so we plant the old way with a planting stick and blessings."

I had heard about the agricultural scientists who had tried to change the Hopi way of farming and to get them to use the corn seed that grew tall in the long, straight fields of Nebraska. Their corn had not even germinated on Hopi land and the scientists had slunk away in shame.

"Up there," Grandmother said pointing to the First Mesa, "the Hopi live near the sun and the Great Spirit. We catch the baby eagle and make him one with our family; we feed the eaglets rabbits and sing their praises. Eagle is anointed with corn meal and clay and given our clan name. But when the cold wind comes and the kachinas return from the San Francisco Peaks, Eagle is sent to join them with important messages of how well he was treated by Hopi."

I remembered from my mother's diary how a few great golden eagles were sacrificed by the Hopi and, like Ellen Allen, I had trouble with that sacrifice despite knowing how important eagle feathers were in the Hopi life and ceremonies.

"Look, see how strong the corn grows in Hopi fields! Corn and rain are the gifts that the Great Spirit gives to his Hopi children."

I had seen Hopi corn fields before and admired them for their lack of order. The corn was not tall as I had seen pictures of it grown in the Midwest... instead it was bunched and thick and low so that the hard Arizona winds would not cause it to topple. It was planted wherever a digging stick punched a hole in the hard, dry soil.

Elvis & Cowboy Charlie

My truck began to labor so I downshifted as we entered an ancient settlement which was a collection of poor, tin-roofed houses all of which had bright green gardens of corn which I knew were watered by hand. I downshifted into low gear to make the last few hairpin turns near the top. We slowly rolled into a village attracting the attention of many children and dogs, but no grownups. The children were smiling and healthy looking but their dogs were mangy and thin.

"Where are we going?"

"Stop here. I need the village's permission to go farther," Grandmother said quietly. "Wait in the truck."

I was more than happy to wait and watch. I shared nothing with these people and I didn't have a good feeling about them, and yet they were Grandmother's beloved people and I respected them for being so independent of the modern white society. I could not imagine living up here in their airy world of stone and dust. Farther on, I knew that the villages were even more primitive.

I killed my truck's engine and watched a girl of about eighteen emerge from a low doorway of thick stone. There was no light inside and I wondered how she lived in such a place and if she had, from birth, developed night vision like a cat. When she saw me she froze in mid-step and studied me for several minutes...like a deer on a remote hillside, curious, but not overly afraid. She wore a purple print dress to her ankles; her feet were bare and around her wrist was a heavy silver bracelet. She was very pretty and her hair was bound up tightly in the traditional butterfly whorl on each side of her head which I knew meant that she was unmarried. She smiled. I smiled. I think she laughed and I know that I laughed and then she ducked back inside leaving me to wonder about her life up here in this ancient, sky place.

Children began to appear as if they were stepping out of stone. I watched, blinking in amazement. My eyes were very keen and yet...yet the children appeared like ghosts. I got out of the pickup and leaned against the fender. I said "hello" and they giggled. One stretched his hands out and vertically widened the distance between and the several of the others raised up on their toes...so I knew they were impressed by my height. I wished then that I could say a few words in Hopi, but then I decided that there was nothing in my mind that they would understand or needed to hear.

Finally, Grandmother appeared with an old man whose hair was long and gray. He nodded to me and I nodded back.

"We have permission to see him."

"Who?"

Grandmother did not answer, but began to walk. I felt a hundred probing

151

eyes on me. A puppy appeared wagging his tail and sniffing at my pants leg. I bent to pet him and he rolled over onto his back and peed on his spotted tummy. Children began to laugh and I laughed with them.

In less than the length of a football field Grandmother halted before a mud and rock house.

"This is where the shaman lives. Wait here in silence."

In Hopi, Grandmother called a name and soon an old man appeared. He wore khaki colored pants cut off unevenly at the ankles. His feet were bare, his shirt was black and shiny and his eyes held me then dismissed me as he spoke to Grandmother.

They spoke a long, long time and I couldn't tell if their animated conversation was going well...or ill. Finally, Grandmother and the shaman nodded. Money changed hands and Grandmother walked away. I hurried to overtake her.

"Is it okay?"

"Yes, he will pray for Stella in the kiva and during all the ceremonies this year."

"How much is it costing?"

"Shhh! Don't talk of money or the prayers will be diminished."

As we walked out on the mesa, it grew narrower. Less than the width of two cars and in some places there were low stone walls along the edges and beyond those walls was nothing but empty blue sky. In these places I noted that the top of the mesa tilted toward the high cliffs and I knew that this red earth, when wet, would be slippery. And when it snowed in the winter, it would be icy and that was why there were walls only in certain treacherous stretches on this soaring and narrow mesa top.

I wondered how many Hopi...especially the children...had fallen to their deaths over the long centuries. Grandmother had told me that this place was the second oldest town in America...dating back more than a thousand years and that only Orabi was thought to be older. The houses were multi-storied pueblos, resting on smooth, solid rock, some leaning out into space and others crouched weather worn and weary from the slow unraveling of centuries in the sun, wind, snow and rain. And bare Hopi feet.

We passed a kiva which I knew was one of the ancient ceremonial places of these people. I wished I could climb down inside, but knew that was forbidden. Ladders made of worn, pine poles jutted from deep within these sacred chambers.

"We're almost at the end of this mesa, Grandmother."

She held up a hand. "Speak softly, Charlie. This is *Phillip's* home."

Phillip! *Stella's real father!* The man that my father had almost killed in a vicious knife fight four years before I was born.

Grandmother called for what seemed a long time. Finally, a small, frail looking man with a disfigured face appeared. I took an involuntary back-step and gasped because the Hopi's face was missing his nose! And there were terrible scars on his cheeks and one ear was cut away. I felt my flesh quiver. Grandmother spoke and Phillip said nothing; finally he pointed at me and Grandmother said my name.

"Cowboy Charlie Coyote." Just like that.

Phillip measured me up and down and I didn't detect hostility or friendship. Just curiosity…like someone might look at a scorpion or a rock painting or a piece of wood with an unusual shape.

Then Grandmother began to speak again and Phillip kept nodding his head, glancing at me from time to time and staring at the sky. After maybe ten minutes, it was his turn and he spoke slowly, voice soft and musical like clear water running over river rocks.

I was captured by the sound of his voice and by where I was and what was happening even though I did not understand what was being said. I just sensed that it was good and I was happy to watch the girl with the long purple print dress who watched me right back with wide, unblinking eyes and just the hint of a seductive smile…or so I vainly imagined.

"Charlie, come shake Phillip's hand and tell him you are sorry for what happened long ago over your mother."

With my heart pounding, I stepped up to him and managed to say, "I am very sorry for that long-ago fight between you and my father."

Phillip studied me for a moment, said, "Do you know that your real last name is not Coyote?"

I glanced sharply at Grandmother who'd raised a forefinger to her lips telling me that I was to answer…then listen.

"No," I managed to say.

"Your father got his name because he was smart and cunning enough to steal your mother from me. Smart and cunning like *Coyote*. So we Hopi called him that and it stuck. I heard he liked that name and took it gladly."

Then he stuck his hand out and we shook. His hand was as hard and dry as the rock on which his sky village was anchored. He turned around without a word and disappeared into his pueblo without a sound, but more importantly without any hatred toward us Coyotes.

Grandmother took my arm and led me away. I turned to see that the pretty Hopi girl was still watching me and when I smiled, she smiled right back. My heart skipped a beat and then I turned away knowing I would never, ever see that pretty Hopi girl again.

We climbed into my truck and drove off down the steep turns onto the high plateau heading south back across the Painted Desert to Route 66. As I drove my mind was at peace and I knew that Grandmother's mind was too.

"I am glad you met him," she said, staring out the window. "He is a good man and healer."

"Is he also a shaman who will make the prayers for Stella?"

She nodded.

"Then I hope he has powerful medicine, because Stella is tough."

Grandmother smiled and I took that to mean that she thought her Hopi shaman's medicine was even stronger than the darkness inside my sister.

# *Chapter 20*

We stopped in Winslow for groceries and gas and then hurried home; it was late in the afternoon when we pulled into our yard. I shut down the truck and we grabbed bags of groceries then carried them inside. That's when I heard snoring, and there, sound asleep on our couch...was Elvis.

I almost dropped the groceries on the floor. Grandmother was right behind me and she *did* drop her bag of groceries. I tried to wake Elvis, but he was sleeping so soundly that even shaking him didn't seem to work.

"Grandmother, get a cold cloth," I said. "He's really out."

"Is he sick?"

"I don't know."

We were finally able to wake Elvis, but he was groggy and his pupils were dilated. "What's wrong?" I asked.

"I...I took some strong sleeping pills after Mark dropped me off. I'll be fine; think you could brew a cup of coffee?"

Grandmother went to make coffee. We got Elvis awake, but even though he soon shared our dinner, he seemed quiet and withdrawn. I had never seen him subdued before and it worried me.

"I'm going to go to bed and get a good night's sleep," he announced, right after dinner instead of coming out on the porch to talk, sing or play the guitar. "We'll catch up on things over morning coffee."

Grandmother and I wished him goodnight and the next morning when he ate breakfast Elvis seemed like an entirely different man. We took our second cup of coffee on the porch and he looked around fresh-eyed and cheerful.

"Good to be back," he said. "Really good. Your grandmother told me that you two were up on the Hopi Reservation yesterday to see a shaman about helping Stella."

"That's right."

"I wished I'd have been there with you and asked him to say a few prayers for me."

"We can drive back up."

"Naw, that's okay," Elvis said quickly. "I'm a Christian, but I've studied religions enough to know that there's something to learn in all of 'em. Next time you go to see that Hopi shaman ask him to say a few prayers for me."

"I'll do that," I replied.

In the clear morning light, I thought Elvis looked extremely tired. He had put on weight and his face had a puffiness I hadn't seen before. He didn't seem to have his usual spark and quick, wholesome laugh, either. I suspected it was due to not enough sleep, too much of that rich casino food and maybe the sleeping pills. Put all of them together and I knew that it was a recipe for an unhealthy life.

Grandmother came out and started talking about everything on her mind. The chickens who were not laying eggs very well, her pottery, the weather and even a little gossip about what was going on in Winslow.

Elvis and I just listened although he did ask a few questions about Stella.

"I'm sorry that she ran off with such a loser," he said. "I thought Stella would know better than that."

"Maybe she is doing okay in California," I offered hopefully.

"California is a beautiful state, but there are people over there who can chew you up fast. I prefer Hawaii. I fell in love with it working on the film *Blue Hawaii* back in 1960 and the people over there are just so nice and easy to be around. I sleep better in Hawaii than I do even in my own bedroom at Graceland...but I think I sleep better out here than either one of those places."

"You'd sleep better if you and Charlie go to work on this place," Grandmother said, surprising us both. "There are fences to be mended and the corrals keep falling down. The barn has some boards dropping off and...."

"Grandmother," I said with exasperation, "I'm sure Elvis didn't come here to be put to work."

Elvis smiled and held up his hand. "When Mark drove me out we saw that Rip was on the porch and we figured you'd be back soon. He returned to Las Vegas. He likes staying there and I like staying here so it works out."

"Can you stay long?"

"I'm afraid not, but it's good to be here with you now. I miss Stella, though. This ranch seems a lot quieter without her."

"It is," I agreed.

"I need to leave in a couple of days," Elvis said. "Cowboy Charlie, will you drive me back to Las Vegas? I'll pay for your expenses and time."

"Sure."

"And if your truck breaks down, I'll buy you a new one."

We all laughed, knowing he'd gladly do just that.

We sat for awhile and just as I was thinking of getting up and getting busy,

Elvis said, "Grandmother, I told my friends that Coyote story you told me and they thought it was funny. Do you have any more of those?"

"Sure, lots."

"How come Coyote is in so many stories?"

"It's because he has things to teach us. We love Coyote and there is so much to laugh about him because he is often the worst of ourselves. Some of The People call him Brother Coyote, Changing Coyote and even Trickster Coyote because he is always trying to fool people. Coyote always tries to be clever and is very lazy. A long, long time ago he was asked by the Creator to make The People out of clay."

"Is that a fact?" Elvis asked.

"Yes, but Coyote did such a sloppy job that he had to throw those people away and start all over. He even tried to make the world and the heavens, but instead of placing each star carefully in the sky he just threw them up and that is why they have no pattern to this very day. Coyote is lazy and that is why he is always getting himself into trouble. He tries to think too much instead of listening to his heart and living the right way…the Hopi way."

"What is the Hopi way…if it's not a secret you can't tell outsiders."

"It is no secret." Grandmother said. "The Hopi way is to live a selfless life…to place society's welfare above your personal welfare…always. It is to be humble and to do things that benefit everyone. In this way we can make a difference for the better even if we ourselves are not rewarded…or even noticed. And finally, it means that we need to understand that the Creator has given everyone what is necessary to live together without hatred, greed or envy."

Elvis nodded in agreement. "That's not so different from what Jesus taught."

"True, but The People believe that Nature and Spirit are one and the same. That all things in the universe have life and are sometimes seen in living form as our kachinas."

"I see. How about a story?"

Grandmother rocked a little faster.

*"When Coyote was young he used to tease a family of crows. The more upset they became, the more Coyote teased them. He finally grew tired of that game, but the crows were still angry. One day three of them waited in a tree for Coyote and began to stare hard up into the sky. Coyote sat down and looked up, too, but he couldn't see a thing.*

*"Why are you crows looking up when I see nothing and my neck is getting stiff?"*

*"There is going to be a big hail storm here soon," one of the crows answered.*

*Coyote looked again. His eyes were very keen and yet he saw nothing. "There isn't even a cloud in this sky."*

*"Well," one of the crows answered, "we are warning you to be very careful."*

*Coyote began to worry a little bit.*

*"If you find a canvas bag, we will help put you in it and then you will be protected from the sting of the hail."*

*Coyote knew where such a bag could be stolen and decided this was very thoughtful of the crows and that he would do it. How nice of the crows to suggest such a thing given that he had always teased them!*

*He ran to get a canvas bag and when he returned the crows told him to climb inside then they would tie him up and he would be safe.*

*"Thank you," Coyote said, climbing into the bag. He was not at all worried about the crows getting hurt by the hail…crows were not as smart or as important as himself.*

*When he was tied up inside the bag, the crows flew off and gathered rocks in their claws and then dropped rocks over and over on Coyote who began to howl because the rocks hurt. The crows finally grew tired of punishing Coyote for teasing them so they flew down and let him out of the bag. He was bruised and bleeding and looking very sad. When Coyote suddenly looked around and saw no hail but only stones, he understood that he had been tricked. He grew very angry, but the crows flew up in the trees laughing at him. There was nothing Coyote could do but slink away in shame and he never teased the crows again although he still hates them for out-smarting him."*

*"And the moral of that story is?"*

*"Don't tease crows. And don't tease people because they may turn around and make you pay."*

"It's a good lesson to remember," Elvis said with a laugh.

Grandmother nodded. "Would you like to hear a Navajo Coyote story this time?"

"Sure."

*"A long, long time ago Coyote was walking down a dirt road with his friends, Porcupine and Skunk. All three were very hungry so when they saw a piece of meat they ran and got to it at exactly the same time. Porcupine and Skunk thought they should all share the meat equally, but sly Coyote wanted it all. So he said, "We will have a race down this road and whoever gets to the bottom of this hill will get all of the meat."*

*"Porcupine and Skunk did not like this idea, but since Coyote was bigger and stronger than either one of them they had no choice but to agree to the race."*

*Grandmother giggled to herself. "And what do you think happened in this race?"*

*Elvis said, "The coyote would be a lot faster."*

*"No, because Porcupine rolled into a ball and then rolled down the hill very fast and won the race."*

*"That wasn't fair!" Coyote cried in anger. "We must have a different contest."*

*Porcupine was very unhappy, but he wanted to be fair so he asked, "What kind of contest?"*

*Coyote smirked because his mind was racing and he already had a plan. "We will each dream," he told his friends. "And the one who has the most beautiful dream to tell can eat all of the meat."*

*So that was what they did. Coyote and Skunk lay down and went to sleep to dream, but not Porcupine because he was still angry about not winning the race.*

*Coyote and Skunk finally woke up and Skunk told of a very good dream. Then it was Coyote's turn and his dream was even better. Oh, it was such a wonderful dream that surely he could not lose!*

*Porcupine saved his dream for last. "I dreamed I already ate all the meat!"*

*Coyote and Skunk looked and the meat was…it was gone! They blinked and rubbed their eyes and finally Coyote asked in anger, "Porcupine, what happened to the meat!"*

*Porcupine rubbed his belly and smiled. "My dream was so good that it came true!"*

Both Elvis and I laughed hard. "So what's the moral of that Coyote story?"

Grandmother replied, "It says that if you don't sleep too much and work hard your dreams can come true."

"Elvis," I said, "there's always work to be done here, but it can keep. Would you like to go for a horseback ride?"

"Yeah," he said, "I'd like to ride back to that high ridge where we can see that mining land. How big is that mining company's claim?"

I thought about it for a few minutes. I knew the approximate boundaries so I said, "About two thousand acres."

"That sure makes my ranch in Memphis seem piddling. Do you think that you could talk them into selling it to me?"

"There's nothing I'd rather do," I answered, "but I don't think they'd sell it to anyone."

"Too bad."

We thanked Grandmother and went to saddle Buster and another horse. An hour later we dismounted beside a barbed wire fence after a hard climb up a mountainside overlooking the neighboring copper country land.

"I don't suppose you'd cut this fence so we could ride out there," Elvis said.

"Afraid not."

"Then let's tie our horses and hike a ways." He pointed to a hill south of us about a mile. "That'd be a fine vantage point."

I wasn't sure hiking that far or climbing the hill was smart thing to do. Elvis wasn't accustomed to our 6,000 plus feet of altitude and he wasn't in good shape.

"Come on," he said, squeezing between the wire strands. "It's a good day for a hike."

There were stands of ponderosa among the pinyon and juniper pines. We weaved our way through the trees and I warned Elvis to watch out for rattlesnakes.

"Look!" he said, pointing at the ground, "rabbit's shit!"

"No, that's the droppings of mule deer."

"Are you sure, Charlie?"

"Yeah, unless the rabbit that dropped his load here stood about eight feet tall."

That cracked Elvis up. "What other animals are living up here?"

"A few mountain lions and bobcats. Mostly mule deer and elk, though."

Elvis was so excited by this news that he began to study the ground carefully as we moved through the pines. Then I heard him shout, "Charlie, look! An arrowhead!"

"That's a fine one," I told him. "We might come on an old Indian encampment and find pottery shards and maybe even a grinding stone."

Now Elvis really got excited. "Are you serious!"

"I am. Long ago the Sinagua and other ancient peoples lived in this country. You can find little rock walls and sunken places where they took shelter underground with roofs made of mud, brush and poles. And wherever you see rock faces covered with a black patina formed by a mineral wash you're almost certain to find pictures etched in stone. They're called *petroglyphs.*"

"Do they tell the stories of those ancient peoples?"

"I'm sure that they do. But only the Hopi, Navajo and other Indians really have a good idea of those picture stories say. And in some cases, maybe rock art has no story at all, but was just something that the long-ago artist wanted to do out of pure joy."

"What a thrill that would be to have watched an ancient Indian artist at work! To be able to talk to him and learn his thoughts…his hopes and dreams. Because they'd have had them too, Cowboy Charlie. Smaller than ours, maybe, but just as important."

"I'm sure you're right about that," I agreed. I had seen plenty of archaeological sites and I'd never stopped feeling that excitement that I now heard in Elvis' voice. Sadly, I'd heard that some people were buying land in the great Southwest and using huge backhoes to unearth valuable old Indian pottery and other archaeological treasures.

As a boy, I'd even found my own unbroken pot, a beautiful thing with black and white designs. I'd been excited to sell it, but then I'd been told by Grandmother that these things should always be left as found because they were sacred and were never to be sold for profit. In school I'd learned that when the great discovery at Mesa Verde had been unearthed many of its irreplaceable treasures had ended up being bought by Europeans including the mummified remains and skeletons of the ancient Anasazi. On the rare occasions when Grandmother spoke of that sacrilege, she cried and prayed.

"Do you suppose I could keep just this one beautiful arrowhead?"

"Okay," I said, amused that such a rich man could get so excited about such a small and reasonably common artifact. "I'm sure that the owner who made and shot the arrow it was attached to wouldn't mind someone like you keeping it as a reminder of a long ago time. Just treat it with respect."

"Oh, you bet I will!" Elvis wiped the arrowhead clean and slipped it into his pocket. "I'll bet if we looked around we could find many more."

"I'm sure we could, but once the copper mine goes into operation, everything changes. The Indian artifacts and treasures will all be either buried, dug up or smashed to pieces."

"They'll *destroy* everything?"

"Sure. They'll come in here with huge earth-moving equipment. Elvis, it's all about profit. If they happen to dig up an old burial or ceremonial site, you can be certain that they'd tell no one because that would mean bringing in Indian peoples and government officials. Copper mining would be put on hold and a lot of money would be lost; that's the last thing any mining company wants to happen."

"What a sacrilege!"

I couldn't hide the anger from my voice. "That's the way it is everywhere.

Destroy the past and make way for the future."

"Charlie, what's the name of the company that owns this land and this mountain we're standing on?"

"Copper Mountain Mining."

"Where are their headquarters?"

"I'm not sure but they have an office in Flagstaff."

"On our way to Las Vegas we'll stop off and ask what it would take to buy this land and save it from mining."

"I doubt they'll sell."


That night Elvis and I played songs until late. He told me that I'd come a long way with my music and figured I was about ready to turn professional.

"I'll tell you what, Charlie. When we get to Las Vegas I'll put in a good word and I think we can get you work in one of the casino's smaller lounges. If you do well, they'll move you up fast into the big money."

"What about a band?"

"No problem. I know a lot of good, hungry musicians in that town."

I suddenly had second thoughts. I really liked and respected my old rodeo cowboy friend, Twister, and he'd invested time in me and money in my training. I didn't want to leave him feeling it had all been a waste.

"Cowboy Charlie, I can see that you've got some concerns. But the very worst that can happen is that you won't like the music business and become a great bulldogger. I'm asking you to at least give music a try. God gave you a fine voice and good looks…so you have the gifts…you just have to want to use them."

*How often,* I thought, *does someone get a chance like this with the help and encouragement of the King of Rock 'n Roll?*

"Alright, Elvis. I'm in."

"Great! Have you written any new songs?"

"As a matter of fact I have."

"Sing one."

"Now?" I couldn't believe he'd asked me to start singing on a mountaintop, but there it was.

"Sure. I want to hear the lyrics. And what's your title?"

" 'Midnight Moon.'"

"Nice title. Let's hear it."

I took a deep breath. "Okay. I'll sing you the chorus."

*Down in Arizona there's a midnight moon,*
*that makes a boy and a girl just wanna spoon.*
*And when the stars at night are all aglow,*
*I'll tell you mister, it's an all night show.*
*We cuddle and kiss, it's some kind of bliss*
*down in Arizona 'neath the midnight moon!*

I was going to sing more but Elvis burst out laughing.

"What's so damn funny!"

He stopped laughing, but I could tell it was a struggle. "Charlie, I hope you never do figure it out."

I headed back toward the fence and our horses. I wasn't sure if my song was supposed to make anyone laugh; I'd thought it pretty romantic, but maybe I missed something.

When it came time for Elvis to leave, he hugged Grandmother, promised to return sooner and we loaded into my truck and headed for Las Vegas. We passed Walnut Canyon where I told Elvis there were some cliff dwellings and dozens of interesting petroglyphs.

"Charlie, in just the few days I've been staying at Coyote Ranch, I feel much better than when I arrived. This country really invigorates me." He was quiet for a few minutes. "One of the things I like and appreciate here is that you and Grandmother never treat me as anything but an ordinary guy. You don't try to pry into my past and bedevil me with questions about the famous women I've dated and all the things I've done since I became rich and famous."

"It's none of our business."

"You're right. But you and your grandmother probably know less about me than a million of my fans. I'd like to keep it that way."

I wasn't sure where this conversation was going, but I could tell it was important to Elvis.

He continued, "My life is very complicated. I have many people who depend on me for their livelihoods...for putting food on the table for their wives and children. I love my fans and I'd never do anything to disappoint them...but I'm growing older. I did a lot of stupid movies for the money and I always tried to do the best I could with the lousy scripts I was handed requiring me to sing sappy songs. I never got a chance at serious roles. But I'm finished with that now and I just want to concentrate on my concerts and showroom work."

"People love your movies, Elvis. They'll be watching them for years and years."

"I doubt that. What I do know is that I'm trying to make some changes in my life. For a long time I've felt like a hamster on a wheel, always running in circles. I'm grateful for the life I'm leading, but what I know is that I've got kind of a love-hate thing with performing. On the one hand when I'm on stage and the music is rockin', it's the greatest thing in the world. But it's wearing me down. I can't sleep right and when I do sleep, I don't wake up fresh. I stay up all night watching television and movies and sleep all day."

"Why don't you just chuck the whole thing and come out here and buy a ranch?"

"I've thought of that plenty of times, but don't you understand that as soon as the word got out that I was living out here the road leading off the highway to your ranch would turn into a freeway with tourists and autograph seekers?"

That thought had never entered my mind…but now that it had I wasn't keen on the idea at all.

"That's why," Elvis continued, "I've gone to a lot of trouble to keep you Coyotes my secret except for my driver. Charlie, I want you to have this."

He took off his gold and diamond ring and handed it to me. It had the initials, TCB on it and I knew that it meant "taking care of business."

"I can't take that."

"You have to," Elvis insisted. "If you ever got in trouble like when we met at that rodeo a few years ago all you'd have to do is show that ring to my bodyguards and the door people and they'd let you right in to see me. My special friends have similar rings. And if I got in trouble, well, you could get in to see me."

I didn't know what he was talking about unless it was some fan that might try to hurt or even kill him to become famous. Elvis reached over and slipped the ring on my little finger and it fit perfectly.

"I gave President Nixon a ring like that, but he doesn't tell anyone. He gave me a lawman's badge in return and made me promise to fight drugs and crime."

"Elvis, are there people who…who would kill you?"

"I expect so, Charlie. Sadly, it goes with the territory. I've gone on stage under death threats. But I have some really good people protecting me. And I've studied the martial arts and I could kill an attacker with a single blow. I'm a good shot with a rifle and a pistol and I watch who I let around me. Having said all that, I understand that a person can't live their lives in fear."

"But why would anyone want to hurt or kill you?"

Elvis shrugged his shoulders. "Anytime you have money, fame or just a lot of success there are those who hate you. Some men hate me for my looks or because their girlfriends have a crush on me. Other men write and ask me to help them get a break in show or the music business…and of course I can't so they blame me. Some church people think I'm the Devil incarnate."

"No!"

"It's true. Many preachers think I'm leading young people to hell and damnation…but they're wrong. I'd never sing another song if that was true."

We rode awhile and I could tell that Elvis was troubled. "You got more to tell me?" I asked. "Anything you say I keep to myself."

"I know that. What I was thinking is that you and your Grandmother and this Coyote Ranch are sort of like an ace up my sleeve."

"I don't understand."

"It's something I could use if…well, if things started going wrong for me."

"Like people trying to kill you?"

"Or my health failing. I think I'm a good man. I love the Lord and try to follow his ways, but the flesh is weak and willing. It's easy to get caught up going down the wrong path. And if I ever felt that I was heading for a bad end…well, I'd have you people to run to and this place to hide."

"Is that the reason you're trying to buy that mining company's land next to ours?"

"That's the biggest part of it…and also what you said about tearing up the land and what has been left by the people who came long before us. It all plays a part in my thinking. If I came here, I could fix it so that I'd really disappear in this country."

"I see."

"Another thing, once we get to Las Vegas, you'll need an alias."

"What are you talking about?"

"You'll need a new name and identity."

"But I like my name and who I am."

"You have to do it for me. So let's pick a name you like for your music career and conceal where you came from and all of your past. Show business people do it all the time."

I didn't really know what to think. This whole thing seemed…well, kind of bizarre…and yet, yet it made sense in a crazy sort of way. I had no trouble believing that there really were nut cases out there that would kill The King to become famous themselves. Still, I wanted to tell Elvis that all those uppers and downers he was taking these days might be messing with his mind.

"How about Johnny West?" Elvis suggested.

"That really sounds phony," I replied after a few moments of reflection.

"Why? One of my favorite basketball players was Jerry West and that name sure didn't hurt his career."

"Yeah, but he's a great *basketball player.*"

Elvis was caught up in this new name business and not listening. "There are a lot of people in the music business named Johnny...most famous being Johnny Cash."

"Ever heard of *Charlie* Pride or *Charlie* Rich?" I asked, unable to keep from smiling.

"Dammit, if you have a better name, then let's hear it!"

"I don't."

"Then Johnny West it is," Elvis said, grinning broadly. "And I can tell you this much for certain...Johnny West will sure look better in the bright neon lights over Las Vegas than Cowboy Charlie Coyote."

"Anything else you want to change about me?" I asked, unable to keep peevishness from creeping into my voice.

"This conversation has gotten way too serious. When are you going to get married?"

"I have no idea."

"Marriage is hard," Elvis quietly confessed. "I tried it but it didn't work and Priscilla was wonderful...every man's dream girl. Let's stop at that mining company's headquarters."

I frowned. "Elvis, if I go in and ask for a price on that land, they're going to take one look at me and either start laughing or show me the door."

"Maybe so, but if I go in there they'll take one look at me and see big old dollar signs," Elvis said. "Their price will jump through the ceiling. I'm rich, but there is a limit to what I can spend. Colonel Parker keeps tabs on my spending and so does my father, Vernon. Both of them are always badgering me about how much money I spend...as if it were their own."

"I have an idea," I said. "I'll ask Twister to go into the mining company and inquire about selling that land. He looks rough, but he commands attention and respect."

"Then we'll ask him," Elvis said, deciding the matter. "But he'd have to be able to keep the secret."

"He would and so would his wife...to their graves."

"Then it's settled."

We stopped at Twister's horse ranch. When he came out to the truck and saw Elvis, his eyes grew wide and a big grin crept across his rugged face. "Well as I live and breathe, if it ain't Elvis Presley!"

We talked for a few minutes. Twister invited us inside for coffee or something stronger, but Elvis begged off and said, "We have a favor to ask."

"Shoot."

Elvis laid out the plan. He emphasized that he wanted to have a safe haven if things went south, but that he also cared about the land and the likely treasures of ancient Indians it held in trust. He ended by saying, "Twister, you'd need some fancy western clothes to wear so you look like a wealthy land investor. Otherwise, you won't get anywhere with those people. I'm buyin' the best western suit we can find for you."

"Well, that's a damned relief because I don't have fancy western duds anymore. And I'll do 'er, if you'll also autograph my wife's Elvis albums. She's a huge fan of yours."

"It'll be a pleasure."

Twister went around to my horse and he returned shaking his head. "What the hell did your sister do to nearly ruin that fine mare?"

I was embarrassed for Stella and managed to say, "She and her new husband fell on hard times while they were rodeoing. Stella rode the mare in too many barrel races and the mare went lame."

"I'll say she did!" Twister was mad and I didn't blame him. "Charlie, where are you and Elvis takin' the palomino mare?"

"Vegas."

"She'll be better off right here with me and the missus. That horse doesn't need to ride in a trailer another mile. We'll get her sound again, but it'll take some time."

"I'll pay you for the feed and care."

"Fair enough. I've already figured out that you're going to try to make it in Las Vegas as a showman."

"I'm…I'm sorry."

"Don't be. You have to find out if you can be famous. I'm guessing you'll be back in my arena bulldogging someday. I can wait for awhile before I decide if I want to take you back or not."

"Thanks," I managed to say, shaking his hand.

We went into the house and stayed for lunch and Elvis autographed Alice McCabe's record albums. I'd never seen the woman so tickled and downright giddy. When it was time to leave, we drove Twister into Flagstaff and bought him a real nice western suit, new Tony Lama boots and a handsome black Stetson hat. He looked like he was worth at least a million dollars.

"There it is," I said, when we pulled up out of sight and about fifty yards down the street from the mining company office. The ruse wouldn't have worked if they'd have seen the wealthy land speculator get out of my dusty pickup.

"Cowboy Charlie," Elvis said, "go inside the office with Mr. McCabe. Remember, if they ever suspect I'm behind this, we'll never get a deal."

"Only one thing bothering me a little," Twister offered. "Why would I ever want that piece of property? It won't carry a lot of cattle and water is as scarce as bird shit in a cuckoo clock."

"It just needs a well dug," I countered. "There's plenty of sweet water under that ground…Elvis and I can vouch for that. And there are some good grasses on the land and lots of elk and mule deer."

"Hmmm," Twister pondered. "Maybe I could tell 'em that I'd like to build a hunting lodge on the land. Bring in big money people with fancy rifles and such."

"That sounds good to me," Elvis said. "You could also say that we've walked and ridden some of that land and it's an archeological treasure chest. Maybe mention something about the Smithsonian Institution inquiring about putting an early American research center on the property."

"That's really good!" I said. "If they think that we might raise a fuss about the petroglyphs and pottery to be found, we'll have them worried as hell."

"Then that'll be our story."

As we headed for the mining office, I saw that Twister had a grin on his face and realized he was enjoying this challenge. "What name are you going to give them, Twister?"

"Good question. Twister probably doesn't cut it, eh?"

"Nope."

He pulled on his mustache for a moment and then laughed. "I'll call myself Mister Rockefeller!"

"No," I said quickly. "That would drive the price up even more than if Elvis wanted to buy it. Pick a common name."

*This is a big day for phony names,* I thought. *I'm now Johnny West and Twister is going to be….*

"Bill Jones." Twister said. "Is that common enough?"

"Sure is. And who am I?"

"You're my son."

"No way," I argued, "I'm too dark skinned."

"So maybe I'm married to an Indian, "Twister countered.

I could see he was starting to get a bit prickly. "Why don't you just say I'm your top cowhand and that you have many…uh…ranch holdings."

"If that pleases you, then it pleases me plumb down to the ground," Twister said, clearly anxious to liberally distribute his fresh load of concentrated bullshit to some mining executive.

Once inside the office which wasn't all that much special to look at we came face to face with a receptionist. She was cute and friendly and she wore a low-cut blouse that made my mouth go dry as desert sand.

"My name is Bill Jones and I'd like to see the company owner or manager," Twister McCabe grandly announced.

"For what purpose?"

"I'm interested in buying some land your company holds title to and it's located about sixty miles east of here south of Route 66. Not much to look at, but I'm looking for...for solitude and...and long views. The property has a nice little mountain top and the elk and deer are thicker than fleas on a dead dog."

"I'm afraid that property isn't for sale."

I was at a loss for a comeback, but not Twister. He leaned forward on her desk, smiled and said, "Miss, are you prepared to tell your employers that... all on your own...you turned down one hell of a lot of money for that itty bitty mountain surrounded by all that sagebrush? Ground that is about as worthless as tits on a bad-assed bull?"

The receptionist flushed deeply and jumped out of her chair. "Please wait here for a moment, Mr. Jones." She gave me a weak smile. "You can wait here, too."

She returned, got Twister and ushered him into a private office.

When she came back, she asked me, "Do you work around here?"

"Sometimes."

"Does Mr. Jones live in Arizona?"

I picked up real quick that she was trying to get me to talk about him and find out all that she could concerning his business and money.

"Some of the time," I said vaguely. "He comes and goes...has his own jet, you see."

She was about to ask another question, but her phone rang and she got busy. I overheard her talking to what I figured was probably her boyfriend and I gathered from the one-sided and tense conversation that they were either breaking up or having some serious relationship problems. I was kind of interested in that because, if she was suddenly free, I'd have liked to have taken her for a ride...on my horses...of course. But then again, that would probably be a huge mistake and it was even more likely she'd turn down the offer so I kept my mouth shut and studied a big black fly tracking slowly across the ceiling.

Twister was in the man's office for about thirty minutes and when he came out, he gave me a close-to-the-chest thumbs up and a quick grin. I followed him out to the truck where Elvis had decided to take a nap. We woke him up and all climbed inside then drove off.

"Well?" Elvis asked. "How'd it go?"

"At first he said there wasn't any way he would sell the company's land. But he changed his mind when I started talking *big* money."

"How much *big* money?" Elvis asked.

"Well, the man said they had about sixty thousand dollars in that land."

"Go on."

"And he said that they expect to put another hundred thousand in it before they can start mining copper even on a small scale."

"Cut to the chase," Elvis said. "Did he name a selling price?"

"He said that he'd have to discuss the matter with the board of directors but that the price would be upwards of three hundred thousand dollars. That seemed very high so I told him again about the Smithsonian's interest and that I was sure that the Department of Old Indian Artifacts would want to look deeply into the matter."

"Is there even such an agency?" I asked.

"Who knows, but probably," Twister said with a dismissive wave of his hand. "Ain't there one for about everything these days?"

"Good point," Elvis said. "Nice work!"

"Copper Mountain Mining Company is not big. I learned that the land you're interested in is only one of six that they own or have an option to buy and mine…depending on the price of copper."

"So you're saying…?" Elvis asked.

"I don't think that the company is rolling in money," Twister mused. "The man running things is not living a high lifestyle. His office is humble and I have the feeling he isn't making a huge salary."

"Sure got a pretty and sexy receptionist, though," I offered.

Both Twister and Elvis gave me a drop dead look and I nailed my eyes to the road and kept my mouth shut for the rest of the way back to the horse ranch.

We dropped Twister off, hugged his sweet wife and headed for Las Vegas.

"So you thought the receptionist was a real looker, huh?" Elvis asked about the time we drove through Williams.

"I sure did!"

"Well, she might have been," Elvis said, "but wait until I introduce you to a few Las Vegas showgirls. They'll set your heart to pounding and…well, you'll see what really beautiful woman look and dress like in the big city of sin."

"I can hardly wait," I said, not daring to even imagine.

# *Chapter 21*

The truth of the matter was that I'd never been west of Williams and when we started down the mountain into Ash Fork, I was amazed at how the country changed so quickly. Where before there had been tall pines and deep forests, at the bottom of the mountain where Ash Fork was nestled, it was all juniper and pinyon pine. Stacks of red, soft brown and pale pink flagstone was being loaded on railroad cars and big trucks.

"Flagstone capitol of the world, I guess," Elvis said as we passed through. "Someone told me they ship this stuff all over the United States to make patios. I ought to have some shipped out to Graceland."

Less than an hour later we were rolling into Seligman which was an important railroad town with a Harvey House hotel that wasn't nearly as impressive as the one we had in Winslow. The downtown wasn't much to look at, but I saw nice little ranches up against the northern foothills toward the Grand Canyon.

Past Seligman we saw signs promoting the Grand Canyon Caverns just south of the highway. "Have you ever been down in those caverns?" I asked Elvis.

"No, I'd go crazy."

"It says that they have a giant sloth that got trapped way below the surface...one taller than a house!"

"I doubt that," Elvis said. "Anyway, we don't have time to look at a phony sloth and someday we'll *all* be underground."

I thought that was kind of a creepy thing to say and drove right past the caverns. Elvis and I were roughly following the Santa Fe Railroad line on Route 66 and less than an hour later we rolled into the sleepy Hualapai town of Peach Springs. I looked for peach orchards, but there weren't any to be found. Besides a little railroad depot, there was a hotel, post office and grocery store, but not a lot of tourists. Maybe without peaches the town had gone into decline.

"Next stop will be Kingman," Elvis told me. "We'll gas your truck up and head on to Las Vegas."

"I can't wait to see Vegas."

Elvis smiled. "You know, I can't either. I told you that I love the peacefulness of Coyote Ranch and that high scrub pine country we ride, but Las Vegas really fires my blood. I've played the showrooms of the biggest and finest hotels there where they treat me like a king."

"That's because you *are* a king."

That pleased Elvis. "That's right, Cowboy Charlie. "I'm the one and only King of Rock'n Roll!"

Later that day we crossed over Hoover Dam which I would have also liked to see on a tour they said we could take, but the closer we got to Las Vegas the more intense Elvis seemed to be so we drove right through Boulder City to the outskirts of Vegas. Even at a distance the tall hotel casinos looked impressive as they lifted right out of the vast desert floor.

"It doesn't look like much in the daytime," Elvis explained. "But at night... man oh man! It lights up like a big Christmas tree."

Elvis popped a Coca Cola and reached into a bag he carried. I glanced sideways as he took a handful of white pills and swallowed them with the soda.

"What are those?"

"Amphetamines," he said. "When we arrive at the hotel I want to be alert and looking sharp."

"You already look alert and sharp."

"Just drive. Everything changes the minute we step out of your truck. I'll do all the talking."

"Okay."

We drove up the Las Vegas strip and I was really rubbernecking. I'd never seen the likes of it with so many monstrous billboards and tall casinos and hotels. And what really got me was that the neon lights were on in broad daylight! What a waste of electricity.

"Keeping this place lit up must cost a fortune," I said.

"Who cares? Hoover Dam generators provide all the juice. It's Las Vegas and she never shuts down. That's why I love it so much."

I couldn't believe all the famous names I was reading on the marquees... Charlie Rich, Ricky Nelson, The Smothers Brothers,Trini Lopez, Johnny Mathis and more.

Traffic was bumper to bumper and there were thousands of people walking around, many with plastic drink cups in their hands. On the marquee of the Las Vegas Hilton, I read, ELVIS IS COMING BACK!!!

The letters were a good twenty feet tall and flashing red, yellow and green. I clucked my tongue in amazement. "Elvis, when is your next show starting?"

"Friday night. Want to watch?"

"Would I ever!"

"Then I'll get you a front row seat. But remember…you don't know me. I sure don't want to lose my ace in the hole."

"I'm Johnny West."

"That's right. I'll make sure that you get a good room and I'll pay all expenses as long as you're there. I'll also have one of my people set up your auditions. But first, you need new outfits for the casino lounges and you'll have to rehearse. I want you ready and well prepared for your first show. This is a union scale town and you should start off at about four hundred dollars a week."

I couldn't believe my ears. "Will you be in the audience on my opening night?"

"I'm afraid not," Elvis said. "We need to keep our distance. Besides, when you go onstage, I want you to be the center of attention…not me."

"I understand." And I did, but I was disappointed. I would have loved to have had Elvis in my first Las Vegas audience, clapping and cheering me on during my performance. "And I want to thank you again for giving me this chance in show business."

"I'm handing it to you, but you have to take it and run," Elvis reminded me. "And besides, I owe you and your grandmother so much for what you've done for me out at Coyote Ranch."

"Our pleasure."

I was about to say something else, but right then we passed a gambler standing in front of a casino yanking the handle of the biggest slot machine I'd ever seen in my life…my gawd, it was the size of a refrigerator! There was a pretty peroxide blonde at his side, giggling and cheering him as he played.

When we drove up to the hotel in my dusty ranch truck, a valet hesitated then slowly walked out to help or greet us although he probably thought we were lost and needed to be sent on our way back to the sticks.

"Drive to the Dunes and take this," Elvis said, stuffing a handful of cash into my coat pocket. "Live it up...but don't go crazy. Meet beautiful women, gamble and have fun like you've never had before. And get a good haircut and some nice clothes…much nicer than we bought for Twister. There are plenty of places that sell quality in this town so don't worry about the money. If you run low, come to this hotel and show the doorman that ring I gave you. It'll get you to one of my staff and all you have to do is tell them that you need another thousand or two."

"Dollars?"

"Sure! What do you think I'm talking about…bananas?"

We both laughed, but I managed to say, "Elvis, I can't take…."

But he didn't wait to hear what I had to say and was out the door. When the valet recognized who was climbing out of my Chevy pickup, his eyeballs nearly popped out of his head. A sharp-eyed young woman screamed and pointed at Elvis as she began to jump up and down in a fit of hysteria. People stared for a split-second and then began to rush him and I saw Elvis break into a run for the hotel.

And just that fast, while I sat in my truck with a handful of cash, Elvis was gone like a leaf caught up by a dust devil.

I used the regular parking lot at the Dunes and I carried my worn satchel with my change of clothes and toiletries into the magnificent lobby packed with people and slot machines. No one smiled at me or gave me any kind of a greeting and I knew it was because I looked like hard times with my long, black hair and battered Stetson, guitar case and scuffed cowboy boots.

At the hotel desk, I registered as Johnny West and asked for a cheap room. I was given one on the third floor that faced the alley and that suited me just fine because I was sure that it would be far nicer than any motel I'd ever stayed in. And after tomorrow, I wouldn't look like Charlie Coyote fresh off a hard-scrabble ranch outside of Winslow, Arizona.

"That ring you're wearing," the registration clerk said, eyeballing it enviously. "It's one of the better knock-offs I've seen in this town. How much did it cost you?"

I glanced down at the gold and diamond ring that Elvis had presented me…the one he'd said I'd merely have to flash to be treated like royalty. And for some reason, I started to laugh.

"Are you alright?" the hotel clerk asked suspiciously. "If you're on drugs or…."

"No," I said, quickly. "I'm okay and I won't make trouble. Is the food any good in this place?"

"You get a lot for the money. Try the 99-cent all-you-can-eat buffet tonight and you won't be sorry."

"Thanks, I will."

"What did that Elvis ring cost you and where did you buy it? Those zircons sure look like real diamonds. I'll bet that cost you…oh, twenty bucks."

"Nice guess," I said, taking my room key and weaving my way through slot machines, cigarette smoke, clanging coins in metal trays and ringing bells.

After I cleaned up I went back down into the casino and bought some expensive clothes at the hotel's big gift shop so I didn't even have to drive around town. Taking the advice I was given by people who dressed sharp and had probably never had dirt under their fingernails or calluses on their hands, I

175

bought three handsome western suits, shirts, ties, an expensive watch, a big silver belt buckle and a pair of beautiful Justin boots that set me back over a hundred dollars and were worth every penny. Back in my hotel room I showered then dressed in my new clothes and decided that I looked like a high roller...a Texas rancher...or at least the son of one. Or maybe, because of my dark complexion and high cheekbones, they'd take me for an Oklahoma Indian who struck oil on his reservation. To be honest, I didn't know what they'd make of Johnny West in Las Vegas...but I supposed I was sure to find out soon enough.

I ate in the casino restaurant buffet and it was delicious, but I overindulged. I walked the casino floor hoping to take in a lounge show, but a sign on the stage said that the evening's performance had been canceled. From the enthusiastic way the people were gambling, I decided they either hadn't noticed the lack of music or they didn't care. I walked the streets to work off my meal and walked them again the following morning after a huge breakfast that I got for only 49 cents.

The Strip's transformation was amazing between night and day. At night, it was a wonderland pulsating with energy and promise...but in the harsh light of the morning sun...I couldn't help but think Las Vegas was sad and shabby. There were lots of empty beer cans, cigarette butts and other trash littering the sidewalks. Someone had puked on the pavement and it stunk and made my own breakfast sour on my stomach. There were people on the street that looked hollowed out and some were desperately begging for money. I gave generously because I knew that someday I might find myself in exactly the same situation and I wanted to think that generosity in life begat generosity.

My hometown of Winslow had its share of losers panhandling at all hours of the night and day. Mostly, they were Indians, but not all. Down and out had no respect for color or race...it could grab anyone by the throat and shove their faces in the shitter.

"Hey, Cowboy!"

I turned to see a young and beautiful woman with hair as black as mine and a smile that made me blush. Her coral-colored dress looked as if it had been painted onto her body's curves. She blew a cloud of smoke, sized me up and down with a bold and hungry smile.

"Yes, Ma'am?"

"You're young, strong and handsome," she told me. "I'd like to show you a good time for only twenty-five dollars. You got a room or a car we can party in? I like to drink Jack Daniels and do 'the pony'...do you?"

I couldn't speak for a moment thinking that I couldn't ride a pony anyway given my size.

She laughed, deep and throaty. "You're a shy one…but don't worry, I'll give you something you'll always remember."

When I still didn't say anything, her smile slipped. "Okay, big boy, twenty bucks and that's my bottom. You can have me do it all and those wild broncos you've ridden will seem like rocking horses compared to when you climb onto me. You won't be sorry."

I finally managed to say, "Why is someone as pretty as you doing this? You ought to be on stage or even an actress."

She blew smoke in my face. "You're a funny man. I like that, but with me, honey, money talks and bullshit walks. Which is it with you?"

"Are you in need of money to eat? If so, there's a good breakfast at the Dunes and I'll gladly pay for it."

She had on these real long, black eyelashes and when I studied them close, I could see what I thought were empty window shutters fronting her eyes.

"You big, dumb asshole," she said before she walked away. Then over her shoulder, she yelled back, "And you ain't no real cowboy…you're just another phoney!"

I watched her walk up the street, swinging her butt and she didn't even get to the next intersection before a man hurried up to her. He was an older guy wearing a shell necklace, a gold bracelet, a flowery Hawaiian shirt with open toed sandals…the kind with their thick soles made out of worn down car tires…and knee-high fuzzy, red socks…a real dork. I watched them talk, saw money change hands and they disappeared.

*So this is the way it is here,* I thought. *Charlie, you had better be damn careful or you could lose your soul in this town.*

I went back to my hotel room and used the hotel stationery to write Grandmother. We didn't have a phone at the ranch and I knew she wouldn't get the letter for three or four days, but I wanted to get it off and let her know that we'd arrived in Las Vegas and I was hopeful about getting a singing job at four hundred a week so we could pay off all our debts and start banking money.

Writing the letter lifted my spirits. Despite all its people Las Vegas made me feel small and lonesome…funny how a lot of people around can make you feel that way sometimes.

I watched television and wasted the day thinking about that woman on the street and how many beautiful girls I'd seen down on the casino floor. Were they all prostitutes or did they have regular jobs, husbands and boyfriends? I was eager to find out…but for some reason I just couldn't find it in myself to go downstairs on the elevator, sit in front of a slot machine or a bar and spin lies about my name and past.

I had a couple of good Luke Short and Nelson Nye paperbacks so I lost myself in the Old West.

For the next three days I wandered around Vegas, soaking up the scenery and watching a few lounge acts. They usually consisted of a drummer, bass player and lead singer and while they weren't bad, neither were they all that good. The musicians I saw were at their best with their constant small talk… banter, I guess you'd call it. They'd play a song or two and then they'd crack jokes and play off the small crowds. I began to wonder if I was cut out for that kind of work as I had never been one to tell jokes…especially the off-colored ones that seemed to be most common here and earned the most laughter.

My favorite joke was this: *An old cowboy who had lived a hard, wild life died and went up to the Pearly Gates and asked St. Peter if he could enter heaven.*

*"Well," St. Peter said, looking at the cowboy and taking his name, "I see that you have been a rounder and a drunkard and womanizer all of your life. I'm afraid that I can't let you into heaven. Sorry."*

*The cowboy had expected that so he was quick to say, "Oh, but I have done a few very fine things in my life."*

*St. Peter rechecked his records and replied, "I have no record of you doing anything good, noble or fine. What are you talking about?"*

*"Well, sir, I did a very noble and brave kindness when I was in a bar and dancing with a lady. We were havin' fun and just minding our own business drinking and laughing and in comes this bunch of rough Hells Angels."*

*"Yes," St. Peter said, "I'm heard of that bunch. Not good people and none admitted up here."*

*"Keep 'em out, St. Peter, they're bad 'uns! Anyway, these Hells Angels began to lay their hands on the lady and sayin' things I cannot repeat. So I told them to leave the lady alone…to keep their filthy hands off of her and their filthy mouths shut! I defended her honor!"*

*"My," said St. Peter, looking greatly impressed, "that was a noble and brave thing to do!" He looked back down at his book with a frown, then back up at the cowboy. "And when did you say you did this brave and noble act?"*

*"Oh, about a minute ago."*

I know. I know. It's a dumb joke, but it's a great cowboy joke and it always gets a laugh in Winslow…but maybe not in Las Vegas.

Finally, a fast-talking fella named Leon Heitzman rang my hotel room and said that he worked for his friend Mr. Presley and wanted to help me make some "connections". He flattered me by saying, "Mr. Presley says you have a damned good set of pipes and can even pick a guitar."

"I'm not that great with the guitar, but I can sing…nothing like Elvis, of course."

"Of course. Can you meet me downstairs? I'm at the bar wearing a red shirt and black pants. No hurry, I've got a room here and there's lovely company sitting on my lap so take your time…and by that I mean an hour or more…if you get my drift."

I got his drift. "Sure."

I took a bath, shaved, dressed and still had a few minutes to kill so I got out my guitar and practiced a little in case he wanted to audition me after he auditioned his "lovely company" somewhere in this huge hotel.

One hour later I was in the bar but there was no Mr. Heitzman to be seen. I ordered a beer, sipped on it and waited nearly another hour thinking that the upstairs "auditioning" must have gone very well. Anyway, Mr. Leon Heitzman finally arrived looking flushed. He slid down beside me, shook my hand with his sweaty one and promptly began to tell me how important he was and how many big acts he'd booked both here and in Tinsel Town, which he explained meant Hollywood, as if I was a complete rube and had never heard the oft repeated term.

"Johnny, Las Vegas is the future! In ten…twenty years at the most Hollywood will be a ghost town and all the movies will be made right here in Las Vegas."

I nodded, but wondered if that meant they'd be doing a lot of movies like *Lawrence of Arabia*. After Mr. Heitzman had a couple more whiskeys, he asked, "Is that your guitar?"

"Yeah, it's a Martin and was given to me by Mr. Presley."

"Take it back up to your room," the man said. "They'll want you to use what they have to play and that Martin guitar would be like hanging a Rembrandt painting over a truck stop toilet."

I had my first audition in the man's upstairs hotel room a few minutes later.

"Sing," he ordered, flopping down on his couch.

"I wrote this one myself," I told him, and started singing.

*Oh I'm just a poor rodeo clown in love with Clara*
*my sweet little honey*
*But she don't like my hugs and kisses…she acts like love means*
*first prize money*
*But I'll keep on wearin' my funny rodeo clown clothes*
*and my stupid red bulb clown nose*

*Until dear Clara sees me for what I really am*
          *And she won't mind eatin' canned spam.*
*Oh I'm just a poor rodeo....*


"Stop!" Heitzman shrieked. "Johnny, you're killing me! How many more songs like that have you written!"

"A bunch."

"You lookin' to do a *comedy* act?"

I clenched my fists. "No!"

"Johnny West, I assume Elvis told you that casino employees are unionized."

"Yeah."

"Well, all the showroom and lounge acts sign contracts to do a certain number of performances for a certain amount of time."

I felt a nagging worry inside. "Go on."

"The point is, I can't just insert you into a lounge and bump some other entertainer that has a contract so we might not be able to get you in rehearsals and then on the stage for awhile."

"How long?"

"Maybe a few weeks...or months."

I was dumbstruck. I'd actually expected to start rehearsing this very day and going on stage to perform tomorrow or the next day. I guess I should have known better.

"You do understand, don't you?"

"I'm going crazy living in that hotel room. I'm not eating right or getting enough sleep."

"Johnny, the best thing you can do is to go back home and we'll call you when we get a slot for rehearsals. We'll try to get you into the Jubilee Lounge. Do you live in Las Vegas or LA?"

"No, I live...." I almost told him what Elvis has asked me not tell...about Coyote Ranch. I cleared my throat and said, "I live on the far side of Arizona."

"I see. Well, do you have a number so we can call when there's an opportunity?"

"No," I told the man. "I'll just call you every few days."

"If that's the best that you can manage."

We shook hands and as I was opening the door, Heitzman said, "Johnny, you've got a helluva fine voice and Elvis says that we can cover your guitar work with good musicians. But...but I think you ought to devote more time to your voice and guitar work than to writing songs."

The meaning was clear. The man was trying to say he hadn't liked my song… he thought I had no song writing talent at all.

Sensing my disappointment, Heitzman quickly added, "Almost every singer I've ever known has wanted to write some of their own songs. Money is a part of it…if they get a recording contract and own the rights to the hit song they can make a lot of money. But here's the thing…you have to make it as a singer and performer *first* and only then you get a chance to write your songs. Understand?"

"Yeah," I said on my way out wondering if I'd ever even see the man again.

When I returned to my hotel room, I locked the door, stretched out on my bed and stared at the ceiling for a long, long time. I've been a fool to think that I'd be singing before a Vegas audience in a few days. I still believed that my voice would carry me on to success, but I was beginning to realize that even with the help of Elvis Presley, making it in this town was going to be far more difficult than I'd imagined.

I closed my eyes and dozed off for awhile and when I awoke the sun was going down. There was a beautiful sunset and I had the sudden urge to go home and think things through. Maybe I'd been wrong to deviate from becoming a champion bulldogger, but Twister McCabe had made it plain that his door was open to me…at least for awhile.

It was time to leave Vegas so I went down to the gift shop, found some nice luggage and packed my new outfits. I didn't want to arrive at Coyote Ranch looking like Roy Rogers or Gene Autry so I pulled on my old working clothes and suddenly I felt better.

"I'm checking out," I called, passing the registration desk clerk.

"Name, Sir?"

I shouted over my shoulder, "Johnny West, Room 402!"

"Come back and visit us soon!"

*We'll see,* I thought, *we'll just wait and see.*

# *Chapter 22*

I left Las Vegas just after midnight with very mixed feelings. I really didn't fit in this city of neon lights…or any big city, for that matter. Yet, I knew that this was where my "opportunity" as the man had called it was to be found.

As I drove south out of Vegas and then crossed the huge Hoover Dam a big smile crossed my face because I was back in Arizona where I'd always lived and expected to die. I gassed up the truck in Kingman and drove along Route 66 feeling somehow lighter inside. Way off to the east I could see the first pink glow of sunrise and by the time I stopped at the little café in Peach Springs, the sun was up and shining right into my face.

Breakfast cost $2.00 and I was reminded that I couldn't expect people outside of the casinos to put out a good meal for just 49 cents. That was fine with me. I gave the short, cute Hualapai waitress a whole dollar for her tip and she rewarded me with a big smile. Then I headed off with my foot heavy on the pedal and passed back through Seligman, Ash Fork and Williams. My truck labored a bit on the hill back up into the high pine country, but the air was cool and bracing and I had my window rolled down and my heavy coat collar turned up.

When I passed through Flagstaff I thought I might stop for a moment to tell Twister that I was coming home, but rejected the idea. I didn't have any solid plans and I still hoped to make some real money singing in Las Vegas so I decided that until I found out what my true destiny was I ought to leave Twister to his own plans.

When I turned off Route 66 onto our potholed, dusty dirt road I drove faster than I normally would have because I was eager to see Grandmother. I needed to use her as a sounding board and see what advice she might have to offer. That old Hopi was wise and she would give me plenty to think about.

But when I pulled into the yard, things were very quiet. Rip slunk out from under the porch and when he saw it was me he got all excited. Grandmother's chickens were still in their pen and I thought that odd because she always turned them out on nice mornings.

"Grandmother!"

No answer.

"Grandmother!" I shouted, throwing the truck door open and striding to the porch.

I tried the front door, but it was locked. I hurried around to the back of the house where we kept a key hidden under a flat rock. I entered a cold house and rushed to Grandmother's bedroom, suddenly terrified that she might have died alone in her sleep.

The bed was empty. I hurried back into the kitchen and with panic starting to clog my throat and glanced at the table where I spied a note. I snatched it up and read,

*Dear Charlie, if you come back before me you need to know that Stella and Lenny were in a terrible car accident and are at the Prescott Hospital. I don't know how to reach you in Las Vegas so I asked a friend to take me to the Prescott Hospital to see if Stella is alive...or dead. Come too! But don't drive so fast that you risk your own life!*

The letter dropped from my fingers and I headed for the door. Having been up all night, I was dead tired but that didn't matter anymore. I was about to jump into my truck when I realized that I needed to fill Rip's water and feed bowl to the brim and also to feed the chickens and horses. Our range cattle would do fine foraging on their own.

I fed everything, grabbed a canteen and filled it with good water then stuffed a couple of apples and a loaf of homemade sourdough bread in a sack and ran to my Chevy. Then I remembered I hadn't locked the back door so I did after lugging my Las Vegas clothes into the house.

By now the sun was way up in the eastern sky and I felt a terrible urgency to get moving. I started the truck, threw it into reverse, then spun the steering wheel and shifted into first gear stomping the gas pedal. Prescott was a good four hours away. I'd have to go back up through Flagstaff and Williams, then down to Ash Fork before I turned south on the highway down to Prescott another fifty or sixty miles.

I would make it there in record time.

I don't remember much about that fast trip. It was early afternoon when I finally found the hospital and it took five minutes to locate my sister and Grandmother.

I burst into Stella's hospital room and there was Grandmother and Homer Yazzie. I glanced at my sister and saw tubes feeding off plastic pouches, machines feeding blood and medications into her body. My sister looked so small that had I not known better I would have instantly thought she was a girl instead of a woman. Her beautiful face was badly swollen and purple and Stella's mouth was open and an oxygen tube was like a thin, yellow snake trailing into her nostril.

"How is she?" I asked.

Homer said, "Your sister lost the lower part of one leg in a rollover with her husband. She has internal injuries and just got out of emergency surgery."

"What are they saying about her chances?"

Grandmother said, "They think that she has a fighting chance. And we both know that Stella is a fighter. I have prayed that she'll live."

"How is Lenny?"

Grandmother's face hardened. "He was drunk and lost control of their truck and it rolled down into a canyon. He was thrown through the window and his head was crushed like a ripe melon."

I looked away, trying to tell myself that I should feel bad for Lenny; after all, he was my sister's husband and she had loved the man. Some people swore that Stella Coyote was the most beautiful woman between Flagstaff and Albuquerque…and I wouldn't have argued the point. Even in Las Vegas, Stella would have been a head-turner especially in her tight Levi's. Now she would limp very badly… I didn't know if she could handle that and thrive rather than just survive.

*Stella the one-legged coyote, they'd snicker behind her back. But gawd help anyone that I overheard say that.*

"Where'd the accident happen?"

"Somewhere between Yarnell and Skull Valley. A driver spotted their overturned truck on the side of mountain. He notified the police. Stella was barely alive, buried in window glass and empty beer cans."

I decided not to ask any more questions.

Two days later it was clear that Stella would recover. I tried to talk to her, but she didn't have anything to say about Lenny or the wreck and I understood and accepted that silence.

"Sun Dancer is with Twister in Flagstaff," I told her one sunny afternoon in the hospital. "He'll get her fit and ready for the barrels in a few months."

"I won't be riding her in any more rodeos."

"I'm sorry to hear that."

"If anyone in the Coyote family makes it big in rodeo, it'll have to be you."

"Stella," I said, "you've only lost the lower part of your leg. You'll get a prosthesis and…."

"Stop it! How am I going to shift my weight in the stirrups going around the barrels with a missing foot? Do you think someone can put a wooden foot in the stirrup and screw my stump into it? Is that what you think?"

I was momentarily thrown off balance and stung by her anger. Thankfully, Grandmother came to my rescue and said, "I have seen people ride well without arms, legs or feet. Even blind people."

"In *professional rodeos!*" Stella harshly demanded.

"Excuse me?"

I turned to see a tall, bespectacled man in a medical coat standing in the doorway. "I'm Dr. Rolland Chandler, Stella's attending physician."

After he made a quick check on my sister, he said, "You're going to be fine, young woman."

"Says you," Stella replied bitterly.

The doctor studied her for a moment. "I'll be in tomorrow at this time. Are your pain medications doing the job?"

Stella ground her teeth together. "I'd rather have a fifth of Jack Daniels, Doc."

He turned to leave. "That isn't going to help anymore, Stella."

I hurried out after the doctor because I had some questions. "Doctor Chandler, could I have a few moments of your time?"

"Sure. We'll schedule a consultation later, but I'm open to some questions that I'm sure you need answered right now."

"How is my sister, *really?*"

"Physically, she's going to be fine…mentally, perhaps not. It's clear that she is underweight and has not been taking care of herself. She won't admit it, but I am sure she is an alcoholic and that certainly needs to be addressed in her recovery."

I knew he was right.

"Your sister has a lot of hard work to do in order to make a full recovery… and the physical part is the least of her challenges. But the other part…the drinking and depression, that will be the real challenge."

"What about the amputation?"

He shrugged. "Thousands of young soldiers came out of Viet Nam with far worse losses and most of them managed to do quite well. But with the alcohol problem compounding things, she's going to need some serious counseling."

"How soon can she go home?"

"She won't be going straight home if you and your grandmother follow my recommendations. Stella needs some time and counseling and that can only be found in a city much larger than Prescott. And the prosthesis also will require considerable attention until she learns to accept and use it well."

"Where are you talking about?"

Dr. Chandler shrugged. "Phoenix would be good."

"What about Las Vegas?"

"That would be fine, too. But...why do you mention it? Do you have family in Nevada?"

"We don't have family in any big city."

"It's a decision that doesn't need to be made for a few weeks," he told me. "Will you be staying here with your grandmother?"

I hadn't even thought that far. "I...I don't know. We have a ranch and livestock to be taken care of."

"Someone needs to be close to her...especially now." He frowned. "When your sister was waking up after the amputation, she started calling for her mother. So, if she could...."

"Our mother is dead...she died long ago."

"Oh. Apparently, your sister still has her very much in mind. However, if I may say so, she doesn't seem to be grieving too much about her late husband."

"None of us are."

"I see."

Then he left.

Grandmother and I went outside to talk. It was a nice day, but windy.

"We have to get her to a big city," I said. "Phoenix is closest, but I think I can make money in Las Vegas."

"Then we'll go there."

"How does that work with our livestock?"

Grandmother thought about it for a few minutes. "I have some Navajo friends that will stay and take care of our livestock. We can trust them. I will give you their names. Make sure you say that we cannot pay much, but we will give them a fat steer to butcher every six months that we are gone. They will be happy to do it for that."

She gave me names that sounded vaguely familiar. I didn't like the idea at all, but it made sense. In Vegas, if I was working the lounge, I'd be making four hundred dollars a week...plenty enough to take care of all Stella's surgical expenses and counseling. If I returned to Coyote Ranch, I'd be making nothing. And then there was our dear friend Elvis. I was sure that he'd help out just like he had when I'd nearly been killed by Buzzard a few years ago.

"Vegas it is then," I said. "We have no choice."

"Find a house outside of the city," Grandmother urged me. "Coyotes need the space."

"I'll do my best."

"Go do it now."

"You'll say goodbye for me to Stella?"

She nodded. I wondered if I was being cowardly by leaving Grandmother to care for Stella. She had the harder job by far. But I had a job too, or at least I hoped I had one. I'd have to put pressure on Leon Heitzman even if that meant asking Elvis for yet another favor.

So I drove back to our ranch, arriving just before dark. I was so exhausted I climbed up into my loft and fell asleep in an instant. I would spend tomorrow checking our cattle and packing up the things we'd need for a long stay in Vegas.

Later, I got out the Martin guitar and played it for awhile noting that my fingertips were tender on the steel strings which reminded me that I needed to practice a lot more often. After an hour, I threw everything in the truck, promised Rip that help was coming and headed back to Winslow where I contacted Grandmother's friends and presented our offer.

They were a sweet, quiet old couple who accepted the offer without discussion. I didn't know if it was because of the meat...or out of respect for my Grandmother and the sad circumstances of the Coyote family. Maybe it was both. They were living in a one room shack north of town that had neither electricity or plumbing. I left them fifty dollars to buy supplies and gas. I had a feeling they would stay at Coyote Ranch as long as they were needed and be grateful for the change in scenery.

A day later I was in Las Vegas and as I drove up the Strip, I seemed to have a world of trouble on my mind. I wondered if I should just go straight to see Mr. Heitzman, or go around him and seek help from Elvis.

But when I looked up at the marquee where Elvis had been featured, his name was gone, replaced by Johnny Mathis.

"Oh my gawd," I said quietly to myself. "He must be in Hollywood or back at Graceland. What am I going to do now?"

Having no particular place to go, I returned to the Dunes and was surprised and hugely relieved when the desk clerk not only recognized me, but had a sealed thick manila envelope with my name neatly printed on it.

"It was left here for your return," the desk clerk said, handing it to me. "Can I get you a room?"

I shrugged. "Sure. Why not?"

Upstairs, I tore open the envelope and in it was a short letter from Elvis.

*Dear Charlie. I heard about the car wreck and your sister. Enclosed you will find cash and a list of some outstanding surgeons and specialists that I've had my people contact and who will help Stella. Sorry I had to leave without even a quick goodbye...TCB...good luck on stage and my thoughts and prayers are with the Coyote family always.*

I sat down on the bed and counted the money. Two thousand dollars in crisp fifty dollar bills. I felt like crying with relief...instead, I offered my prayers and thanks to my friend Elvis and took the money down to the casino cashier and said, "Do you people have a safe place to keep cash?"

"We sure do, Mr. West."

Ten minutes later I was on my way to see Leon Heitzman and determined to bully or bribe him into getting me on stage and into the union so I could start making money. Once I was working, I'd go find a house out in the desert for Grandmother and my sister.

It was a lot to do and even more to think about...but I'd never been more determined to do my part. Elvis believed in me and I needed to believe in myself.

# Chapter 23

Mr. Heitzman was out so I wandered around in the casino for awhile noticing most of the gamblers played the nickel and dime slots.

The Jubilee Lounge seated maybe fifty people at ridiculously small tables that were meant to hold four drinks and an ash tray. The stage was tiny; a set of drums and the sound equipment was crammed in the back and covered with a black vinyl tarp.

A tall cocktail waitress in a small dress came over and asked me if I wanted a drink. I declined. "Who's playing here now?"

"They're called 'The Ramblers' and they go on at nine o'clock. They're a country and western band and from the looks of you, Cowboy, I'm sure you'd enjoy their music."

She didn't speak with much enthusiasm and I wondered if she was on the last leg of an all-night shift. She had a blonde pony tail and long legs with black mesh stockings and black high-heel shoes. Had she not appeared so worn out she would have warranted a second and even third look.

"I expect I would."

Her badge read, GEORGIA and she seemed friendly and was probably from Georgia because she had a nice southern drawl that I found very appealing. "Georgia is sure a pretty name."

She laughed…a laugh softer and smoother than Southern Comfort. "I'll call you Cowboy because you really look like one."

"I am one."

"Give me your hands, please."

I hesitated only a moment and she examined the calluses on my palms. "You're a working cowboy, alright, and I do admire a *real* cowboy."

"I nearly got killed riding the bulls, but I wised up and now I'm bulldogging."

"So you're both a working *and* a rodeo cowboy?"

"That's right."

She sized me up from heels to hat and must have liked what she saw because she winked and said, "Well, you can bulldog me any old time I'm not working this casino floor."

We both laughed at her bold joke. "Cowboy, you're not drinking or

189

gambling. What are you here for?"

"I hope to sing in this lounge."

"You're kidding."

"Nope. I'd hoped they'd said something about me coming."

"Nope, but that doesn't mean a thing. I just serve drinks and collect money and tips."

"Georgia, I think I will have a drink after all."

"What's your pleasure?"

"Coca Cola on ice."

"From your rugged good looks and size, I was thinking a cowboy like you might ask for sarsaparilla. You remind me a little of John Wayne when he was young…only you got that long, black hair. Same manly good looks, though."

I blushed. "Thanks. But I never tried that sarsaparilla stuff."

"That's what the cowboys wearing white hats in the old movies always drank."

"I see."

She walked off to get me a drink and after I'd admired her south end I took it upon myself to climb up on the little sound stage. It actually bent and creaked under my weight.

*Hell, I've stood on wooden pallets stronger and higher 'n this.*

There wasn't much of anyone in this part of the casino so I pulled back the tarp to look at the sound equipment. I noticed a switch and a microphone. I turned both on and they screeched so I turned down the volume knob and tapped the mike. I walked around silently mouthing a song just so I could get the feel of what it could be like singing in a casino lounge.

I spotted Georgia taking drink orders, batting a drunk's hand off her behind and coming to me with a tall cola beverage. She looked so tired that I had a powerful urge to sing her a song…maybe to lift her spirits. Just then I felt inspired and thought of the great Ray Charles hit, *Georgia*. I didn't exactly remember the lyrics, but I didn't think she'd mind with me being a song writer if I made up some lines on the run.

So in a low, husky voice I sang to her.

*Georgia, Georgia, it's you the whole night through, just the thought of you brings Georgia to my mind. Other women may come and go…but it's you, I'll always know. Other hands reach out to me, but it's only you that brings out the Georgia peach in me….*

She froze while I murdered the classic, but I could tell she was pleased and flattered. I finally ran out of words to think up so I turned off the mike and got off the little stage.

"What'd you think?"

"I liked it a lot, Johnny. You have a *beautiful* voice. You can sing to me any time you want. "

"So you thought it was pretty good, huh?"

"I sure did. You wouldn't believe how many drunks here have seen my badge and burst into that song trying to impress me with their terrible renditions; you're one of the very, very few that have done the song proud and made my heart go pitter-patter."

"If I get to sing here regularly, maybe you'd come and see me."

"I would."

I took my drink. "Where are you from?"

"I'm from a little town due north of Memphis."

"What a coincidence! I've a very good and famous friend that lives in Memphis."

"Let me guess. That friend wouldn't just happen to be Elvis Presley, would it?"

"Why, how'd you know?"

"I've heard that line a thousand times. But that's fine because I love the way you look and sing."

I was going to thank her, but some people at the closest slot machines started yelling at Georgia for more free drinks.

"I'd better get busy or they'll fire me. Will I see you around?"

"You bet." I tipped her five dollars and she stuffed it in between the top of her bulging, and nicely tanned breasts.

"Thank you!"

I finally did catch Leon Heitzman in his office and to my surprise he'd heard from someone…maybe Georgia or a casino patron, I don't know…and they'd raved about my impromptu singing in the Jubilee Lounge.

"You'll start tonight," Heitzman said, "but you gotta join the union first."

"How do I do that?"

"I'll take care of it." He found a form and told me to sign it on the bottom which I did.

"Be there by nine-thirty," he said. "If you do well, we'll work you in and get rid of the damned *Ramblers* who couldn't carry a tune in a corked jug."

I won't go into a lot of detail but The Ramblers quickly accepted my role as lead singer and I took over their stage and name. Earlier, I'd given Georgia fifty dollars and asked her to invite all her friends to hear my first performance while they enjoyed free drinks…strong drinks, not the watered-down ones that casinos grudgingly give you.

I received standing ovations after each of my songs and I didn't even bother to really play the Martin guitar…I just made it look like I was pickin' a hot lick. The lead singer whose voice sounded like the death rattles was a fine guitarist. Now, they had a real singer in the lead spot.

*Why shouldn't we all stick to what we do best?*

Within a week, we were drawing large crowds every night and I was learning songs as fast as I could. I changed our stage name to 'The Coyotes' and while there was some resistance at first, the name caught on big. When my girl Georgia wasn't on shift, she was always at the front table and I was beginning to feel something strong for her. Miss Loretta Hickey seemed like a lump of pure ordinary compared to this kind, happy and mighty sexy woman.

Leon Heitzman was also becoming a regular and one night after the last show he pulled me aside and said, "I'm going to find you a much bigger lounge."

"Does that mean a lot more money?"

"Of course it does! The word is out, Johnny…you're in demand!"

"And the other guys?"

Heitzman shrugged. "They'll do for awhile. We'll up their pay, but not as much as the jump you'll get. And if we can get a record made, we'll have to use studio musicians who really know how to play."

I wanted to argue out of some sense of loyalty, but knew better. Also, I had found a completely furnished house a mile outside of Las Vegas for Grandmother and Stella. It was a nice, big ranch-style on an acre of the hardest, rockiest ground I'd ever seen. The vegetation was mostly sage and creosote brush…with not a blade of grass and plenty of scorpions and rattlers prowling around outside a block wall that surrounded our swimming pool and spacious backyard. The air conditioning was so good you could cool meat and out by the pool we had a fine view of some bare black mountains. I had the feeling that Grandmother didn't mind living there at all.

Stella, however, was difficult from the start. When I could, I took her to her appointments with the physical therapists and mental health counselors. She got her prosthesis and hated it. She was too embarrassed at first to wear a bathing suit because then you could see that the lower part of her leg was a stump. And she found liquor…enough to float a boat. But Grandmother and I decided that we had to ease her back slow and that if we started browbeating her about the alcohol, she'd either find a way to run off to only God knows where and end up dead or she'd drink far heavier just to show us that she was still her own person making her own bad decisions.

So we gave her space and after a while she did find it in herself to put on a swimming suit and then she'd float for hours on an inflatable mattress and stare up at the hot Nevada sun through big, dark glasses.

"She's doing better," Grandmother kept saying to me. "I know it doesn't seem that way, but she is."

"She hates the prosthesis."

"Wouldn't you, Charlie?"

"Sure, but...."

"We'll get her a better one. The man said that it all just takes time. How's the playing and singing going?"

"It's going better than I'd ever dreamed, I'm making a lot of money and building a following."

"Don't get big headed."

"I still wear the same hat size."

"You know that's not what I meant."

I kissed her wrinkled brown cheek. "I love you and I'll be fine."

"Bring that woman around again."

"Georgia?"

"Yes. I really liked her."

"Stella didn't seem to."

"Stella doesn't even like herself right now. Bring Georgia around more. She makes me laugh and she's fun to be around."

"I will."

And so I did and Georgia began to sleep in my bed when neither of us was working the casino. I rubbed her feet because they hurt after long hours at the casino and while I wasn't making much headway with my guitar playing, I was sure learning to be a lot better at making love.

# *Chapter 24*

Little by little Stella began to talk and then to confide in Georgia. And one day around the pool I heard them laughing. I pulled Grandmother to the window and we watched the two young women enjoying themselves.

"She's very good for Stella."

"Good for me, too."

"Do you know anything of her past?"

I thought about that for a minute. The truth was that Georgia had a mysterious and quite troubled past. I gathered that she'd had a rough childhood including a stepfather who'd molested her and a mother who never wanted a child. She'd been a straight A student and loved science and math classes, but had quit school just before her high school graduation and had taken a Greyhound bus out to Las Vegas hoping to catch on as a showgirl or marry a handsome movie star.

Because of her looks and long, lovely legs, Georgia had gotten on a chorus line of dancers and had done well until she'd twisted her ankle so badly that she couldn't walk for months. The doctor had warned her that the ligaments in her ankle had been torn and stretched and that she'd never dance again. Discouraged, she'd gone through hard times and several boyfriends who also worked at the casinos. A blackjack dealer fed her a long line, but he turned out to be just as abusive as her Tennessee stepfather. She'd gotten a job as a cocktail waitress and found that her looks, southern drawl and pretty smile could earn her more money in tips than any other job she could hope to find.

She'd dreamed of becoming a veterinarian in her childhood days. Georgia loved animals and I'd promised her I'd take her horseback riding at some local rent stable when the weather cooled down and time permitted. I didn't know if horses could stand the summer heat here, but I suspected they could.

"I knew at first glance that you loved animals too," she told me one night as we sat in chairs out by the pool. "And were a real cowboy who rode bulls and broncs."

"Not anymore. If I get back into rodeo, it'll be as a bulldogger."

"You were big and strong enough to bulldog me, Cowboy Charlie. I'm sure you could make a good living at it." She looked off for a moment. "You

194

got a cowgirl hidden somewhere waiting for your return?"

"Not anymore," I said, thinking of Loretta.

"Stella tells me that she was a barrel racer...and a good one."

"My sister is poetry on a horse." I waited, wondering how much Stella had told her about Sun Dancer and Lenny. And when Georgia didn't say anything, I added, "I just hope she'll ride horses again someday."

"I'm sure that Stella is going to be alright. I've no doubt that she'll ride lots of horses in time. And have you noticed how she seems so much healthier?"

"I have noticed that she's put on weight and seems to have a big appetite," I said, "but Grandmother says that she still has darkness deep inside."

"Maybe lightness is blossoming inside your sister."

I had no earthly idea what *that* meant.

"Stella told me a little about your mysterious mother and that diary that was chronicling her life's sad story among the Hopi. She wants to finish the diary...it's preying heavily on her mind."

"I was surprised that Stella had opened up that much of our past and especially our mother. "Did Stella say anything else?"

"I know all about you and Elvis...and her and Elvis."

I didn't know what to say. I was curious if Stella had told Georgia that she'd loved Elvis. And I wondered if the time came when Elvis met Georgia, if he'd steal her heart away from me. He could do that without half trying.

Georgia kissed my lips. "Don't worry so much about Stella. I think your sister is going to turn out fine. Her appointment with the plastic surgeon went well. Isn't that wonderful?"

"It sure is."

Actually, with a tan added to her already dark skin, Stella's few and minor facial scars had vanished. And my sister had recently received a new prosthesis; when she was wearing long pants or a dress, you barely even noticed her slight limp. Physically, Stella was looking better and better and I believed she was transitioning into a happier and healthier person day-by-day.

Grandmother and Stella joined us out at the pool with a tray of iced tea and we sat around talking.

"Grandmother," Stella said, "I don't suppose you poured some vodka in my glass, did you?"

"You don't need it anymore."

"You're right. I need to take care of myself. And I have a confession to make."

Georgia raised her hand, as if pleading for Stella not to say any more, but my sister wasn't one to be silenced.

"I know that the police and everyone believe that when Lenny and I had that rollover, *he* was driving…but *I* was at the wheel."

Grandmother groaned. I caught my breath.

"Lenny and I were both drunk…he drunker than me. We almost crashed a couple of times driving up the mountain through this little town called Yarnell. We bought more beer at a gas station and I insisted that I was driving on to Prescott. Ten or fifteen miles later Lenny became really angry and started slapping me. I lost control of our truck and…well, you know the rest of the sad story."

"It wasn't your fault," I said. "Lenny dragged you down."

"And I dragged him down as well. We'd gone to see his parents over in California. They treated me like dirt and refused to give us any money. That's part of what the fight was about. Lenny was yelling about what an awful mistake it had been to get married. He was going to get rid of me the first chance he got and said that was going to happen in Prescott the next day. I was crying and well…with being slapped and the tears…I missed a curve and drove over the side of that mountain."

"And you never told anyone that you were driving?" I asked.

"I told Georgia and now I'm telling you. If I'd have confessed to the police, I'd have probably gone to jail…maybe even prison. I couldn't do that. I couldn't stand to be caged. I'd have shriveled up and died."

Grandmother and I were at a loss for words. And then, quite suddenly, a red-tailed hawk swooped down and landed on the green branches of a Palo Verde tree and began to tear apart and devour a kangaroo rat. The hawk kept glancing at us to see if we minded his bad table manners. Grandmother was pleased by the fierce bird's presence. She puckered her lips and made some red-tailed hawk sounds and the bird answered. It seemed to me that she and the hawk communicated silently, each with their black, piercing eyes. Then the hawk swallowed the rat except for its long, bushy tail which dangled from its sharp beak and rose silently into the hot sky.

"I like this place," Grandmother said. "But I miss our ranch."

"Me too," Stella agreed with a faraway look in her eyes.

My mind was still on what Stella had confessed. But later, Grandmother told me the red-tailed hawk was a sign of Stella's soaring, and indomitable spirit and that her confession was the freeing of guilt that disappeared with the hawk that had really been a kachina.

"If that's the case, any idea what the poor kangaroo rat represented?" I asked.

"The last of her darkness which the hawk swallowed. And the rat's tail we saw as the hawk flew away was a reminder that there is something always left of our pasts…good and bad…a reminder of life's most important lessons."

Two days later I made a quick, solo run to Coyote Ranch to check up on things and bring our dog Rip back to live with us in Nevada. Grandmother needed some clay so she could start firing pots and we all thought she could sell them in Las Vegas. Stella wanted to know about her horse and I promised I'd stop and see how Sun Dancer was getting along at Twister's place. I also wanted to lay some spending cash on the old Navajo couple that had settled in nicely.

When I arrived at Coyote Ranch, I immediately noticed the emptiness and silence of our ranch yard. "What happened to Grandmother's chickens?" I asked the Navajo couple.

"Run out of chicken feed…so not many eggs," the old man said in his stoic way. "We boil and eat chickens. Rooster tough as rawhide."

I know my jaw dropped. There'd been at least twenty hens and a rooster. My oh my was Grandmother going to be upset with this couple! But the Navajo didn't seem a bit concerned. I figured they'd decided it was the best thing to do and that unfed chickens would just wander off into the brush…better that Navajo ate the chickens than coyotes.

"I see," I said, deciding to tell Grandmother that she was going to have to buy a new flock when we got around to coming back home.

After digging up some clay and packing it into buckets, I stopped in Flagstaff to see Twister and his wife Alice. Sun Dancer was sure doing well.

"I'm thinking of taking the mare to Las Vegas for Stella," I told my old friend.

Twister didn't look pleased. "That horse was in real bad shape when you dropped her off. If your sister uses her…."

"She won't," I interrupted. "You know Stella lost some of her lower leg."

"Yeah, I'd heard that. Me and Alice are awful sorry."

"I'm confident the palomino mare will be good medicine for Stella," I told him. "And I did leave our stock trailer here."

"You got a good place for the horse over in Vegas?" Twister asked.

"We're renting, but it's fenced and I can throw up a shade. Don't worry, we'll take care of her." I took out my wallet and gave Twister two hundred dollars. "I hope this is enough."

"More'n enough, Cowboy Charlie. My wife and I became fond of the mare while she's been here. We even got to talkin' around the table and I think that Sun Dancer could make an easy switch from barrel racing to being the horse I'd use for hazing."

I could tell that he really wanted to buy this mare. "Twister, I need that palomino more for my sister's state of mind than the money, but I appreciate your offer."

"Alright, we'll load 'er up then."

"I may take on a new student," Twister said after Sun Dancer was in the trailer and I was ready to pull out. "If I do you can always come back if the singing business doesn't work out."

"Thanks."

"I've seen a lot of young cowboys come and go. And I've seen quite a few strong young men try to win money bulldogging. But I have to say that you have the quickest hands and the most natural ability and raw power I've ever come across."

"Ah, I don't know about that."

"I do," Twister said, looking me straight in the eye. "You're a natural athlete. You could have been a professional at any sport you chose. You don't even know your own strength and the physical gifts you were given. If I'd have had your size, quickness and power, I would have been world champion bulldogger for another ten years."

I was so embarrassed I changed the subject. "I'm making good money in a Las Vegas lounge. I've got a band and we call ourselves The Coyotes."

I thought Twister was going to die laughing and I didn't bother to tell him the size of my last few paychecks.

Twister finally said, "I've been in contact with Elvis for awhile."

"You've called him?"

"We've been back and forth quite a few times about the copper mining property. He told me that the next time you stop by he wanted you to call him from our house…he wants to talk to you in private."

"Should I call him right now?"

"Be a good thing to do."

I nodded and we went into the house. Twister's wife said, "Cowboy Charlie, are you finally going to call Elvis!"

"Yeah."

"I'm glad. He has some big news that he wants to tell you personally."

I couldn't imagine what that might be, but I wanted to find out before I died of curiosity. "Where's your phone?"

They pointed the way into the kitchen and gave me the number. My heart began to pound fast as I dialed. A stranger answered and when I told them I was Cowboy Charlie Coyote, he asked me to wait until he could find and rouse Elvis.

I held the phone for a good twenty minutes. I was nervous, anxious and wondering what was taking so long. It was noon in Flagstaff so it would have been two or three o'clock at Graceland.

Finally, a sleepy, slurry voice came on the line. "Hey, Cowboy Charlie. How you doin', my friend?"

"I'm fine."

"I hear you're a hit at the Jubilee Lounge. I knew you'd do great. When I get to Vegas next time, we'll have dinner together and talk about the record making business. I'd like to see you in the recording studio."

"I'd like that a lot," I told him.

"Charlie, are you sitting down?"

"I'm leaning on the kitchen counter."

"Did Twister tell you anything about that mining property next to your ranch?"

"No."

"Well, that just shows he and his wife can keep a secret. I'm not telling anyone else, but Twister bought that land for me about a week ago."

"What!"

"I'm your new, mystery neighbor, Cowboy Charlie. Ain't that a kick in the butt!"

"Well damn, Elvis! That's the best news I've heard in a long, long time."

"I knew you'd be happy. Twister and his wife were beside themselves trying to keep our secret so I could break the news to you personally."

Elvis was sounding more alert and happy by the moment. "Hey," he said, "I've got my spies in Las Vegas and they tell me that you're seeing a cocktail waitress by the name of Georgia."

"That's right."

"Is it serious? You know I had it in mind to introduce you to some famous actresses…some of 'em are old girlfriends. I mentioned your name and described you to a couple of beauties and they started panting with a burning love."

I knew Elvis was joking, trying to get a big laugh or reaction.

"Aw, you know I'm not going to live in Hollywood. I'm doing well in the music business, but I sure miss the wide open spaces and the silence of Coyote Ranch."

"That's what I figured and what I really hoped to hear."

We talked for a few minutes about Stella and Sun Dancer. Elvis wanted to know how she was coming along in her recovery.

"She's doing better and better," I assured him. "And I'm taking Sun Dancer down to Las Vegas to try and get her back in the saddle."

"Give her all my love."

I didn't think that message was going to do my sister any good so I changed the subject. "Now that you've bought the land next to our ranch, when are you coming out for a visit? And are you going to start building a ranch house?"

"Whoa up there, Cowboy! Things take time. And besides, I was hoping you might bring that woman of yours out to Memphis so I can meet her. You could stay together right here at Graceland and we'd have a lot of fun. I'd put you in a recording studio and you could make a record, if you don't insist on writing the song yourself."

I chuckled. "Okay, you find me the song and some musicians and I'll do what I can to make a decent record."

"I think that would be a fine idea. But I want to meet Georgia. My spies tell me she is quite a looker."

"If you start looking at her too much, I'll have to do something physical about that," I warned, only half in jest.

"Don't worry because I'm fine in that department. Do you think you'll marry her?"

I had always appreciated the way Elvis got right to the point. And his question was one I'd been thinking about for some time now. "I do."

"That's wonderful news!"

"Thanks."

"Let me know when you intend to visit and I'll send you and Georgia first class plane tickets. Or better yet, I'll send one of my private planes to pick you up."

"You bought *planes?*"

"Yeah, I'm doing over a hundred shows on the road a year now so that I can't take the time to drive. I bought a Jet Commander to take me from city to city."

"What's that?"

"It's a corporate jet. Faster'n hell, but small so I bought a four-engine jet from Delta Airlines that can carry a hundred passengers; I had it completely gutted and outfitted just for me by a firm in Dallas. I'm calling it the *Lisa Marie* after my daughter. It has a queen-sized bed, three closed-circuit televisions, a six-seat conference room, a lounge with a bar and every seat on the plane has gold-plated seat belt buckles…oh, and there's a fake fireplace and a couple of half-baths. I even had my *TCB* logo painted on the tail."

"Elvis, you're really flying in style."

"I deserve to, as hard as I work. I had a chance to do a movie with Barbara Streisand called *A Star is Born,* but they couldn't meet my price so I passed. I think Kris Kristofferson is taking my role and he's a great actor so it doesn't matter."

"Was it a good role? One that would have finally shown the world what a fine actor you are?"

"Sure, but it's all about money now. I got people depending on me and I'm done with movies. I can make a lot more doing performances. Easy come and easy go."

Even as he said that I wondered. When I'd first met Elvis all he talked about was how he wanted to be a great actor as well as singer. He admired the really fine actors like Paul Newman, Robert Mitchum, Cary Grant and Gregory Peck and considered most of them his friends. Now he was talking about fast money. I just couldn't help but think that he'd lost sight of his dreams and why did he need a jet that carried a hundred people and had its own fireplace and gold-plated seat buckles? And I'd seen some of those super market tabloids showing pictures of a fat, tired-looking Elvis and read how he was heavy into drugs and had even been found unconscious a few times…very close to death.

When my silence grew uncomfortable, Elvis said, "Don't worry. I'll have enough money to help you out if you ever need it."

"I wasn't worrying about that. How is your *health?* "

"I'm tired, but making a ton of money and taking care of business just like I always do. Charlie, are you worried that I won't have enough money to build a nice ranch house?"

"No, I'm a little worried about your health, that's all."

"Don't. I got some fine doctors close at hand and plenty of loyal friends that take real good care of me and set up all the road shows. Last year I gave away fourteen Cadillacs, one to a complete stranger I met in the showroom because she'd decided she couldn't afford one. You should have seen the surprise and joy on her face when the salesman handed her the keys and said she owned it thanks to Elvis Presley!"

I didn't know what to say. Elvis Presley was legendary for his impulsive generosity.

"Do you want me to send a plane out to get you and Georgia?"

"No thanks."

"Your choice," Elvis said, abruptly hanging up at his end of the line.

"How'd he sound?" Twister asked.

"Not too good."

Twister and his wife exchanged glances.

"What is it?" I asked.

"We're really worried about Elvis," Twister said. "Putting that land deal together wasn't easy. I had to talk to Elvis a half dozen times or more and sometimes he didn't even make sense."

"He takes drugs to sleep and more drugs to bring himself back up."

Twister was quiet for a moment. "Elvis is not the only one that I've talked to from Memphis."

"Who else?"

"There's a fella said that he knows you. He said he used to drive Elvis across the country in a limousine. I forgot his name but...."

"His name is Mark."

"Well, he got fired awhile back. Said it was alright because he couldn't stand to be around Elvis anymore. He told me that Elvis was killing himself. Some of his best friends have tried to get him off the drugs... but when they push it too much Elvis threatens to fire them, too."

"I see."

Twister's wife said, "We were wondering if there was anything you could do to save Elvis."

"I...I don't know what I could do," I stammered. "Elvis and I are close friends...but he's always kept his show business and personal life pretty much to himself. He told me right from the start that he really appreciated that I never tried to pry into his personal affairs. So we've kept it that way from the beginning."

"Have you read the tabloids?" Twister's wife asked worriedly.

"You can't believe them, Alice. They'll say whatever they have to in order to hype their sales."

"I've read enough about Elvis to know that he's nearly died a couple of times in the last year."

"How?"

"Overdoses! His pilot had to make an emergency stop in Dallas because Elvis wasn't able to breathe."

I was so upset that I knew I had to leave. "I'll be in touch," I told them.

"You better be thinking of some way to save him or he's going to die before long."

"I'll...I'll put some thought to it," I promised. "But really I don't know what I could possibly do."

"Just think about it, Charlie. Alice and I have a feeling that no one back at Graceland or close to that crowd is going to be able to save Elvis. Maybe it will take someone like you."

I didn't think so, but I nodded and hurried out their door. I whistled Rip into my pickup and high-tailed it down to Route 66 looking forward to seeing my family and cooling down in our swimming pool.

"Rip, you've always loved to swim in the stock pond at the ranch," I said, reaching over and ruffling the dog's coat. "My guess is that down in Vegas where it gets so hot, you're going end up spending more time in the pool than any of us people."

Rip's thick tail drummed hard on the truck's seat. He stuck his nose out the window and I could tell he was happy to be back with me again. He'd probably figured we'd abandoned him to the old Navajo couple and his days of being a cow dog were sadly in the past.

# Chapter 25

On my way back to Las Vegas I should have been thinking of how Elvis had made me come to the decision to ask Georgia for her hand in marriage. But after listening to Twister and his wife telling me how Elvis was in such bad shape and how at times he was even too drugged up or down to make sense on the phone, I couldn't get Elvis and his failing health off my mind.

I had seen a lot of alcoholism in my life. It was everywhere on the reservation and you frequently saw it in the rodeo crowd. Lenny and my sister had partied and drank to excess and look at the pain and loss that had resulted... Lenny dead and my sister maimed. They'd gone over a mountainside, but they could just as easily have done a head-on with a family.

*They could have killed children.*

I decided to present the rapid physical decline of Elvis to my family and Georgia and see if they had any radical ideas. Twister had told me that he thought the only thing that might save *The King* was to get him to come and live on his new Northern Arizona ranch property...and to go into permanent seclusion, changing his complete identity. As I drove through the old railroad towns on Route 66, I decided that it was likely the only possible chance to save Elvis Presley.

*And he said he was doing over a hundred shows a year?*

I'd only been performing at the Jubilee Lounge with The Coyotes for a few months, but it was already taking a significant toll. I was accustomed to getting up early and working through the day at physical labor...breaking horses, fixing fence, roping, branding and doctoring cattle...hard work...but healthy, outdoor work in clean air.

Being in a casino with all that smoke and noise, the crazy all-night hours and how you got keyed up after the last show around two o'clock in the morning so you had trouble falling to sleep before sunrise...these things would kill anyone's vitality. I was younger and stronger than Elvis and show business was already taking a physical toll. So it was easy to understand why Elvis was failing, given the incredible number of performances he did each year.

The three musicians in my little band were a good ten years older than me and they'd been performing in the casinos for eight years. Sure they made good money, but each of them looked far older than their ages. They smoked too much between sets and they drank too much every night when we finished in order to calm down. It wasn't all that difficult for me to imagine what I'd look like after a decade of playing in smoke-filled casino lounges.

I was worried about Elvis and I was also worried about myself. If Elvis, with all his intelligence and talent was going down the tubes, what made me think that I wouldn't end up the same way…only much sooner?

I didn't have a good answer and as I drove over the Hoover Dam and looked out toward another beautiful desert sunset, I realized that becoming rich and famous wasn't all that it was cracked up to be. I wanted in the worst way to never have to worry about money again…to build a nice house on our Coyote Ranch property and to sink a deeper, sweeter tasting well. To buy a new tractor with a front loader and own fine horses. In short, I wanted to have a secure financial future… but now found myself asking, *at what cost?*

*The cost Elvis is paying?*

I knew of a jewelry store in downtown Kingman and I had three hundred dollars in my wallet. So I stopped, checked on the palomino mare to make sure she was okay and then went inside and looked at the diamond rings.

"Hey, there, Cowboy," the owner said, his eye on a television set. "How are you doing today?"

"Just fine." I looked up at the television and saw that a tall horse ridden by a very small jockey was being led into the winner's circle. "Big race?"

"Oh yeah! That horse Seattle Slew just won the Belmont Stakes to become only the tenth horse in history to win the Triple Crown!"

"He's a beautiful animal," I said, admiring the Thoroughbred and watching the crowd go crazy in the stands.

"Yeah, I'll bet that you wish you had that race horse in your stock trailer."

I grinned. "I doubt Seattle Slew would work out well on a ranch."

The jewelry store owner laughed. "I'm sure you're right! What can I do for you today?"

"I want to buy a wedding ring."

"Congratulations! You came to the right place. Come over here and let me show you what we have to offer."

I picked one that cost $299.95 and convinced the friendly owner that, if he wanted the cash, he should eat the sales tax. It was an easy argument. Someday, when I had more money…*if* I had more money…I'd buy Georgia a much bigger and finer diamond. But I had a hunch she'd take this small one for now and be overjoyed.

Buying Georgia a ring really perked up my low spirits. Rip sensed it and wagged his big, shaggy tail. I gave the dog a hug and said, "It's going to all work out for the best."

Rip thought so too…I could tell by the way he squirmed all over the seat.

I arrived at our rented place just after dark and when I pulled in, all three of the most important women in my life rushed outside. I took them in my arms and hugged them and kissed them one-by-one.

"How is Sun Dancer!" Stella asked, running around to the back of the stock trailer. "And look at you, Rip! You've lost some weight, but you look good!"

Rip was beside himself with joy at being back in the family. I think he'd been fine with the old Navajo couple, but he was our dog and always would be. Now, he was jumping around and yipping with happiness.

We unloaded Sun Dancer and the women had filled a big round galvanized tub with fresh water. The horse was thirsty and drank gallons. Stella's saddle and tack were in the pickup's bed and I hoped she'd find the courage to put them to use. The air was hot and dry and the early evening stars were a brilliant blanket in the heavens.

"How's our ranch looking?" Grandmother wanted to know as I grabbed my bag and headed for the house.

"It looks about the same."

I needed a beer or two and I wanted to talk over some serious business with these smart women. We all settled down at the kitchen table. Georgia got a beer for each of us and Grandmother and Stella chose coffee.

"Tell us all about it," Grandmother said.

I drank Coors from the bottle and it tasted wonderful. "There's a lot to tell. Not all of it good."

They frowned with concern. Grandmother tapped her forefinger on the table. "Did you bring me clay for making pottery…or forget?"

"I brought the clay. Enough to keep you busy for a month."

"And our house is still standing?"

"Yes. But…well, the old Navajo couple ate your chickens."

"Dammit!" she cried, slamming her little fist down on our table. "Why?"

"They claim that your chickens had stopped laying and they'd run out of chicken feed."

"They should have bought some feed."

"I don't think they have any money," I told her. "You're going to have to buy new chickens."

"And my handsome red rooster?"

"He was the last to go into their pot. They said he was really tough...but tasty."

Stella started laughing, then Georgia and I couldn't help myself and joined in. Finally, even Grandmother saw the humor in the situation. Then I told them about the rapid decline in Elvis' health, but also the good news about him buying the Copper Mining Company land next to ours under an alias.

When I was done talking Stella said, "So what are you going to do about helping Elvis?"

I threw up my hands. "I don't rightly know yet."

"But you will do *something*, won't you?" Georgia asked.

"I was hoping we could all think on it and come up with a solution."

"There's only one solution," Stella decided. "You kidnap Elvis and bring him back to our ranch in Arizona. Then we keep him on the ranch until he wants no more of that show business life. The carrot is that he has his own Arizona ranch property now and has a solid dream to build upon."

I looked at the others and they were nodding. "Okay," I said, "we'll have to plan it out, but that's what we'll do."

Then I took Georgia's hand and led her out into the moonlight. Bending down on one knee with Rip crowding us close, I said, "I'm not much at making speeches, but I'd be mighty proud if you'd be my wife."

She cried and we hugged. Then we went into the house and made the announcement and went straight to my bedroom.

"It's all going to work out for us, Charlie," Georgia whispered in my ear after the lovemaking. "Every wonderful bit of it."

"Including saving Elvis from himself?"

"Yes."

We were quiet for awhile listening to a pack of coyotes out in the sagebrush as they howled at the warm golden moon. And holding my fiancé, I began to think that we really could save Elvis...if for no other reason than he richly deserved a long happy life.

# Chapter 26

A whole bunch of good things came to our family in the next few weeks. Georgia and I were married in a simple Las Vegas ceremony and of course, Stella and Grandma cried with happiness. And with her mare back, Stella found the courage to go riding and once she started, she was up before daybreak every morning and heading out into the desert to greet the sunrise. Rip, glad to have something to do, always accompanied my sister and Sun Dancer.

"That horse has made a world of difference in Stella," Grandmother said one morning over breakfast. "It's the *real* medicine your sister needed."

"You're right," I agreed.

We didn't hear from Elvis for awhile and I was worried as we tried to figure out how to grab and shove him headlong into obscurity. I knew that Elvis loved his fans and even though he was on a steep, slippery slope toward an early grave, I wasn't at all sure that he'd willingly give up his incredible fame and fortune.

Then one night at the casino, things took an ugly turn. I was onstage when out of the corner of my eye I saw Georgia cornered by two large men that I recognized as bouncers at a nearby casino. They were pawing her and I tried to ignore what was happening out on the floor…for maybe five seconds…then I jumped off the stage and charged across the floor.

"That's my wife you're messing with!"

One of them had a bull neck and sloping shoulders. He was as tall as I was and at least thirty pounds heavier. He turned and sneered, "We're just having a little fun."

"Not anymore," I growled, planting my feet and burying my fist in his nuts. He bellowed and doubled up in agony. I grabbed his hair and slammed his face into a slot machine so violently that it shook out a jackpot of nickels. His nose broke and smeared the front of the slot machine as he collapsed.

A heavyset woman who'd been playing the nearest machine screamed and I turned just in time to take a punishing overhead right to my jaw that corkscrewed me completely around.

I was dazed and the second bouncer would have destroyed me if Georgia hadn't grabbed a drink from a patron's hand and tossed it into the man's eyes. I shook off my daze and shot a straight right hand into his mouth, knocking out teeth and cracking my knuckles. When he staggered I drove a left uppercut to his gut followed by a punch that broke his jaw. People were screaming, blood was flowing, both bouncers were down and one of the big bastards vomited all over the carpet.

"Georgia, let's get out of here!"

"I could have handled them!"

"Only after they'd had some fun handling you," I said through clenched teeth as we sprinted outside.

I knew that the casino would be furious with me for busting up the bouncers. I also realized that there would be repercussions both from the casino I worked for and possibly from the bouncers and their rough friends. But right then I didn't care. We were out in the cool night air and headed for my truck.

Once inside, I drove down The Strip toward an all-night pawn shop. "Georgia, please wait here."

"What are you doing?"

"I'm buying a hide-out gun."

She jumped out of the truck and got into my face. "Don't just buy one, buy two! Six-shot, short-barreled .45 caliber revolvers."

"Are you any good with a pistol?"

"I'm a Southern girl, remember? I used to hunt coons."

"If those people decide to come for us, they'll be a lot harder to kill than any raccoon."

"True, but at least with guns we'll have a fighting chance."

I yanked open the door and almost yelped with a pain that shot up my arm.

"Are you alright!"

"I hurt my hand."

She looked and it was already badly swollen. "Then how can you play with your band?"

"I messed up those goons pretty bad and we'll probably lose our jobs."

"How will we pay…."

"Let's buy two revolvers and talk about it later," I suggested.

And that's what we did.

Two days later a letter arrived from casino management that they'd been sued not only by the bouncers, but by the heavyset lady who claimed she was knocked to the floor which seriously injured her back. The casino was "temporarily" laying both of us off until they decided to either settle the damages which they assured me were serious in respect to the pair of bouncers

I'd beaten. The lady had been offered two thousand dollars for a quick out-of-court settlement and was expected to take the money.

"We're done working there," I told Georgia, wadding up the letter and tossing it in the trash basket.

"Cowboy Charlie, I've saved up a good amount of money."

"So have I. So let's just write them back a letter saying we quit."

"Then what?"

"We do whatever it takes to save Elvis."

Georgia thought that made all the sense in the world so we wrote the letter and sat each evening on the porch with Stella and Grandmother talking about The King and about almost everything else.

"I have another story for you," Grandmother announced one evening.

"Let'er rip," I said.

Georgia was smiling. "Yes, please. Charlie has told me about your stories and I'd love to hear one."

Grandmother started rocking and began.

*Once there was a rancher who found a dead eagle near its nest. There was only one egg so they took it to their ranch and placed it under a hen sitting on her nest of eggs. In time the eagle hatched with the chicks and since it had never seen another eagle, it believed it was a chicken."*

"Wait," Stella said. "You never told us this one before. Wouldn't the baby eagle know it was not a chicken?"

"No," Grandmother said, "and that's because it had never been able to see itself."

*In time the eagle grew up in the chicken pen very big and strong, but still thought of itself as a chicken. It was happy and wanted to act like all the other chickens. But then one day another eagle flew over the chicken yard and all the frightened chickens went clucking and running into the chicken house where they huddled very afraid.*

*And guess what the eagle who thought it was a chicken did?*

I chuckled, pretty sure I knew the answer. "It flew up into the sky and became another eagle and soared over the Hopi Mesas?" I asked.

"Nope. It ran squawking and afraid into the chicken house until the eagle flew away."

"But why?" Stella asked.

Grandmother folded her arms and said, "Because the eagle in the chicken pen did not believe how strong and beautiful it really was. And that it had wings to carry it up into the sky."

"You're saying…."

"I'm telling you this story so you know that we all have choices we may not even be aware of. The big choice we have in life is to decide if we are eagles…or chickens."

We all went to bed that night probably thinking about the lesson of the eagle who was convinced it was only a chicken with lowly abilities and ambitions. I wondered if someone like Elvis had thought he was even more than an eagle and had flown nearly to the sun and gotten blinded.

"Your grandmother is pretty special," Georgia whispered sleepily just before she dozed off.

"I know."

"We must be eagles if we are to save Elvis. All of us."

I nodded in the darkness before finally falling asleep.

# Chapter 27

The Las Vegas spring of 1977 was one of the hottest months on record. People were constantly talking about the recent death of the reclusive billionaire Howard Hughes who'd had quite an impact on Las Vegas. And when they weren't talking about that they were talking about some crazy New York serial killer nicknamed "Son of Sam".

I was making frequent trips to Coyote Ranch to check on the Navajo and to dig more clay for Grandmother's pottery which was selling for high prices in Las Vegas. So high that she needed help and so Stella and Georgia began to learn how to throw and fire pots. They were making us a ton of money and I began to see that we had a "cottage industry" on our hands. I handled the deliveries and took the payments, kept track of our in-store inventory and thought about applying for a singing job in one of the casino lounges, but was enjoying being around the women so much that I hated to go back to the nightclub work. And the casino had never called either of us back. I assumed they'd settled the lawsuits out of court and decided that I wasn't worth the risk of having another public relations and legal disaster.

When Georgia and I had hatched up what was probably a hare-brained plan to kidnap Elvis and bring him to his new ranch, I'd realized that by doing so I'd never have his pull and get into a recording studio…never make a record and probably never become anything close to being rich or famous.

"Cowboy Charlie, you ought to come back here and start working on bulldogging," Twister always told me when I stopped by their place. "Your hand is healed up and we could get back into the swing of it."

"I'm pretty busy in Las Vegas," I'd tell him. "Did you find another student?"

"Nope. Still hoping you'll come back."

"I'm giving it some serious thought, Twister."

"And what about saving Elvis?" the old bulldogger asked.

"We're all giving that a lot of thought."

"If I can help in any way, don't hesitate to ask."

I'd have told Twister that we would keep him posted and up-to-date on our plans to rescue Elvis, but we really didn't have any concrete plans. Georgia, being raised in Tennessee, knew the lay of that land around Memphis, but it might just as well have been Switzerland for all I knew.

Through rumors and the tabloids, I'd read that Elvis had broken up with his long-time girlfriend, Linda Thompson, and quickly taken up with a twenty-year-old beauty named Ginger Alden. Elvis had played his last and by all accounts disastrous engagement at the Las Vegas Hilton and yet he hadn't bothered to call or look me and my Coyote family up. It gave me a very bad feeling about what was going on in Elvis' life and a sense of urgency that something had to be done or he was going to crash and burn.

And then one day right out of the blue Stella said, "I want to go home to our Coyote Ranch."

I knew we all did. We could make and deliver Hopi pottery from the ranch and the heat on the low desert was starting to get tedious even with a swimming pool. And I could start working with Twister again and concentrate on bulldogging.

Stella, however, was another matter, so I asked, "What are you going to do up there?"

"I'm going to college," Stella announced. "I've been thinking about working for a degree in Alcohol and Drug Counseling. Since we're still Arizona residents, I won't have to pay out of state Nevada tuition."

"That's a wonderful idea," Georgia said.

"Yes," Grandmother agreed. "You will find plenty of our people who need your help. But there are things you can also use that I've taught you...spiritual things."

"I know. And to realize I'm an eagle."

At that remark, Grandmother beamed with pleasure.

"Then you're not going to take up barrel-racing and rodeo?" I asked.

"I don't think so. Maybe some weekend rodeos, but not like I did with Lenny...what about you?"

"I'll give Twister a call."

"Don't give up that singing dream," Stella urged. "But I think that with Twister's help and coaching, you'll make a lot of rodeo money."

I agreed. Stella's tragedy and how she'd finally come to grips with her role in the death of her late husband had been almost miraculous. We'd all talked about how she'd let the police think that it had been Lenny behind the wheel and maybe that was wrong...but none of us thought she ought to change that story and risk going to prison. Sometimes you have to look to the greater good and let someone believe what they want to believe.

"Then we'll go," I said.

"What about the old Navajo couple?" Stella asked. "We can't just send them packing back to the reservation…I don't think they have anyone there that will give them much help."

I had been thinking about that couple. Navajo and Hopi take care of their own and since we had both of those bloods in our veins, I thought we should do the same. Maybe the couple had family somewhere on the rez, but maybe not. Or maybe they'd gotten into a clan squabble and there was no support for them at all. It really didn't matter. We would keep them around and see that they had food enough and warm clothing. They were nice people and willing to help out whenever and as best as they could.

"I'll buy them a motor home or travel trailer with a good generator," I decided. "I'll rent a backhoe and dig a septic so they have everything they need to be comfortable. They'll be safe and can dig clay for the pots and gather yucca for the plaques…something I sure won't miss doing."

"We need to keep all our retailers supplied in Las Vegas," Grandmother said. "We're making good money now that I have so much help." She grinned at Stella and Georgia. "Good, fun help to be around."

I thought that was just perfect and our family had come to an agreement. We'd leave Las Vegas. Maybe next fall I'd come back and see if I could get another lounge job that paid union scale since I was now a paid-up member, but likely not. There were so many more pressing things to worry about… namely Elvis.

And then just the day before we were leaving, Elvis called.

"Charlie, when are you and your bride coming to Memphis?"

His voice sounded weak…even a little desperate and I suddenly knew that it was time not only to go home…but to go to Graceland.

"We could come right away."

Elvis' voice was heavy with depression. "Thanks, Cowboy Charlie. I've been thinking about the Coyote family. I want to see Stella. Is she doing okay?"

"She's doing remarkably well."

"I miss her and our horseback rides. Your sister is one hell of a woman."

"I know."

"And…and I need to hear more of Grandmother's great stories. I want to go up to the Hopi Mesas with her and maybe in the sky with the world all around below I'll be closer to God and heaven. Maybe up high I can find deeper truths…some real answers and meanings. I've been praying for help every day and night. I've been constantly dreaming about my twin brother, Jesse. And I want you to tell me all about my new ranch. We can talk about all the things I need to do to make it a quiet hideaway. *Come quick, Charlie!*"

The desperation in his voice was so real and so unfamiliar that it was all that I could do to stammer, "Elvis, we're as good as on our way!"

He didn't say anything more. I heard him start to wheeze and choke on the other end of the line and then it went dead.

"Grandmother," I said, "Georgia. Stella. Let's pack it all up and get out of here today. I'll hook up the stock trailer, load Sun Dancer and Rip then we'll roll out by sundown."

They stared at me so I explained, "Elvis is in bad trouble. He asked for our help and it can't wait."

Without a word or a moment's hesitation they flew into action.

When we got back to our ranch, we learned that our barn had burned down. The old Navajo couple was very sad and felt guilty, but it was not their fault. At first morning light I did an inspection. A high-mountain lightning strike had given the old wooden barn a direct hit. Everything inside was lost, but the animals had all been saved.

"We can rebuild a bigger and better barn," Grandmother said with grim determination.

Stella and I exchanged glances and I knew we were both thinking...not of the lost barn for it had been old and drafty...*but of our mother's destroyed diary.*

"What is wrong?" Grandmother asked, noting our overwhelming sadness.

With tears spilling down her cheeks, Stella told her and Georgia about Mother's precious diary that we had almost, but not quite finished reading.

"Do you really want to know the ending?" Grandmother asked softly as she motioned for us to all sit down at the kitchen table. "For it is sad."

"Then you *know?* Did Father kill her or maybe Phillip...or did she just disappear leaving us behind?" I asked, afraid of the answer.

"It happened this way," Grandmother said.

And then she began to tell us the secret of why our mother had never been seen or heard from again.

"Your mother left us and returned to live with my Hopi people. She went back to see if she still loved them and Phillip. Then she learned about the priests who were killed on the mesa tops and their chapel destroyed."

"What...." I didn't want to ask, but had to. *"What* priests?"

"The Franciscan Catholic missionaries from Spain first arrived on the Hopi mesas in 1629 determined to save our souls and change our pagan ways. They made us abandon our ancient Hopi ceremonies. They and the Spanish soldiers did the same to the Pueblo peoples east along the San Juan River in New Mexico. So in August of 1680, the San Juan and the Hopi rose up against all Christians and slaughtered them; the village priests on the Hopi Mesas were thrown off the cliffs. Years later, a bolt of lightning destroyed their chapel near Awatowi. So they are all gone."

Stella asked, "Our mother learned of this the last time she visited the Hopi?"

"Yes, and she couldn't take that so she went to the place where the priests were thrown off the mesa and...and joined them...probably as an act of penance. Your mother, Ellen Allen Coyote, jumped to her death off the mesa to fall on the rocks where the priests were sacrificed."

I had to know. "And where is our mother buried?"

"She was not...her sun-washed bones still lie on those rocks at the base of the cliff with those of the long ago Spanish priests. It is where she wanted to die and so my people left her untouched."

"No burial?"

"She should remain there forever."

I exchanged glances with Stella and realized we were both nodding in agreement. "So that was the end of our mother?"

"No," Grandmother said, "the end of her begins with her strong and beautiful children. And now, I will give you a very old Hopi prayer that I learned as a child. Remember it when I am gone."

Grandmother closed her eyes, bowed her head and began to whisper.

*Do not stand at my grave and weep. I am not there, I do not sleep. I am a thousand winds that blow. I am the diamond glints on snow. I am the sunlight on the ripened grain. I am the gentle autumn's rain.*

*When you awaken in the morning hush, I am the swift uplifting rush of quiet birds in circled flight. I am the soft stars that shine at night. Do not stand at my grave and cry.*

*I am not there. I did not die.*

# Chapter 28

Georgia and I were ready to drive out of the mountains and down to Phoenix for a flight to Memphis.

"Here," Stella said hurrying out to my truck. "Take this and give it to Elvis! Tell him it is special from me to him."

She handed me a picture that had been taken last Christmas. Stella was wearing a Santa Claus hat and sitting astride Sun Dancer decorated with a huge wreath around her neck. Both horse and rider looked to be in the holiday spirit.

"It's a wonderful picture of you and your mare," Georgia said. "Elvis will love it!"

"I sure hope so. I want him to remember the time we spent together. I want him to remember the good times we all had here at the ranch...and my hope is that it will bring him back with you for keeps."

Looking into Stella's clear black eyes, I was reminded again of how much she had loved Elvis. Back then, she hadn't been half the woman she'd been since losing her husband and a part of her leg. My beautiful sister was more whole and alive now than ever before.

We flew into Memphis and caught a cab to Graceland. I found that the contrast between the western desert and the South was almost overwhelming.

"Tennessee is a beautiful state," I told Georgia. "I've never seen so much green grass in my life with flowering trees and water everywhere."

"It's a big change from Arizona, alright." Georgia blew out a breath and said, "I'm really nervous, Cowboy Charlie."

"So am I."

"Why? Elvis is your friend and he wants you here."

"I think he's looking for a miracle, but I'm just a cowboy."

"You're a cowboy for sure, but you're a lot more that."

When we arrived at the gate, I got out and showed the guard my TCB ring. He sized me up and down and pronounced, "You even look like a real cowboy."

"That's because I am," I said, getting back in the cab.

We drove up to the Graceland mansion. I was overwhelmed by its beauty and wondered if Elvis really could ever leave such a magnificent home and property.

217

We were ushered inside. Elvis wasn't waiting.

"He's upstairs in his bedroom," the man at the door whispered. "I'll take you to see him."

"Thanks," both Georgia and I said at the same time.

"I should tell you that he is not doing at all well," the man said on the way up the stairs.

I wasn't prepared for what I saw when we were led into the room. Elvis was pale and overweight. He was dozing and there was a beautiful young woman sitting in a chair near his bed reading.

"Can we wake him?" I asked.

"You can try," she told me as she left closing the door softly behind her.

Georgia and I stood gazing down at the The King. He was still incredibly handsome, but Elvis Presley was not anything like the man I had known and loved back in Arizona.

"Is he alive?" Georgia whispered.

"Of course I'm alive!" Elvis said, his eyes suddenly popping open. "But I'm close to death. Real close. Cowboy Charlie, your wife is beautiful. Glad to meet you, Ma'am."

"It's an honor," Georgia said, wiping away tears.

"I have it all figured out," Elvis whispered.

"What?"

"To leave and never come back again. To have a chance at a full life. I have it planned and almost no one knows except a few of my best and most loyal people here at Graceland."

I was dumbstruck, but did manage to ask, "When?"

"At midnight. I've got a friend who owns a new motor home. I bought it from him and it's loaded and ready to roll, parked outside my gates. We'll go to Arizona and my new ranch."

Elvis closed his eyes with just the hint of a wan smile on his lips.

I can't tell you exactly who helped us at Graceland or how it went. I will say that we left just after midnight, me behind the wheel, Georgia as my navigator out of Memphis and Elvis snugged in on the rear bed.

We were out of the state of Tennessee before someone discovered that he was missing late the next morning. Elvis had planned it out well and we had boxes of cash and his most treasured possessions. We drove straight through Arkansas, Oklahoma, the Texas Panhandle and New Mexico. Elvis never left the motor home so he was never seen. Georgia and I bought fast food all the way to Winslow and then to Coyote Ranch.

The sun was just coming up when we pulled into the yard and Rip immediately started barking.

"Welcome home, Elvis," my sister said, kissing his face. "Welcome to the country and to a new life."

"Thank you. Have you still got Sun Dancer and a good horse for me to ride?"

"I sure do."

"And maybe a bush blanket for us both?" he asked with a wink.

Stella blushed and for one of the first times in her life, was speechless.

Elvis was very weak and unsteady. Grandmother shoved a warm muffin into his mouth. "We're going to live together, Elvis. And we'll find the right way."

"I believe we will," Elvis said quietly. "Yes, I do believe that we will."

I could tell that Stella and Grandmother were as shocked as I'd been upon first seeing him at Graceland. We were going to take him into the bedroom, but Elvis said, "I want to sit on the porch in a rocking chair and listen to the silence…and to nature. Maybe you could bring me another muffin and cup of coffee."

We all got stuck in our doorway trying to see who could get to the kitchen first. Seeing us jam up like that, Elvis laughed and that's when I knew he was going to make it.

# *Postscript*

*To protect Elvis, we've temporarily moved away from Coyote Ranch, but the old Navajo couple is still living there in that big motor home and I am certain that they will die there happy. Elvis kept the former Copper Mining Company land that he bought through Twister McCabe and we often ride it and look for pictographs, petroglyphs and old arrowheads and pottery.*

*To the north of Coyote Ranch the Navajo and Hopi Reservations combined are the largest in America and there is a world of beautiful country to hide in out by Monument Valley. Indians can tell stories and keep secrets...I expect that we will be privileged to grow old and be laid to rest in this ancient and sacred red ground.*

*Stella and Elvis got married, but they never had kids. Georgia and I made up for that with five of them, two boys and three girls.*

*Elvis and I have been chewin' on this story for a lot of years and we finally agreed that it might just save someone else who is travelin' down that same bumpy road of life toward an early grave. So I wrote it and Elvis swears that my story writing is a lot better than my song writing...but you can be the judge of that.*

*Elvis and I have both had our times in the limelight, him of course, infinitely more. But, looking back, what memories we keep are the good and very best ones.*

*All of us Coyotes hope you just follow the Golden Rule...be happy and healthy and thankful for every single day...'cause we sure are.*

*Your friend where the wind blows free and clean.*

*Cowboy Charlie*

# Author, Gary McCarthy

 *Gary McCarthy* is the author of fourteen published American historical and thirty-four western novels in addition to his very enjoyable and informative four-volume *Our American West* series In 1993, his *The Gila River* won the Western Writers of America's Golden Spur Award as the best historical paperback novel of that year. His 1991 *Russian River* California historical novel, and 2003 Arizona Western novel *Restitution* were Spur Award Finalists. McCarthy received widespread recognition for a series of novels relating to our national parks. All of his novels have been adapted to the audio format.

The author is well suited to writing about the American West; he grew up riding horses and received a B.S. degree in Animal Science and an M.S. in Economics from the University of Nevada. Before becoming a full time novelist, McCarthy was employed as an economist. He has a keen interest in Native American cultures, especially the Navajo, Hopi, and Hualapai who live in his beloved Arizona. His *River Thunder* is set against the harsh background of Arizona's rugged northern mountains and the magnificent Grand Canyon and is the winner of the Western Writers of America's 2009 Spur Award for Best Historical Audio Book. *Maddie O'Brien's Christmas Donkeys* is the heartwarming story for all ages of a how a small band of donkeys arrive one snowy winter night and transform the lives of the entire O'Brien family in ways that Maddie could never have dared to dream.

Gary McCarthy has over three million books in print. McCarthy enjoys hiking and horseback riding in the Grand Canyon Rim Country when he is not traveling the Southwest in search of new stories upon which to base his next novel.

Gary McCarthy has always been a huge and devoted fan of Elvis. He hopes if you enjoyed this novel as much as he loved researching and writing it, you'll write a short review and give *Elvis & Cowboy Charlie* a *four or five star Amazon rating* and try some of his other novels. If you have any comments, please email Gary at garyccbooks@yahoo.com.

CPSIA information can be obtained at www.ICGtesting.com
Printed in the USA
LVOW11s2341160715

446587LV00032B/739/P